Murder Most Fowl

Swansneck Village Mystery Series
Book 1

V S Vale

PENLAND
PRESS

Illustrations created by V.S. Vale
Formatting by Polgarus Studio

ISBN 978-1-9996565-1-5 (mobi)
ISBN 978-1-9996565-2-2 (epub)
ISBN 978-1-9996565-3-9 (print)

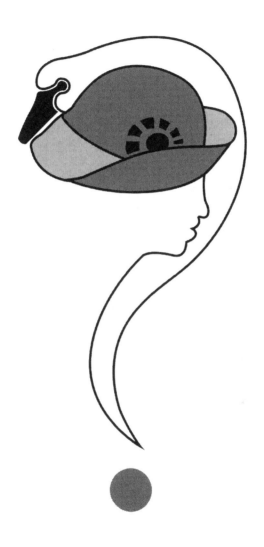

SWANSNECK VILLAGE MYSTERY SERIES

Please Note

As a British author, I aim to retain the 'British flavour' of my work, so have written this book with British English spelling. Words such as: Mum, colour, centre, neighbour, pretence, organise, travelled, etc., should not be considered typos. In consideration of US and Canadian readers, I have adhered to US English rules of punctuation, so as not to cause confusion.

There is also a Glossary of British Terms at the end of the story.

www.vsvale.com

Be sure to visit my website to receive an exclusive copy of **Old Mother Bradshaw's Cook Book**, featuring the Lancashire recipes enjoyed by the Swansneck characters! It's free when you join my newsletter... PLUS you'll be first to hear about brand new releases, sneak peeks and exclusive giveaways.
You'll also find links to follow V S Vale on social media:

Facebook: https://www.facebook.com/vsvaleauthor/
Twitter: https://twitter.com/VSValeAuthor
Instagram: https://www.instagram.com/vsvaleauthor/
Pinterest: https://www.pinterest.co.uk/VSValeAuthor/

"I'd love to hear if you enjoyed reading this first book in the series, and would be delighted if you left a review on the platform where you purchased it. I appreciate you taking the time. Many thanks!" V.S. Vale

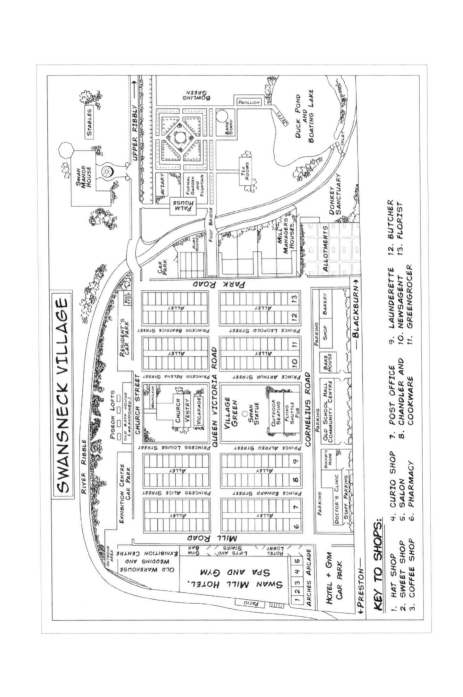

SWANSNECK VILLAGE

KEY TO SHOPS:

1. HAT SHOP
2. SWEET SHOP
3. COFFEE SHOP
4. CURIO SHOP
5. SALON
6. PHARMACY
7. POST OFFICE
8. CHANDLER AND COOKWARE
9. LAUNDERETTE
10. NEWSAGENT
11. GREENGROCER
12. BUTCHER
13. FLORIST

CHAPTER ONE

I would never have guessed I'd be fighting for my life with a murderer only days after my thirty-fourth birthday. Had I known, there would have been a legitimate reason for my panic attack. In hindsight, it was most likely the culmination of guilt and stress that had switched my brain into overdrive...

My heart pounded in my chest and spots swam before my eyes. Was this the 'buried alive' feeling Mum had referred to so often? The misery she suffered before I left Swansneck to go to University *down south?* London is what the locals meant, but any place in England south of Manchester was referred to as *down south.*

Back then, I had no idea what Mum meant when she said, *"she felt buried alive in Swansneck village."* I thought she was being melodramatic. But, since my return four days ago, I knew exactly what she meant. To think, before her death she endured close to thirty years working behind this counter at our family bakery. God bless her, I had never truly understood her pain.

That's probably why she insisted I study hard at school and earn a degree, to enable me to leave the village where four generations of Bradshaw's had lived. All bakers—until now. That was my fault. The usual male offspring of the Bradshaw Bakers line ended with me.

"Hard graft being a baker... no job for a girl." Dad's opinion on that point never wavered.

But maybe that was the opportunity my mum had recognised?

"Get out while you can, Jen," she'd said.

So I did. Although I wasn't sure *why* I was getting out.

As a youngster, I thought Swansneck was a wonderful place to live. Set in the East Lancashire countryside alongside the River Ribble, Swansneck was a Victorian model industrial village, the proud creation of its founder, Cornelius Swan. A dwelling place for the 400 or more workers needed to run his cotton mill in the mid-1800s.

Wise move. Owning the mill, the village, the houses, and the park meant he controlled the workers. Hey, you must admit the man had his head screwed on... No wonder he excelled as a Victorian Industrialist.

"Jenny, what are you doing, girl? Mrs. Scrogham needs serving."

My grandmother, Hilda, jolted me away from my budding anxiety attack. With lips compressed she expertly wrapped a bloomer loaf in white tissue paper and passed it to a customer waiting in line.

At my end of the counter stood Mrs. Scrogham, anxiously shaking her head as she studied the warm savoury pies that filled the shelves of the glass display unit.

"What can I get you, Mrs. Scrogham?" I coaxed, not wanting to agitate her further in what appeared to be a momentous decision.

"I'm not sure... What do you suggest?"

"Well, the Hot Pot pies are selling well today, and there's one left." I pointed to the golden crusted pie that glistened under the lights of the cabinet and smiled to hurry the sale.

More lunchtime customers came into the shop. Several familiar faces from way back, but mostly strangers. People made their choice of freshly baked bread from shelves mounted on the two side walls, then queued at the counter to pay.

Mrs. Scrogham—a renowned ditherer all her days—held up the line. With no sign of a decision set to emerge on her care-worn features, I upped the ante.

"What about a steak and kidney pie? Delicious with the potatoes I guess Bert—Mr. Scrogham—still grows at his allotment?"

Within earshot of my sales patter, Hilda gave an approving nod, but Agnes Scrogham only sighed.

"Oh for heaven's sake Agnes!" bellowed Maud Higson from further along the queue. "Make a decision, woman, or we'll all be in our graves from starvation at this rate!"

The other customers chuckled at Maud's no-nonsense tactic to get the line moving.

"My Bert's not very well at the moment, he has a bad chest," Agnes explained. "That's why I'm not sure..." Her voice drifted.

Hilda tuned in and took up the cause. "Ah, in that case, why don't you give him his favourite?" Without hesitation, she reached into the cabinet and pulled out a cheese and onion pie. Not waiting for Agnes to confirm or refuse, Hilda had the pie wrapped in a jiffy.

"That's on me," she whispered as she handed it to a startled Agnes. "Tell Bert to get well soon." Without waiting for a reply Hilda eyed the line and barked. "Next!"

"Thank you," said Agnes. But before leaving the counter, she smiled at me. "It's wonderful to see you back in Swansneck, Jenny. Bert will be ever so pleased to hear you are home."

"Thanks," I uttered as brightly as I could muster—not pleased one iota to be *home*.

I then focused my attention on helping Hilda to shift the lunchtime rush.

As usual, the baked creations my father and his apprentice,

Carl, made fresh every morning were sold by early afternoon. Only the cleaning chores within the bakery remained.

My grandmother—who had always insisted I call her Hilda since she hated every Gran and Nana term I'd ever tested upon her—looked at me quizzically.

"What's wrong, Jen? You don't seem yourself today."

"Probably because it's her birthday!" my dad called out from the inner sanctum of his baking empire. The familiar slosh of water echoed as he mopped the floor.

"Jenny shouldn't be working on her birthday... not on such a lovely sunny day."

That was a typically thoughtful comment from Dad—at the end of the working day.

"Tell her to leave any chores and get outside in the sunshine. We'll see her later." He transmitted his message via his mother—as though I couldn't hear him.

"Will do, Bob." Hilda ushered me toward the shop doorway. "Go on, Jen, go for a walk, we'll meet you later."

"But I need to do more unpacking at the house..." I argued limply. "I can't go for a walk."

"A walk will do you more good. Now go..." Hilda shooed me away from the shop as she would Fat Cat, the bakery mouser, who nowadays stalked the Bake House living quarters.

Ushered onto the sidewalk, I stared down at the familiar grey stone paving, mellowed with age and worn into ruts by 162 years of footsteps.

Such accuracy was due to the Bake House being built in 1855, along with the rest of Swansneck village. Attached to the bakery and shop, stood the house where I was raised. A modest home with no commute to work, precisely what you need when your day starts at 4.30 a.m.

The straight length of Cornelius Street stretched before me and I gazed toward the mill. Everything about Swansneck village was straight, except for the huge horseshoe bend in the River Ribble into which it was set.

As befitting a Victorian industrial village, the layout of Swansneck conformed to an efficient grid pattern of eight narrow streets. Linear lines of terraced houses faced one another across the cobbles, which created—as many like to think—a very close knit community.

Although for the majority, the village layout provided the perfect opportunity to watch the comings and goings of their neighbours, to find out their secrets.

The eight streets were named after each of Queen Victoria's children: Princesses Helena, Beatrice, Alice, and Louise plus Princes Alfred, Edward, Arthur and Leopold. They were bordered in turn by four main roads. Mill Road, the blindingly obvious choice, ran in front of Swan Mill to the west; and Church Road fronted the church to the north. Then to the east spanned Park Road, considered the best road in the village, because it was closest to, you guessed it, the park.

On one side it held a row of terraced houses, and on the other, a few semi-detached homes, set aside for Swan Mill managers. Whether from their front or rear windows, the houses on this road overlooked the river and the park beyond it, making them the most prized in the village.

At the top end of Park Road, there were a few compact bungalows, called almshouses. An old English philanthropic concept, almshouses were reserved for the *'elderly, poor and distressed.'* Loom workers rarely lived beyond the age of seventy after a lifetime of toil in a Victorian mill; which was possibly why they'd only built four of them.

Then, edging the village on the South side was Cornelius Road, the commercial heart of the village. It boasted a handful of essential shops, plus the old Infirmary—now a clinic—and the old school hall, now a community centre of sorts. But slicing through the middle of the grid was Queen Victoria Road which faced the neat village green. Here, the statue of Cornelius Swan stood stern and erect in its centre.

I always thought Cornelius Swan had seriously sucked up to Queen Victoria by naming practically everything in the village after her and her family. Maybe he'd thought she would award him a knighthood? But Sir Swan never came to pass, so evidently, Queen Victoria was no pushover.

As for the Swan family, Cornelius built a splendid elevated Manor House on the other side of the river to enjoy the grand vista of his success. Although, their view didn't directly span the village's terraced housing. First, they'd see the elaborately wrought iron gates that led to the stunning formal park he'd created with its palm house, aviary, band stand, lake, and pavilion. Not to forget that most Victorian bastion of polite society: the Tearooms.

Back then, the mighty success of the Lancashire cotton industry financed this grandeur, but as with so many great eras, the impressive rise was followed by an unimpressive decline.

I glanced at my watch and frowned; it was past two o'clock.

With a churning stomach, I walked the length of Cornelius Road toward the mill, unsure if I was prepared to face a personal interrogation from my old school friend. But any further delay in seeing Greg was no longer an option.

CHAPTER TWO

The bright August sunshine was a stark contrast to the dimly lit baker's shop with no modern frontage, and I regretted not having my sunglasses with me. Again, I thought of my mother's buried alive analogy and shivered involuntarily.

The short ten-minute walk brought me to the junction with Mill Road and childhood memories came flooding back.

Scooting around the neighbourhood on roller skates, I'd stop and gaze in awe at the huge five-story sandstone structure that dominated the village. Except when I was a child, it was no longer the cotton powerhouse of employment as it had once been.

Unlike Hilda and those of her generation, I'd never seen the mill used for its intended purpose. Closed in the 1980s, the mill building had become small business units, rented out by the Swan family. Clearly, their fortunes had declined, along with everything else during those times of economic recession.

To think, if I'd stayed in Swansneck as a teenager, my only employment options would have been the bakery counter like my mother, or the textile wholesalers and print shops that re-purposed portions of the vast space.

But now...

Standing on the corner of Mill Road I looked up at that same building. I found it hard to believe the once shabby sandstone facade and rows of square paned industrial windows could be transformed into something of splendour—like a butterfly released from the prison of its cocoon.

Oliver and Alex Swan, the great-grandsons of Cornelius, had remodelled the old mill into a contemporary hotel, spa and event venue. Although, I made a face as I read the ornate lettering of the signage: The Swan Mill Hotel. The Swan family's propensity for choosing uninspiring names hadn't changed.

In a phone call last year, Hilda had told me of the mill conversion, but I couldn't have visualised such a transformation. Swansneck had become an attraction, a 'must-see' destination for anyone interested in Lancashire's Industrial Heritage. Portrayed as a quaint Victorian time warp, visitors would be unaware that it was still a real village—and not a backdrop to a TV costume drama.

But who was I to complain? As a tourist attraction, my once dead-end hometown was breathing again. It had a strong pulse and was now safe to take off life-support.

After crossing the road to the hotel car park, filled with cars and a day-trippers coach, I pushed open the double doors to The Arches Arcade. Another enterprising idea created by the younger generation of Swans.

Previously called the boiler house, this side of the mill was once home to the huge engine that powered the looms after converting from water-power. Now stripped out, the area had become a small parade of five shops, each with an arched fascia. Hence the name The Arches Arcade, I surmised. The roof of the parade held a vaulted glass atrium allowing the bright summer sunlight to pour into the space. Decorative Victorian gas lanterns adorned the raw brick walls, and the polished original flagstone floor shone in a myriad of natural tones.

Situated in the centre of the row, I spotted Greg's

business—The Arches Coffee Shop. After weaving through several carefully arranged bistro style tables and chairs placed at the entrance, I pushed open the door.

Inside, the raw brick wall theme continued, interspersed with pictures of coffee in its various stages of production. Comfy tub chairs sat invitingly around low coffee tables and padded bar stools circled high perch stands. The tantalising smell of freshly brewed coffee hit me full force, and I headed directly to its source.

Greg hadn't changed in the years since we last met. An unruly mop of honey blond hair still fell over his eyes. Glancing up from operating a complicated looking coffee machine he gave me a huge lop-sided grin.

"Jenny!" he said, too loudly for my liking, as everyone in the room turned to see me, wondering why I warranted such a greeting.

Greg spoke to the waitress at his side. "Cover for a while, will you? I'm going to take my break."

He waved toward the room. "What can I get you, Jen? Choose a table and I'll bring our drinks."

"A cappuccino would be perfect, thanks."

I chose a quiet spot in the corner so we could talk, and Greg appeared with two steaming cups of coffee. Bending to place the cups on the table he continued the move to swoop me into a hug. Guilt washed over me.

"Sorry I haven't had a chance to come and see you sooner, Greg." I sipped the foaming coffee appreciatively. "What, with the funeral, and the move..."

"No need to apologise, I thought you'd have your hands full for a few days. But you're here now, that's all that counts." He picked up his cup. "I was sad to hear about your Great Uncle Wilf passing... a real character that chap. How old was he exactly?"

"Ninety-one. Wilf was a rare breed. It must be where Hilda gets her quirky ways—in the genes. It sounds as if her big brother used to torment her something rotten when they worked at the mill. Those were the days, to still want to act the fool after a twelve-hour shift."

"So... what's your plans?" Although Greg's question was casual, I heard the tension in his voice.

"Wilf has left me his house," I said flatly.

He gasped. "Wow, I didn't see that coming. I thought the Swans owned everything in Swansneck."

"Apparently the Swans offered some houses for sale to help cover the cost of the conversions. Hilda said Wilf had worked hard as an over-looker all his days, and never married, so he must have saved enough to afford it."

"Hey, lucky you, getting a house on Park Road."

"It's a three-bed terrace Greg; not the Swan Mansion!"

"Yeah, but even so, it has a bay window..."

"Albeit a single story bay window." I tried to diminish his reference to the ground floor bay window bestowed upon the homes of the mill over-lookers to elevate their status in the workforce. Back then, the next step up the corporate ladder was to achieve a mill manager's home, on the opposite side of Park Road.

"A big improvement on the other streets around here," grumbled Greg. "Not like me, having to put up with the nosy neighbours on Prince Edward Street."

"You're still with your mum then?" At once I regretted what sounded like a dig at his independence. Quickly I attempted to retract its harshness. "No sign of reconciliation with Karen?"

Greg shrugged. "Oh no, we're finished... both moved on. Karen went back to her parents in Preston, took Adrian with her. Though my being back at Mum's does have its advantages, there's room for Adrian when he comes to stay."

"Adrian was only a toddler in the last photos you emailed; he must be growing up fast." During those intervening years, life interrupted and our emails dwindled to an eventual stop.

Although, speaking with Greg now proved as easy as it had always been.

"Yeah, Adrian is becoming more of a handful every time I see him. Surely we weren't that bad when we were ten years old?"

"Probably worse," I ventured.

Greg winced at the thought. "So..." he said, switching the conversation. "What's wrong? Something is troubling you, I can tell."

"You know me far too well." I moaned, gulping the last of my coffee. Where did I begin? I launched into a random list. "It's being back here, serving at the bakery. Thinking about Mum's accident and missing her funeral. Thinking about my old job, thinking of Paul, thinking of London, and on top of all that, I'm thirty-four today and look at me."

I flapped my arms in despair, and an involuntary tear tracked along my cheek. Irritated by my show of emotion, I rubbed it away, then pulled a tissue from my pocket and blew my nose.

"Whoa, that's a heck of a lot of thinking. That has to stop for a start," he quipped, patting my hand that held the soggy tissue. "More coffee is called for, and then we'll take this one step at a time, eh?"

He darted off to refresh our drinks and then returned with an air of friendly efficiency. "Okay, let's start at the beginning. What's happening with you and Paul?"

"The marriage is over, we're getting divorced... Not that I'm sorry."

Paul and I had studied at the same University. A handsome charmer, I'd fallen for him instantly and a mutual understanding grew between us. Paul thought we made a good team because we both planned to work in London and enjoy the cosmopolitan life of that great city. The problem lay in that we—and the plan—quickly morphed into another kind of lifestyle. Employers termed us *career focused*, the polite expression for workaholics.

We never discussed starting a family because I never visualised Paul and I as parents—strange that. And now, with no man on the horizon, I wasn't prepared to consider children. Kids were part of other people's lives, not mine.

I tried to explain my current mood to Greg. "I'll miss being in London more than I will miss Paul. But renting anywhere decent on a single wage is impossible nowadays."

"Ah, so that brings us to my next question Miss Bradshaw." Greg made a twisting motion of an invisible moustache to add to the effect.

A smile tried to lift my lips although the corners maintained a downward angle.

"And your job..." he continued, "what's going on there? Didn't you have a sparkling career as a high-flying entrepreneur's P.A.?"

"Oh I did, but make no mistake, that's not as glamorous as it may sound. I enjoyed the freedom of working on my own initiative, but the guy made me jump through hoops, I was at his beck and call day and night."

Sipping the coffee I detected an extra shot Greg had secretly added.

"Between my boss's constant demands on my time, plus Paul's frequent after work meetings with clients from the ad agency, we drifted apart." I shrugged. It all looked so obvious in hindsight. No marriage could have survived our lifestyle. "Although, we did make a final attempt to rekindle our early relationship. One of Paul's clients owned a villa in the Maldives and offered it to us for a 'get-away-from-it-all' trip. That's why I was halfway around the world and unreachable when Mum died—and the reason I missed her funeral. Paul and I had agreed on a total communication shut-down so work couldn't get in touch."

That pointless trip had prevented me from saying a final goodbye to Mum.

"But even the magic of the Maldives couldn't work the miracle we needed. It was obvious... we were simply no longer a couple. From then on, the only reason we stayed married was for the convenience of sharing rent on our London flat."

"So... What made you decide to leave?"

"After Mum's death two years ago, I threw myself even more into my work. Not wanting to accept reality. The tactic succeeded for a while until Paul announced he'd met someone else, which forced us to re-evaluate our convenient arrangement. And then... Great Uncle Wilf passed away. The old curmudgeon really knew how to put the cat among the pigeons... He forced my hand, which brings us to the unusual terms of his will."

"This sounds interesting. Working class families such as ours don't usually have intricate wills and legacies. Fire away, I'm all ears."

"Well, as you said, Wilf was a character... so wait until you hear his cunning ploy. He bought the house shortly before he died and left it to me along with the residue of his savings. Trouble is, according to his will, I can't sell the house for three years, nor rent it out." I shook my head in disbelief. "The old schemer decided there'd been a drain of youth in Swansneck and forcing me back here was a way to counter it."

"But... you don't want to stay here?" Greg murmured.

I tried to explain. "It's just that I've become so used to living in London, the things to do, the grand architecture, the events, the theatres, the hugeness of it all..."

"There are exciting cities up here too, you know, Jen. We're not exactly swinging from the trees." He sounded wounded.

"I know, I'm sorry," I blurted. "Maybe I'm over romanticising London; it's just that... being at the bakery counter again brought back what Mum wanted for me. I told you what she'd said before I left for University. I'm wracked with guilt, as though I'm betraying her memory by returning to Swansneck."

"Ah... guilt relating to the promise you made to your mum I can understand—but declaring love for the bright lights of London? I don't buy it. Times are changing here, Jen, you shouldn't be so negative about Swansneck. The village isn't a victim of the recession anymore. The Swans invested heavily and the changes are huge. If your Mum lived here today, she wouldn't hate it with such a vengeance."

Sitting back in his chair, I could tell he thought my depressive reasoning held no water.

I tried again.

"But working behind the bakery counter long term, I couldn't handle it, Greg. No natural daylight in that windowless shop..."

"So don't work there," he answered. "Find another job... or better still, open a business. You said you enjoyed working on your own initiative, and with your own business nobody could breathe down your neck."

Stunned by the suggestion, I sat up in my seat. "I suppose I could handle three years here if I wasn't in the bakery. Then I could sell the house to make a deposit on a flat in London. A single wage could pay a mortgage..."

I spoke my thoughts aloud, but at my assessment, his shoulders drooped.

"Well, if that's what keeps you in Swansneck for three years." He stood to clear the cups.

I grasped his hand to stop him from leaving the table. "Oh, I'm sorry, Greg, I didn't mean it to sound like that. Please, sit. Give me some local knowledge. What are my choices if I don't work at the bakery?"

Mercifully, he sat down again. "Well, I was thinking, I know how much you like vintage clothes and stuff like that." He rocked his head to indicate my dress, a lightweight floral effort that hinted at the 1950s. But before I could comment he continued.

"There's a girl who works here in The Arches, comes in for coffee—she reminds me of a younger you."

"Gee, thanks, and I thought you were trying to lift my spirits?"

Greg chuckled. "No, I mean, she's into all that old style clothing. Nice girl, her name's Marilyn. Anyway my point is, where she works is up for sale." With eyes to the ceiling, he looked reflective. "Marilyn said she was worried about losing her job when the shop has a new owner."

"So come on..." I said, exasperated by the building tension. "What business is it?"

"The Hat Shop at the end of the row, here in the Arcade. They rent out hats. They put some very odd stuff in the window sometimes, all nets and feathers..."

His perplexed expression made me laugh. "Oh Greg, you've hit the jackpot with that idea. I wonder how much they'd want. Wilf left little cash, and the divorce costs swallowed anything I had saved."

"The business can't be very expensive, as the premises are rented, and none of the Arcade shops have traded for more than a year. So I guess you'd only be purchasing the stock and shop fittings."

Pulling his phone from his pocket he scanned the contacts list. "Iris Elston is the owner, my mum knows her. Iris's daughter just gave birth to triplets, and she lives in Kent." He grinned. "Iris said she's got to move to Kent to help with the babies because her husband's a klutz."

Entertained by Iris's derision of male baby care skills he hit an icon on the phone screen. "I'll just call my mum. Maybe you can meet Iris tomorrow? She's in a hurry to sell—which will be in your favour."

Despite a twinge of jealousy for Iris Elston moving *down south*, I wore my broadest grin in years.

"Greg, you're a genius. Arrange for ten o'clock tomorrow morning, will you?"

Greg nodded as his mum answered, and his expression reminded me of a cat that had deliberately knocked over the cream.

CHAPTER THREE

I left The Arches and walked back along Cornelius Street, heading home to change before for the small gathering planned for my birthday.

The talk with Greg had lifted my spirits. My enforced three years in Swansneck now held the seduction of being my own boss. And not only that, the prospect of expressing my passion for fashion too. Being optimistic about my future was something I couldn't have visualised only a few hours ago.

I decided not to stop and see Dad and Hilda as I'd be meeting them at the hotel soon. Besides, I needed to think out a strategy on how to reveal my plans to Dad. Turning the corner I strode up Park Road to reach Wilf's—or, as I should learn to call it—home.

The red brick terraced houses stood as strong and erect as old Cornie's statue, as the villagers referred to it. Passing the symmetrically arranged windows and doors that opened directly onto the pavement I stopped at the end-terraced house and slid the key into the lock. Number twenty-two, my house... The thought made me feel good.

The narrow hallway retained the original terracotta tiled floor, with an elaborate border design of rich blue and white diamonds. The walls showed their age and needed redecorating. Painted brown below the dado-rail and dark blue above, it did nothing to enhance the delightful floor tiles. The first doorway from the hall led into the sitting room, or as Great Uncle Wilf used to call it, the parlour.

Cluttered with my unopened packing boxes, the room looked a mess.

Of course, Wilf's taste in furnishings was not exactly mine, but the solid oak sideboard and two occasional tables were undoubtedly beautiful, in their own way. A tiny couch and two winged armchairs faced the main focal point of the room—a cast iron fireplace. Helping Wilf to polish the intricate fruit artwork of the fireplace and canopy had been a satisfying way to earn pocket money.

As it was summer, the grate had been cleared of coal cinders and replaced with an old bowl of faded potpourri. Hilda probably instituted that feminine idea many years ago, and Wilf just continued the habit.

The late afternoon sunlight was restricted by faded lace curtains that covered the bay window. They must go at my first opportunity, although for now, I'd better stop redecorating in my head and take a shower.

I climbed the narrow, steep staircase to reach the sparkling new bathroom installed in the tiny box bedroom only twelve months earlier. Prior to this I'd be wrestling with the tin bath in front of the fire or taking a visit to the bathhouse. Not to mention having to use the outside loo, or privy as we'd called it. Located in the backyard, the privy outhouse was separated from the kitchen by the coal shed. Those realities I had conveniently forgotten from my childhood.

God bless the Lancashire County Council Planning Department, I reflected as I turned on the shower. Hilda told me they'd refused to grant Oliver Swan planning permission to convert the mill into a hotel unless he installed modern bathroom facilities into every home in the village. He was obliged to agree to these upgrades to achieve his deal, but the unexpected additional expense to his project forced him to sell off some village homes—creating the perfect opportunity for Wilf to hatch his plan.

After my shower, I headed to the front bedroom to dry my hair at the small oak table in front of the window. The shabby white net curtain covering the sash window irritated me, so I swept it aside to let in the early evening light. Luckily this house wasn't overlooked, as Greg had said, so if I wanted to leave the window bare I needn't worry about privacy issues and 'inquisitive' neighbours. Having the end-of-terrace corner position, my new home gave an uninterrupted view of the footbridge, over the river and onto the lush park. The net curtains will be going for sure, I told myself.

Just then, I saw Bert walking down the opposite pavement. I'd recognise the tatty old tweed jacket he wore any day. His flat cap pulled down as always, it seemed strange to think he looked the same as nearly twenty-five years ago when I used to play tricks on him in the park. Well, not just me, there would also be Greg and Kim egging me on to do something terrible, like putting soap in the fountain.

Bert was a park keeper and caretaker of the aviary. He loved those birds like family. But most especially, he loved the peacock. There was always one that held court at the aviary over the peahens, fanning its tail in proud displays. And, for every peacock that ruled the peafowl roost over the generations, Bert had always named him Derek.

I looked down at Bert as he trekked along toward the allotments at the far end of Park Road, a trip he'd always made at the end of his working day, having completed his chores in the park. I laughed. Nothing had changed. A peacock still trailed behind him like a loyal dog. The large bird dragged its colourful train of tail feathers along the paving flags like a giant floor sweeper. Whether in the park or in the village, *a Derek* would follow Bert wherever he went.

With a light heart, I finished dressing; however, the clock admonished my tardiness as it flashed 5.15. Time to get a move on to attend my birthday party. Grabbing my handbag, I stuffed essentials inside and left for the hotel.

"Happy birthday!" a chorus of voices chimed as I walked into the first-floor bar at the Swan Mill Hotel. I neared the table and the small group got to their feet. Greg seemed to take the lead, followed by Dad and Hilda, who'd brought along an old friend, Nelly Worsley, to pad out the numbers. Granted, it was a tiny gathering, but so considerate.

"Take a seat, Jen," Greg said before heading toward the bar. "I'll be back in a moment."

I settled down between Dad and Hilda, and she promptly extracted a small wrapped gift from her handbag.

"There was really no need," I fussed, opening the bottle of perfume to spray a mist on my wrist and sniff the floral notes. "Thank you, Hilda, it's perfect."

A delicate hint of pink flushed her rounded cheeks, showing her pleasure at having correctly gauged my preference in scent. Although she was no shrinking violet, Hilda's forthright ways meant you knew where you stood. At seventy-seven, with a robust figure, she was still a handsome woman. Her hairstyle remained the same—always short, although the colour was apt to vary. Over the years her hairdressing adventures had ranged from raven black to flaming copper to purple plum, although she never considered any dye-job a mistake. At the moment, she was white grey with a prominent black streak, rather like a badger.

I glanced across the room to see Greg chatting amiably to the barmaid, who I recognised as Kim Renshaw. Kim spotted me and waved, then set about her work as Greg returned to his seat.

Having my childhood friends around me after all this time was unexpected. I hadn't realised Kim was still in Swansneck, let alone working here.

Although the hotel bar was busy, guests chose to sit at the stylish lounge chairs and tables that filled the room. The long expanse of bar was devoid of people, except for a man sitting on a bar stool at one end. He watched Kim intently as she came around from behind the bar, carrying a tray to our table.

Greg had ordered a bottle of champagne.

"Happy Birthday, Jenny!" Kim announced, putting down the tray.

Still the blonde bombshell, she'd hardly changed.

"Kim, you look terrific," I remarked.

Popping the bottle on our behalf she filled each glass. "Well, I don't know how I've managed it because I'm never out of this place..." Kim dipped her head closer to me and lowered her voice. "I'm now the bar manager—which just means I work longer hours." She laughed at her own joke.

"But, what nice surroundings to be in." I added, surveying the room.

The bar decor was as I expected from entering the hotel foyer; slick and stylish. Modern furnishings contrasted with the building's industrial history. One wall of the lounge bar was entirely glass, with sliding doors leading to a balcony patio that overlooked the river, revealing dramatic views of the rolling fields and hills on the horizon.

"Yes," said Kim in a whisper. "I love it, but don't tell the boss that."

"Is he your boss, seated at the end of the bar?" I pointed to the guy with the shock of dark curly hair and smouldering looks.

"Oh no—that's Jack—my boyfriend." Kim dismissed my error with a wave. "My boss is Oliver Swan. He's not here tonight... thankfully," she added meaningfully. "Anyway, enjoy your evening, Jen; I must get back to the bar. There's only me and Danny on shift and the restaurant is filling up, so the drink orders will be flowing." She squeezed my hand. "See you soon."

At that, she returned to her post and got busy.

"That was a surprise," I told Greg. "Why didn't you warn me?"

"I didn't think," he said, raising his glass.

"Cheers," everyone hailed.

"Many happy refunds, Jenny," said Nelly Worsley, taking a sip of fizz.

"Returns, Nelly," corrected Hilda. "Not refunds dear, returns."

The group laughed but Nelly shook her head in confusion. Then from what seemed to be out of nowhere, Greg pushed a small plate in front of me bearing a pink cupcake with a single candle in it.

"I didn't think you wanted to see all the candles!" He smirked.

Dad pulled a face. "Cupcakes," he grumbled.

Hilda shook her head. "Your dad doesn't agree with the invasion of American cupcakes. If he had his way, you'd be given an Eccles cake with a candle in it!"

"Oh, Hilda!" I laughed, and I made a big show of taking a deep breath to blow out the lone candle.

After the champagne, followed by a couple more drinks while we chatted, I walked out to the balcony to take in the view. A low glass balustrade surrounded the deck, allowing a panoramic view of the river bank and water.

The mill had been built precisely on the edge of the river bank, for access to the natural water supply. The river current would drive the huge waterwheel—which in turn, powered the looms. Retained as a historical feature, the vast wheel was a disturbing vision close up. Guests with vertigo would feel uneasy out here for sure.

Leaning on the chrome post I looked down to the river below the deck. The flow was low and slow, as always during a summer drought, and the large boulders usually buried within the river were menacingly exposed.

Suddenly, I felt a hand on my shoulder giving me a gentle shove, pretending to push me over the rail.

"Tell your mother I saved you!" Greg taunted, recounting what we used to shout as kids when we mocked a lifesaving event.

I spun around from the glass balustrade, and gave him a stern, reprimanding glare. "Don't be daft," I said, shaken by his antics. Then seeing Greg's crestfallen expression I gulped what remained of my drink and sought to change the subject. "Anyhow, what's with Kim? Is she serious about that Jack guy at the bar? Will we soon be hearing wedding bells?"

"Jack Nabb? I hope not, he's bad news." Greg dismissed the idea.

"Nooo..." I said. "He's not a member of *the* Nabb family— the same Nabb family we avoided like the plague as kids?"

"Yep, the one and only... But there are more of them now, they breed like rabbits."

We both giggled, and the tension eased.

"I've no idea what Kim sees in him," Greg added. "Jack's always so moody... and it certainly can't be his money, because he's only a window cleaner."

"I think he was jealous when you were talking to Kim at the bar earlier. So, you'd better be careful. He must have a possessive nature."

Greg smirked and waved his glass. "Well you know me, mister lady killer..."

"What do Kim's mum and dad think about her dating a Nabb?"

"Not sure if they know. They moved to Nottingham to work in the lace industry a few years back. So Kim lives alone. I bet Jack Nabb finds that handy," he added caustically, then drained his glass as my father came out to join us.

"It's good to have you back home, Jen," said Dad, putting an arm around my shoulder.

Obviously, it was the drink talking. Dad wasn't known for conversation or demonstrating affection. He was old school, withdrawn and private—typically English and awkward when it came to showing emotion.

We still hadn't talked much about Mum's accident or confessed how much we missed her. Like politicians, we could both skirt around an uncomfortable issue with ease. Maybe Dad and I were more alike than I thought.

"Ready for another drink, Bob?" asked Greg.

"Not for me, I'm off to bed... Early start."

Greg raised an eyebrow at me.

"No thanks, Greg, I'll call it a night too," I said. "But it's been a lovely evening, thanks for arranging it."

Greg went back inside and Dad turned to me.

"Wilf did us a good deed in bringing you back here. I know your mum would have been pleased that you've returned to live in Swansneck."

I bit my tongue. How could I answer truthfully without hurting him?

"Yes, Dad, she would," I lied. "It's good to be home, but there's something I need to tell you..." I wondered how to broach the topic, but then considered I was jumping the gun. What if buying the business didn't work out? Now was not the right time to unveil my plans, but I did need to escape from bakery duty tomorrow while I attempted to hatch those plans.

"Dad, I'll need tomorrow off from the shop... I should finish unpacking all my moving boxes." I embellished, just for good measure.

"Yes, all right," he said vaguely, not focusing on my words. "Jen, I wanted to ask you a favour. Wilf left me his homing pigeons. Not sure why, because he knew I'm not a big fan... Another of his jokes, I suppose." He smiled weakly. "There's no time in my day to care for them. And with the hotel increasing their bread roll orders for the restaurant, plus that wedding this weekend, I'm rushed off my feet."

"But, you've always said..." I faltered, certain he was about to ask for my help with the actual baking, but he interrupted.

"So, up until now, I've had Carl leave the bakery an hour early to see to the birds, but that lad has no clue. I was thinking, Jen, will you take care of the pigeons? I know you used to like them when you were a kid. You, Wilf and Bert, were constantly talking about the birds."

I exhaled a massive sigh of relief. How wrong could I have been?

"Yes, of course, Dad, that's the least I can do."

He looked wistfully at the sunset that glowed on the horizon, preparing to drop below the distant peaks and fells of the Lake District like a penny in a slot. "Remember how pleased you were when Bert named a new racing pigeon Princess Jenny?" Dad smiled at the thought. "Proud as punch you were."

"I remember. That little bird was a beauty, with twinkling eyes and beautiful markings."

I slipped my arm around his sturdy waistline, suddenly aware I'd never been so familiar with him before. Together, we stared across the landscape—lush green fields that led to the edge of the Forest of Bowland. I thought about Mum and her thwarted sense of adventure but tried to shut out how I missed her funeral.

Instead, I focused on our phone calls over the fifteen years since I'd left Swansneck. How delighted she was to hear the trials and tribulations of my student life at University, and then my elopement to Paris.

Later I regaled her with tales of attending high-powered

meetings with my boss and visiting glamorous hotels and exciting locations. Mum believed I was living the dream and thrived on those calls. I didn't have the heart to tell her it wasn't all she envisioned. That life with Paul was emotionless, and I was tired and lonely. It would have been cruel to destroy her illusions.

In the early years of our marriage, Paul and I visited Swansneck, but he hated every trip and did nothing but complain about the lack of modern plumbing. Eventually, we stayed over less and less, until our visits to see my parents 'up north' consisted of a rushed meal at a restaurant in Preston before we jumped back on the train.

Sporadic phone calls with Mum became the norm, and despite my offers, Mum and Dad never came to visit us in London. She always condemned the bakery for ruling their lives. I would fret over my long work hours preventing me from seeing them more often, but she would re-enforce her view that I shouldn't give two thoughts about Swansneck. Every call confirmed that Dad, Hilda, and Wilf were fine and sent their love. And so the years passed.

I took hold of my father's hand as it draped around my shoulders.

"Mum would have liked this hotel, and standing here with you to watch a sunset."

"Aye, she liked this kind of stuff." He gave a heavy sigh. "Her time was cut short, Jen. That day, she said she wanted to go to Blackburn for the afternoon. I should have offered to join her, but I was busy with the bakery as usual." His voice cracked a little.

"Dad, you can't blame yourself for not being with her."

"But the witnesses said she stepped out into the road... she mustn't have seen the van coming. If I'd been there at her side, I could have pulled her back..."

I gave his hand a squeeze. "You have to let it go, Dad. Nobody can foresee the future."

"Blackburn..." He said. "Not even ten miles away from home." He turned to me, sadness in his eyes. For the first time, he let me see into his soul. "Jenny, you know how your mum always talked about wanting to travel, and grumbled about being tied to the bakery? Well, what you don't know is that whenever I suggested catching the train to London to see you, she refused. How peculiar is that, after all the times she complained?" He looked away, back to the horizon. "In the end, I stopped offering and kept my head down with work. Over time, I understood why she behaved that way. She preferred to imagine the world outside of Swansneck—but didn't want to see it—in case it failed to meet her expectations."

Stunned into silence, I gazed at the setting sun with him. I hadn't realised Dad could be so perceptive. He truly understood Mum... much more than I did. He wasn't the cold aloof man I'd marked him as all these years. He was a deep pool, with wise emotional depths that he hid well.

His words now helped me to understand what he'd whispered when we scattered Mum's ashes. As soon as I returned from Mauritius, he and I travelled to the Lancashire coast. There, on the beach, he gently tipped the urn into the lapping outgoing tide. "Now you'll finally see the world and travel far," I heard him quietly say.

Dad released his arm from my shoulder and I sensed him shutting down. This rare moment of closeness was coming to an end, so I tenderly hugged his waist once more. "Come on, Dad," I said. "Let's go indoors."

Re-entering the room I could see Greg at the bar, talking with Kim again. But this time, it didn't look like a friendly exchange. Kim appeared anxious, and Jack Nabb was scowling at them from his end of the bar.

Before I could go over to check on the problem, Greg returned to our table. He seemed ruffled.

"What's wrong?" I asked.

"Kim made an error with the bar bill." He shrugged. "I'm used to tracking orders in the coffee shop. I know for sure we only had one bottle of champagne and three further rounds of drinks, but she said it was four rounds."

"Did you tell her?"

"Yes, but she got into a real flap about it. Said Danny must have added the drinks to our tab when she'd already done it. They're pretty stretched. Two people can't cover the bar and a busy restaurant. Anyway, she deducted it from the bill, so all's well."

"I'll be happy to share the bill with you, Greg. I don't expect you to cover the whole evening."

"No, no, consider it a joint birthday and welcome home party."

"Well, I for one have had a fabulous time, and I can't thank you enough for making it so special." I pecked him on the cheek and a slight blush coloured his face, which he attempted to cover by talking briskly.

"Oh, I forgot to tell you, Iris Elston agreed to meet you in the Hat Shop at ten tomorrow morning."

I grinned. "This is a terrible thing for me to say, but fingers crossed she's desperate enough to take my offer!"

CHAPTER FOUR

Beams of bright morning sunshine bounced off the walls of the old bathhouse, which—thanks to the new bathroom installed within every home—was now an unused relic.

The four pigeon lofts were still situated along the rear wall of the bathhouse, providing an uninterrupted flight path across the river bank and out to the distant countryside. A perfect location for the birds.

As I rounded the corner of the building I was met by the bustle of daily pigeon care. Three men attended to their lofts, cleaning out the coops and refilling seed and water trays. I knew Bert in an instant, but the other two men were strangers.

Bert was focused on checking a bird's wing as I approached.

"Of all the places, in all the towns…" I joked.

"Jenny!" Bert glanced up and smiled. "Agnes said you were back. How are you, Luv?"

"Good, thanks," I said and meant it. "Apparently my dad inherited Wilf's pigeons."

I gazed at Wilf's loft. Built from wood, doweling and wire mesh, it hadn't changed from my days here.

"Yeah, but your dad isn't a true pigeon fancier, is he? And that bakery apprentice lad just tossed feed through the wire mesh and got off home." Bert took the insult to our feathered brethren personally. "The birds will be pleased to see you though."

He pointed to Wilf's pride and joy, and I stepped closer to peer through the wire mesh frontage. There weren't as many birds as Wilf previously owned. From the usual twenty birds he treated like royalty, less than ten remained. An array of cube-shaped nesting boxes fixed to the back wall was chiefly empty, but as if on cue, the remaining birds housed within cooed their greeting. Sparkling eyes glinted in the morning light. Pigeons were such engaging birds.

"Well, you know where everything is. Nothing has changed. The water tap is over there, and feed containers there." Bert pointed to two large white plastic tubs the fanciers used for feed storage. It obviously remained a communal expense charged per pigeon.

Bert continued. "And, the mucking-out tools are there. Remember to keep the droppings for the allotment, it's good manure."

I shook my head in quiet disbelief. It was as though I'd been away from the Swansneck lofts for only one day.

"Oh, and this is Nick Faris." Bert pointed to a tall, gangly guy roughly my age. "And he's Tim Yates." He referred to the other man who possessed a pale, jowly face and receding hairline. I placed him in his late-forties.

"Hello," both answered to my nod of acknowledgment.

"Racing men," added Bert. "And Tim is taking part in the training race this weekend."

"Are you still racing your birds, Bert?" I asked.

"No, and I've not entered them into training this week either..." An abrupt hacking cough cut off his words.

Bert didn't look like a well man. Not the robust chap I used to torment.

I turned to the orphaned pigeons now in my care. "Did Wilf continue to race his birds?"

Bert recovered enough to speak and then pointed to Nick

and Tim. "No, Wilf gave that up some time ago. These two are flying the flag for the Swansneck Loft now."

I turned to the men. "And how are your birds doing?" I enquired with genuine interest.

"Not too bad," said Nick. "I've been increasing the distance, up to 100 miles now and they're picking up speed. But Tim's birds are really performing well." He pointed to the impressive specimens Tim was inspecting. Carefully he checked the number identification rings on their legs and placed each bird into a racing transport crate. Deep in concentration, Tim said nothing, so I didn't distract him.

Gathering the things needed to clean Wilf's coop, I attended to the bird's creature comforts.

At the next-door loft, Bert hunched over in a body-shaking coughing fit. "Are you okay, Bert? Agnes said you had a bad chest."

"Yeah, I'll be okay." Typically he dismissed any fuss. "It'll take more than a dose of bronchitis to see me off... might take it easy today though... not sure, we'll see. I'll speak to Agnes about my park chores..."

It appeared Bert was having an internal argument about his work commitments. He locked his loft, and prepared to leave.

"See you soon, Jen."

The sound of a truck pulling up on the road announced the bird conveyor's arrival. Bert turned to Tim and Nick.

"Good luck with the training, Tim. I'll try to get back here for clocking their return time in the morning if I can."

Nick helped Tim carry the precious cargo around the side of the bathhouse to the conveyor vehicle, and I peeped around the corner to watch the crates being placed in the truck. It was a specialist lorry, the kind I'd sometimes passed on the motorway. This one had a lively red and purple livery with Maloney's Haulage emblazoned across the side.

Once Tim had handed over the crates, he went on his way,

but Nick returned to collect his rucksack.

"So you're not entering the training event?"

"Not this time, I'm treating the wife to an anniversary dinner tonight. Going over to Preston and then meeting up with friends afterward."

"That sounds nice."

Nick swung his rucksack over one angular shoulder.

"I'll probably see you in the morning."

"All being well..." I grinned.

Now alone, I finished cleaning Wilf's loft and left the correct quantity of feed and water for my lovely little charges. Double checking I had securely locked the door latches, I made my way past the other lofts.

The tread worn grassy path was dry and dusty, but something on the ground not far from the lofts caught my eye. It appeared to be a small lump of white stone. As nobody would want to risk a pigeon eating it by accident, I picked it up. Only, it wasn't a stone. On inspection, I found it to be a screwed up, slender strip of paper, the sort used during the World Wars to convey messages on a homing pigeon's leg.

On it someone had written in large letters: THE CLOCK IS TICKING

What did that mean? A pigeon racing joke between the lofts, perhaps? I stuffed the paper into my jacket pocket and checked the time. 9.45. Oh no... Cleaning the loft had taken far longer than I'd expected. There was no time to go home, freshen up and meet Iris Elston by ten.

I glanced down at my outfit. My clothes were acceptable. But then I studied my hands. Ugh. I couldn't attend a life-changing meeting in a mucky mess. Iris Elston might take an immediate dislike to me as a potential owner of her business and refuse to sell no matter what the offer. I bit my lip while pondering the dilemma. It would be quicker to use the ladies washroom in the hotel reception and then cut through into The Arches Arcade. With this brilliant time-saving idea, I left the lofts and hurried along Mill Road.

The polished marble reception desk expressed the classy hotel statement the management wanted to portray. I glanced around and spotted a sign directing visitors to the gym and spa, then noticed a single access door labelled Ladies and Gents washrooms.

Discreetly, so as not to draw unwelcome attention from the staff, I darted over and nudged open a door. It led me down a small corridor toward the facilities. Mindful that cleaning the pigeon coop was not the most hygienic of tasks, I leaned against the heavy oak door so as not to touch the handle and tumbled into the ladies room.

As expected, the amenities were spotless and sumptuous. Wash basins moulded from a continuous creamy block of stone gleamed below an expansive run of mirrors and flattering lights. Lulled by the hypnotic rhythm of the nondescript music, I pumped copious amounts of rose-scented soap onto my hands and it frothed under my nails. Finishing with the available hand cream, I examined my hair.

Deftly raking my fingers through it, I was grateful I'd had the foresight to get a decent haircut before leaving London. The jaw length bob with chopped layers survived a dash along Mill Road with no ill effects. Okay, I may be an uninspiring natural brunette, but an easy-care cut worked wonders for me.

Fortunately, my outfit hadn't suffered from the early morning foray. The cropped blue canvas trousers and flat red pumps showed no signs of pigeon. I peeled off my jacket—thinking the striped sailor t-shirt looked better without it—then slung the long strap of my handbag across my body to create a casual, carefree effect.

Leaving the ladies room I entered the short access corridor again and noticed the utility storeroom door was now slightly ajar. As I passed, I heard muffled voices in stern disagreement. I couldn't make out the words—but one voice belonged to Kim.

"No! This has to stop," she hissed, then something clattered as though knocked from a shelf and she fell silent.

"I'll say when it's time to stop," snapped a man's voice I didn't recognise. "Do you hear me?"

"Yes," Kim replied in a whisper.

What should I do? Should I enter the storeroom to check on her? Something had been knocked over, but Kim seemed to be okay because the man continued talking to her, well, warning her... Maybe it was a romantic tryst and she liked him dominating her? Should I interfere? I hesitated. I certainly didn't want to catch anyone in a compromising situation.

Besides, I had no time to get involved. Iris Elston would be waiting for me. So I quickly left the scene.

CHAPTER FIVE

As yesterday, the glass atrium bestowed shafts of daylight to cascade into The Arches Arcade. Mindful I was about to buy a business with what remained of my inheritance, I was reassured by the hum of activity from shoppers and visitors alike.

Thwarted in my attempt to wave to Greg because he was busy working at the counter, I passed on to the 'Little England Sweet Emporium'. There, a clutch of tourists mused over the 'olde-worlde' period charm of the window display, and then I came upon the uninspiringly named 'Hat Shop'.

Akin with the other shops it had a charming, double arched frontage, with the entrance set in the centre. Releasing a deep breath, I pushed open the door. A cute bell tinkled alerting the girl at the counter to my presence. Judging from both her age and flamboyant clothing, I surmised her to be the famed Marilyn. She flashed a broad friendly smile, enhanced to megawatt status by her bright red lipstick.

"Hi. Can I help you?"

"Yes, I'm here to see Iris Elston," I said, just as a lady emerged from a doorway at the rear of the shop. She waved and called out to me.

"You must be Jenny Bradshaw... come into the office."

I entered the office and Iris set about clearing a plastic

camping chair of random papers then unceremoniously dumped them on the floor.

"Take a seat, Jenny."

She perched on a matching folding chair angled against a cluttered shelf that substituted for a desk. I thought this make-do affair would be useless to a toddler, let alone a business.

Once we were settled into the shambles she called her office, we made small talk about her daughter's triplets and then got down to the matter at hand.

I enquired her asking price for the business.

Iris hesitated, then gave me a figure.

I'd attended enough meetings with my prior employer to know the first pass at an asking price was always wishful thinking for the seller. But it gave a jumping off point to begin the negotiations.

"I am interested in purchasing the business, Iris, but not at any price," I said. I had to stand my ground. "My capital is limited, and considering the turnover, investment in expansion would be essential if I am to continue employing Marilyn. I'd need to create a website and consider advertising..."

Iris gave a knowing smile. "Greg's mum said you'd be no pushover. So what's your offer?"

"I'm truly not trying to drive a hard bargain, Iris." Although I was intrigued to hear I was presumed shrewd, I didn't want anyone to think I was a callous negotiator. "I appreciate you're only selling to be with your daughter, but my offer is 70 percent of your asking price."

She held my steady gaze, nodded, then announced, "Make it 75 percent and we have a deal."

Thrusting her hand out for me to shake, I took it and smiled.

"Give me your bank details and I'll make an online transfer to your account this morning."

At once she noted down her bank details. It seemed I wasn't the only one who wanted to get things moving.

"Jenny, why don't you return around lunchtime? We've a busy afternoon ahead as there's a wedding in the village tomorrow. It'll provide the perfect opportunity to show you the ropes—and you can get to know Marilyn."

"That sounds wonderful," I agreed, excited to make a start. "I'll see you later."

Passing Greg's coffee shop, I caught his eye through the front window and gave him the double thumbs up sign. He grinned, returning the gesture.

Then I walked home to make the bank transfer.

With a spring in my step, I passed each of the flat-fronted shops on Cornelius Street, interested to know how they presented themselves and their window displays. The pharmacy window showcased health related items plus a haphazard gathering of toiletries. The post office fared little better, but the chandlers surprised me with its inventive display of copper pans and jelly moulds. I deduced they were trying to tempt the tourists with a Victorian twist on modern cookware and wondered if it was a successful tactic.

The final shop in this first retail block was the launderette. As I passed the doorway, the heat from within carried the familiar scent of freshly washed laundry. I peered inside and saw two women working together to fold a large bed sheet. Their choreographed movements formed a rhythmic dance, and the sight evoked memories of Mum and Hilda doing the weekly wash.

They were delighted when the new launderette opened, especially Hilda who thought the launderette was a beacon of advancement for Swansneck. In reality, the launderette was not simply a place for the village women to efficiently complete the family laundry, it was gossip headquarters.

Although to be fair, the men in the village were not immune to gossip either. Except their chit-chat would take place under the roof of the building next door. The one and only pub in the village—The Flying Shuttle.

Originally built by Cornelius Swan, The Flying Shuttle was a men's club that provided educational evening classes to the workers. Old Cornelius was a staunch Methodist, and alcohol, along with the other demon doings it enticed people to partake in, was banned. But time had marched on from old Cornie's rule over the villagers and the building had become a pub.

Popular it was too—judging by the hubbub I could hear as I passed the uncompromising period building. I chuckled to think it now housed all the horrors that Cornelius had railed against.

I crossed the junction with Prince Arthur Street and glanced along the narrow cobbled road of flat-fronted terraced houses. A man up a ladder caught my attention as he cleaned the upstairs windows of a house a short distance away. Not noticing me, he slowly and methodically wiped the glass with his chamois leather. At least, that was the impression he tried to convey. He appeared more interested in what was behind the glass than any smears that may be upon it. But perhaps I was just being unkind about his diligence.

As I reached the other side of the road, the man lowered his head to descend the ladder. I recognised his dark smouldering looks in an instant. It was Jack Nabb, Kim's boyfriend. Why was Kim attracted to him? Now that she was an adult, did she have a taste for men with a brooding persona?

Every brick of the final block of shops felt familiar to me because they were straight opposite the Bake House. The newsagents, greengrocers, and butchers still looked the same with their typical timeless array of goods. But most colourful of all was the florist on the end, bursting with life.

I rounded the corner onto Park Road and vowed that we needed to create a killer window display at the Hat Shop if it was to attract more attention from passers-by.

CHAPTER SIX

I arrived back at the Hat Shop with both confidence and trepidation, an impossible combination, and I wondered which would win out. As I entered the shop and several customers turned to face me, trepidation edged ahead and won by a nose.

Swallowing hard, I pasted a smile on my face. To think, only an hour before I'd hit the payment confirmation button on my laptop screen and become a proud business owner.

Marilyn chatted with two customers, and Iris was busy completing another transaction. She waved me over as the customer left the shop carrying a striped hat box.

"I told you we'd be busy this afternoon." Iris grinned. "The wedding tomorrow has cleaned us out. Some purchase-only hats are still in stock, along with our vintage range, but our biggest turnover comes from rentals. It's convenient to rent a hat for a singular occasion. Not to mention more economical for the customer."

I somehow felt this piece of information was superfluous as I'd already bought the business. Perhaps Iris was trying to re-enforce my decision.

"Thanks for the speedy transfer," she acknowledged in a low voice. "You won't regret buying the shop, Jenny, I promise." At that, she grasped my elbow and steered me over to Marilyn and the two customers, who I guessed was mother and daughter.

"Ladies, may I present Jenny Bradshaw, the new owner."

I'd forgotten I had bought a village business, and such a simple, candid approach to announce new ownership would be normal.

"Hi, I'm Marilyn Ginty." Spontaneously, Marilyn wrapped her arms around me. Her hug felt genuine, not just an attempt to ensure her job security.

A pretty girl, but not in an obvious way, Marilyn worked at bringing out her best points with artful skills. As Greg had commented, she had a talent with her choice of clothing. Not only did she seem authentic, but she'd be an asset to any business, most especially this one. I considered myself lucky to have her.

"And this is Sharon Yates and her daughter, Amy," continued Iris.

Sharon nodded hello, but seemed distracted by her own thoughts. Amy gave me a friendly smile.

"If it wasn't for Amy, we wouldn't be half so busy," laughed Marilyn. "Amy is getting married in the village church tomorrow and nearly everyone will be wearing one of our hats!"

"Except for the men," giggled Amy.

Witnessing their conspiratorial chuckles, I guessed Amy and Marilyn were friends, which wouldn't be surprising as they looked similar in age, maybe twenty-one or twenty-two.

The physical contrast between the girls was similar to Kim and me.

Marilyn was blonde and vivacious with skilfully styled hair and makeup, whereas Amy had a more natural sultry style, with dark curly shoulder length hair and olive skin.

Iris and Sharon were in deep discussion and invited me to join their conversation.

"Sharon would like your opinion, Jenny," said Iris. "She's

having second thoughts about the hat she's chosen."

Sharon studied herself in the mirror. She wore a small pale pink arrangement of flowers with a side net, and to be honest, I didn't think it was the right choice for her dyed blonde hair. In fact, it looked insipid.

"I know I'm only the mother of the bride, and I shouldn't cause such a fuss," Sharon explained out of Amy's earshot. "But this is my one chance to shine at a wedding. Amy is my only child."

I communicated my understanding with a smile. "I think something of a richer shade would be better with your skin tone. What colour is your outfit?"

"Shell pink."

"Then let's find something in fuchsia pink for you." I gazed around the shop and my eyes fell on a wide-brimmed hat fashioned from lace in the shade I was visualizing. It had a contrasting pale pink ribbon band that would coordinate well with her outfit. "Here, try this." I handed it to her.

Sharon tried it on and gasped in delight. "Oh! I look ten years younger," she gushed, checking her reflection.

"And you're not even forty yet, so don't overshadow me will you!" Amy laughed, admonishing her mother.

Marilyn tilted the hat on Sharon's head to test different angles. "Oh yes," she purred, deciding on the best position, "and you should use a fuchsia pink lipstick too, Sharon, it'd look absolutely fabulous on you."

Iris came over to lay her hand on my shoulder. "You're a natural at this," she whispered. "My little business is in good hands, I can tell."

I let out a small sigh of relief. It seemed trepidation was doped and disqualified from the race. Confidence was now the declared winner.

"So will your mum be able to make it as your plus-one tomorrow?" Amy asked Marilyn as she boxed up the hat.

"Afraid not, her auntie's still not able to walk after the op.

She asked me to pass on her apologies." Marilyn extended the box to Sharon. "But—would it be okay if I brought Jenny instead?"

Marilyn turned to me with an expectant expression, the kind you see on a child you don't have the heart to disappoint.

Sharon was the first to answer. "Oh that's a terrific idea, yes, why don't you come instead, Jenny?"

"It'll give you chance to meet people from the village, now that you're back to stay," prompted Iris, with a *don't hide from the inevitable* expression. Obviously having gleaned details on my state of affairs from Greg's mum.

Helpless to defend myself from the tsunami of good intentions headed my way, I gave in.

"That's extremely kind of you," I replied. "I'd love to. What time?"

Amy spirited a blank invitation from her handbag. "Three o'clock. The reception is at the hotel function room afterward. The details are all on there." She passed me the embellished card.

"It sounds like it will be an amazing day," Marilyn enthused. "Amy's dad has really pushed the boat out—and you too, Sharon," she added with great diplomacy.

But Sharon didn't seem offended. "No, you're right, Tim has relished the chance to go overboard on Amy's big day." She circled an arm around her daughter. "Nothing is too much for his angel, eh?"

Amy tilted her head to rest on her mother's shoulder, and as she did, her luscious dark waves tumbled around her face. She would make a beautiful bride.

For a moment I watched their display of genuine mother–daughter affection and fought a lump in my throat. By eloping, I'd denied my mother the opportunity of attending my wedding. At the time, it seemed romantic to escape abroad and do the deed without informing our families. I hadn't realised how selfish that was.

I fought to keep my equilibrium, by moving the conversation along.

"Your husband, Tim... I think I've met him."

Sharon regarded me in surprise. "Have you? He sells office furniture so perhaps you've had dealings with his firm?"

"No, nothing like that." I shook my head. "I met Tim this morning at the pigeon lofts while I was cleaning out the coop."

The group of women giggled.

"You keep pigeons?" gasped Marilyn. "Honestly? Someone like you keeps pigeons?"

I wasn't too sure how to take her remark, but I nodded and smiled at their amusement. "I'm caring for the birds while my dad's busy at the bakery," I explained, returning to Sharon's comment. "Tim sells office furniture? Well—I may be in the market for a decent desk and two office chairs."

Iris feigned shock and then laughed. "No, you're right, office work was never my strong point, and anyhow, it's your business now. You do whatever you need to do, Jenny."

"Well, I'd like to bring my laptop here, as I'll only need the tablet at home. But that shelf you're using as a desk would almost certainly collapse under the strain!"

Iris chuckled. "Computers are beyond me," she said, "hence my chaotic accounts and filing system. Marilyn has been onto me for months. She wanted to drag me kicking and screaming into the twenty-first century." She turned to Marilyn. "But, you now have a boss who can build a website and do all that promotion stuff on social media—just as you wanted."

Marilyn looked at me as though I was the second coming. I tried to lower her expectations. "Well, I can set up accounting software and put together a passable website for the shop. But although I've got experience creating presentation documents for meetings, I'm not so hot with social media."

"Oh, I can help with that," said Marilyn. "It'll be great."

She seemed buzzed by the anticipation.

Sharon joined in the discussion. "I'll speak to Tim for you, Jenny. He often gets good deals on used office furniture after they've completed a refurbishment. Those fittings would be ideal for you."

"Thanks," I said. "That'd be incredibly helpful."

This day was jam-packed with progress. I was on a runaway train.

Sharon and Amy left the shop, and Iris and Marilyn continued to show me the ropes. We talked about the range of stock carried, both new and vintage. Iris said there was a growing trend in vintage, being much sought after for themed social events. During the afternoon several ladies popped in to collect their hats for the wedding. Candy-striped boxes left the shop at a pace all afternoon.

While Iris cleared her belongings out of the office in preparation to leave, Marilyn disclosed she'd already posted images of a few hats onto her social media account. Just to test her promotion theory, she assured me. But then she proudly announced she'd made a sale. A customer from Bristol had purchased a hat and needed it sent by express delivery today. Marilyn asked me to prepare an address label for the hat box to be ready for the courier collection later this afternoon.

I was happy to oblige. I sensed I'd met a kindred spirit in Marilyn.

Finally, Iris announced she was ready to leave. She made her farewell to Marilyn, and I helped to carry the boxes containing her belongings out to the car park.

Having packed everything into her car, she handed me her set of keys for the shop.

"I'll be travelling to my daughter's tomorrow morning, but you've got my phone number, so call me if there's anything you need. Marilyn's a good girl, she has a kind heart. And if you can accept her transformation into a different film star each week, well..." She laughed. "You'll get on fine."

"Greg mentioned her fondness for flamboyant dressing," I said. "But I didn't think it was over-the-top when I met her today."

"Oh, she toned it down for you," Iris smirked. "Wait until she feels you can handle it, you'll get it full throttle."

My shocked expression must have amused Iris as she continued, "Oh don't worry. I see you're not immune to expressing a unique sense of style yourself." She nodded to my Capri pants and striped t-shirt. "Very Bridget Bardot in St Tropez, I would say."

"Except for several extra pounds of padding." I smoothed my hands over my hips, conscious of my curves.

"Don't knock yourself, Jenny, you look fabulous." She climbed into her car and switched on the engine. Then, before driving away she called out through the open window. "You've become part of a new world now, Jenny—enjoy it!"

I watched her pull out of the car park and considered how perceptive Iris's parting comment was, then rejoined Marilyn in the shop.

"I hope you don't mind, but I must leave you now," I told her. "There are things I need to straighten out... everything happened so fast."

"You're telling me. No problem, you get away. It's near to our usual closing time, anyway." She tapped her fingers on the hat box I'd labelled for her earlier. "I just need to wait for the courier to pick up this parcel. I received a text to say there's been a delay in collection. '*Traffic issues beyond our control*,' they said." She cast a rueful smile. "As soon as he's been, I'll lock up."

"So I'll see you at the church tomorrow then, shall I?" I collected my jacket and handbag from the office.

"Oh yes! I'll be there fifteen minutes before. You know the

shop is closed tomorrow, don't you?"

I looked at the bald mannequin heads that adorned the shelves. "I guessed as much—there's barely any stock left!"

CHAPTER SEVEN

On my way home I decided to contact Hilda to ask if she and Dad would be at the Bake House later. I didn't want the news of my shop purchase to reach them from anyone else's lips. Events in Swansneck never took long to reach Hilda or her circle of friends.

"Why don't you come around for your tea?" Hilda offered during my call. "I can just as easily cook for three. Besides, we're having pie."

"Left over stock?" I joked, knowing all too well it was. History was repeating itself. Mum and I always joked about eating the unsold stock on our calls.

"Waste not, want not," Hilda reprimanded, although not seriously.

"My hips might disagree with you... they want to be smaller."

I heard her familiar chortle down the phone.

"So, what time do you want me?" I enquired.

"It'll be on the table for five-thirty as always."

After a shower, I went into the front bedroom. I'd left the net curtain hooked back from the window and sat at the small table I now regarded as my dressing table.

I combed my hair and contemplated how I should break my difficult news to Dad about leaving the bakery. Then, from the corner of my eye, I saw Bert and a loyal Derek again on their daily travels from the park, headed down the road toward the allotments.

He must be feeling better. Agnes serving his favourite pie last night must've done the trick, giving him the strength to complete his daily duties. I chuckled at the healing abilities of my father's baking while I dressed. Then I grabbed my bag and padded downstairs.

I strode toward Cornelius Street. It was a beautiful evening once again with a mellow warmth and light breeze. At the corner by the florist's, a lady dressed in jeans and t-shirt with Flora Laura written across her back was locking up the shop. With a smile, I greeted her as I passed. Perhaps I would see her at the wedding tomorrow. These people were now part of the world I inhabited, as Iris had said.

Well, for the next three years, anyway.

I crossed the road to reach the Bake House and pressed the brass doorbell to my childhood home. The glossy dark red front door shone as it always had, and the fan shaped stained glass skylight above still depicted ivy and roses.

The door swung open and my dad greeted me.

"You're here then," he said, in our typical Lancashire way of stating the obvious.

He stared beyond me, spotting something in the road. He nudged me aside to step forward for a clearer view.

"Will you take a look at that?" He grumbled, pointing to a vehicle parked in the narrow bay in front of the bakery.

I turned to observe a transit van emblazoned with 'Swan Mill Hotel' on the side, but with no sign of a driver in the vicinity. At that moment I realised the problem.

"What time is your delivery due, Dad?"

The bakery took late delivery of product ingredients several times a week, and this van was blocking the space the truck would normally use.

"Seven o'clock. They'd better have it shifted before then, or I'll be ringing the hotel and having words."

He turned on his heel to lead me along the hall corridor to the kitchen at the back of the house. I grimaced. I wasn't too pleased with that van either, mainly because it had rattled my dad, and I hesitated to think how he would react to my news.

In the kitchen stood a large wooden table with four chairs that had always served as a combined work table and dining table. The house possessed a small dining room, but it was reserved for special occasions. Swansneck's older generation still maintained this Victorian tradition. A room—generally a parlour—was only used when the vicar or a school teacher came to call... but they very rarely did.

I considered it a waste of precious space.

Hilda had laid the kitchen table and now busied herself with the dinner plates. My father returned to his seat at the head of the table and thumbed the pages of his newspaper. Sitting down to join him, I noted his stern expression, so said nothing. Grateful the noise from the radio masking the silence of the room. Voices of a Noel Coward play chattered away in the corner, although none of us paid it any real attention.

Hilda placed a mismatched china plate in front of me.

"There we are."

The plate was piled high with mashed potato, carrots and, what I recognised as a steak and kidney pie with golden gravy. I hesitated, but there was nothing I could do. Had it been any other season, I would have relished this traditional dinner, but on a warm summer day?

I picked at the meal, and although it was delicious, I had little appetite. The prospect of announcing I was leaving my work at the bakery had my stomach twisting into knots.

Hilda and my father finished their meals before me, and she got up to clear the plates into the sink. Dad stood to leave the table, saying he should check on that van, and I panicked. I didn't want him distracted by the errant vehicle or the delivery arrival, so I knew this was my moment.

I pushed my plate away, mumbling something about having had a large lunch, and asked them to sit down again. Hilda wiped her hands and returned to her seat.

"What's on your mind?" asked Hilda. "I can always tell when there's something on your mind."

Was I that easy to read? Why did everyone seem to second guess my thoughts?

"Is this about the shop?" asked Dad bluntly.

Oh no, had someone already told him about the Hat Shop? Was nothing a secret in Swansneck?

"Well yes... it is," I hedged.

"I'm glad you've raised the issue of the shop, Jen, as I wanted to ask you about your plans..." Dad hesitated. "Because it's like this..."

"Oh Bob, get on with it," groaned Hilda.

But Dad merely hung his head and stared at the table as he spoke. "You know how I've always said being a baker is no job for a girl?"

"Yes, Dad," I replied, perplexed.

Was he going to say he was wrong? That nowadays there were many famous female bakers? That I had a gene—the Bradshaw gene—so was destined to be a TV personality baking exotic northern delights? Tantalising the nation with recipes from Old Mother Bradshaw's cookbook?

My heart sank as I waited for him to continue.

"Well, it seems working in a baker's shop is not the job for you either."

"You're hopeless in the shop, Jenny!" Hilda announced frankly. "And we can't afford to employ someone who doesn't put their heart and soul into the work. There, I've said it." She finished and got up to wash the dishes.

"You mean I've been sacked?" I said, astounded. "I didn't even realise I was employed! I thought I was just helping out."

"But you couldn't be 'helping out' forever, Jen, you need an income. A bright girl like you... all educated and such, we couldn't afford to pay you the rate you'd expect." Dad picked up his newspaper from the table and folded it in half.

"I don't believe this," I said quietly. "I've been sacked from a job I didn't even have!"

But why was I so enraged by this announcement? It was the *out* I needed. I should grab it and run.

"Well, you should know that I purchased a business today, a hat shop, in The Arches Arcade. And I plan to build it up to be a great success."

"That's excellent news, dear," said Hilda, drying the dishes. "Something you can concentrate on. I hope it will be very successful."

Despite her supportive reaction, her accusation of being hopeless in the bakery shop stuck in my craw.

"I know I can do well in retail... you'll see." I jutted my chin to re-enforce my determination.

Dad was silent after my announcement and didn't congratulate me on my decision to buy the Hat Shop. He simply flipped his folded newspaper over to study the back page.

To think I'd been feeling guilty about leaving them in the lurch with the bakery, and it turned out they didn't even want me there!

"I'll be going to Amy Yates's wedding tomorrow, where most of my stock will be on display at the ceremony," I stated this proudly, not sure who I was trying to impress.

"You are?" said Hilda. "That'll be interesting. You must come to the Tearooms on Sunday and tell us all about it. The girls will be delighted to receive a first-hand account of the ceremony. I hear Tim Yates has pulled out all the stops on this event."

By 'girls' I knew she meant her old mates from the mill days. They were over-active bloodhounds when it came to gossip. I studied Hilda's face, as open and friendly as ever. I could hardly refuse without seeming churlish.

"Okay," I relented. "What time does the Clan meet on Sunday?"

"Noon, dear." She smiled.

"Bye Dad," I mumbled as I left the kitchen, and received another of his silent nods.

I closed the front door and walked down the path. The hotel van had gone, so Dad would get his delivery, but why I should care, after the treatment I'd just received was beyond me.

I headed toward Park Road and rounded the corner then noticed a police car parked in front of the allotment gate. I shook my head. Break-ins at the allotment sheds must still be a regular event. Although what value people put on their random spades and trowels was beyond me. Whatever the item, it seemed to warrant a call to the police.

I strode off to my house, unsure why I felt the shine had gone off my business announcement. Had I expected them to weep and wail and wring their hands when I told them I was leaving?

Apparently, the old fogies were more independent than I thought.

CHAPTER EIGHT

Early next morning, my sleep was rudely interrupted by a loud knock on my front door. Whoever it was, didn't opt to rattle the polished brass door knocker, but to bang it so thunderously it could have stirred the dead.

I toppled out of bed and pulled on my robe and fluffy slippers. The bedside clock showed it was just past seven a.m. Not exactly dawn, but it was Saturday and not everyone had to be up so early.

I quickly padded downstairs and wrenched open the front door to investigate the commotion. Two men stood on my doorstep, cleanly shaven and dressed in suits. For a moment I thought they looked like agents for the FBI, although, I couldn't be sure as I'd only ever seen them in the movies.

"Sorry to disturb you, madam," one began. "I am DI Kenon, and this is DS Turner. May we have a word with you, please?"

He flashed an identification badge, and I instinctively tugged my robe closer across my body. Why did I do that? I was cocooned in more fabric right now than I wore all day.

"Yes... yes of course," I said, but didn't invite them in. "How can I help you?"

"As you may be aware, there was an incident last night at the allotments." DI Kenon took the lead, and his partner stood there—studying me with interest—as though I was an insect under a microscope.

"Yes, I noticed the police car at the allotments as I left my father's house last night." I frowned, remembering the hullabaloo at the allotment gate, then let out my breath, although I hadn't realised I'd been holding it. DS Turner seemed to find that interesting and flipped open his notebook. I straightened my back.

"Your name, please?" asked DS Turner curtly, and I obliged for his notes.

"And did you spot anyone suspicious in the hour or two prior to seeing the police car?" Inquired DI Kenon.

"Nothing unusual. I returned home from my business premises." Announcing I owned a business bolstered my confidence as I continued to retrace my memories of the previous evening. "I had a shower... Oh, and I saw Bert and Derek walking from the park to the allotments as usual." I released a light laugh at the memory.

"Derek?" queried DI Kenon in a serious tone. "Does he have a surname?"

"Peacock." I grinned. "Derek the Peacock. Bert has always named the current peacock in park residence Derek. That's Swansneck tradition for you!" I presented them both with a wide smile, but neither seemed to get my joke. I sighed. "Other than that, I walked to the Bake House—that's my dad's house," I added this for DS Turner's benefit, as he had become engrossed in jotting down my every word. "Then I passed Flora Laura locking up her shop."

DI Kenon looked quizzical and gave a slight shake of his head.

"Flora Laura—the florist," I enlightened him and received a slight nod in return.

"And at what time was this?"

"About 5.25," I said irritably, tiring of all this before I'd even had my morning cup of tea.

I indicated DS Turner's scribbled notes. "Isn't this a tad much for a shed break-in?"

DI Kenon ignored my comment. "At what time did you see Bert Scrogham?"

Alerted to the fact that I hadn't given him Bert's surname, I became concerned.

"Is Bert all right?" I frowned at him.

"Just answer the question please."

"Well, it must have been around five o'clock, or a few minutes later. Why? What's happened? Please tell me..."

"A body was discovered at the allotments, and we suspect foul play."

"Bert?" The blood drained from my face.

"No, madam. It was Jack Nabb. Did you know the victim?"

"No, no... I didn't," I whispered. "When you say foul play, you mean it was murder?"

"We suspect so..." DI Kenon replied.

Murder in Swansneck? Less than a hundred metres from my dad's house—and not far from my house come to think of it.

"Did you hear anything as you walked to the Bake House, perhaps shouting or an alarm?"

I shook my head.

DI Kenon seemed to register the effect his revelation had on me and reached into his pocket to hand me his card.

"Thank you for your assistance, Miss Bradshaw. Here's my number, should you recall anything, please call anytime."

DS Turner nodded at me, then turned away and headed next door for another round of questioning.

DI Kenon granted me a hint of a smile. "Have a good day," he said, pivoting to follow his partner.

Fat chance.

I closed the door and rested my back against it. Jack Nabb, dead?

And why were the police so interested in Bert?

I arrived at the pigeon lofts ready to attend to Wilf's—Dad's—my—birds, forgetting there would be men waiting to see the racing pigeons' return.

Watching the birds arriving to be time checked was always an event for the fanciers.

Nick Faris and Tim Yates were busy at the clocking device noting down return times to a background of chatter from the visitors. I had hoped Bert would be present, but he wasn't.

Before long the number of birds returning to Tim's coop dwindled. So, no longer having an excuse to linger, I busied myself with cleaning and feeding. Besides, the activity helped to distract me from my concerns about Bert.

Once I'd finished my tasks, I overheard the talk change from pigeons to Jack Nabb's murder. I gave it my attention.

"Well, it's hardly surprising," said Nick. "Over the years Jack was always sniffing around some girly. He must've slept with half the village—and it didn't matter to him who he upset in the process."

The others laughed at Nick's broad brush stroke statement.

"That's an exaggeration don't you think?" said another man. "The bloke wasn't that much of a stud."

"Well, there must be something about him that appealed to women for him to notch up so many conquests." Nick shrugged.

"Women go for bad boys, or hadn't you heard?" Tim checked the leg ring of a late arrival and entered its return time on his notes.

I was feeling invisible during this 'male locker-room' discussion. Had they forgotten I was there, or did they simply not care?

I wondered how Kim felt right now. Should I contact her? Perhaps not. We hadn't rekindled our old closeness, and it could seem like snooping if I contacted her now. It might be best to let her reach out to me.

Tim Yates packed his kit and prepared to leave.

"Are they all back, Tim?" Nick asked.

"Yeah, they did well. I'll enter the timings on my logs at home." Tim picked up his bag. "It's a busy day for me today... my girl's getting married. I'm a little nervous about the father of the bride speech—I hope I don't make a fool of myself and let Amy down."

I reminded the men of my existence. "Amy kindly invited me to the wedding, Tim, so I'll witness your public speaking skills."

Tim laughed nervously. He appeared tense and distracted.

"Aw, you'll be fine." Nick slapped him on the back. "Take a couple drinks to loosen you up beforehand, and you'll knock 'em dead."

At that, the small gathering disbanded, and I checked on Bert's pigeons before leaving. If he wasn't here for the training race, I guessed he wouldn't arrive until later... or not at all today. Whether it was because of his health or—err— other allotment associated reasons, I owed it to him to give his feathered companions food and water. I rotated the latch on the door to access the trays.

Restocked with rations, the birds cooed and pecked away at the seeds, reminding me I hadn't eaten breakfast. The police visit had shaken me and I'd only had a cup of tea before leaving for the loft. I stooped to secure the lower latch on Bert's coop. I didn't want to be responsible for the local cats having a pigeon fest.

While tidying up, I planned the rest of my morning. I would stop at home to wash, then take a stroll in the park to clear my head. A visit to the Tearooms would enable me to grab a light snack that would sustain me until the wedding reception.

It was at that moment I spotted another stone-like

crumpled lump of paper on the ground. I picked it up and carefully unravelled it.

THIS IS THE START—NOT THE END

How odd. Talk about cryptic messages! What on earth did that mean? The starting point of a race... not the end? This messaging lark must be fun for the pigeon fanciers for them to keep send so many. Did they relay coded script among the lofts to keep their hand in should World War Three break out? If Britain's staunch brigade of homing pigeons be conscripted to carry encrypted messages for spies? Was that the reason our queen had her own prize winning pigeon loft?

Suddenly I visualised a line of pigeons—each wearing a military cap—and preparing for take-off with a coded message strapped around their skinny legs. I grinned at my notion of using homing pigeons to win a war in these days of nuclear missiles.

My imagination was in ludicrous overdrive. I needed to eat.

CHAPTER NINE

After stopping at home to freshen up, I crossed Park Road to reach the footbridge that led over the river. The footbridge was mid-way along Park Road, allowing the villagers to access the park, instead of using the elaborate park gates in front of Swan Manor.

I had a notion the arched footbridge had been constructed for two reasons. Firstly, it prevented the need to trail to the top of Park Road, then cross the road bridge to reach the park gate—an obvious time saver. But I considered there to be a second possibility. That the footbridge was to discourage mill workers from walking in front of—or rather, standing to gawk at—Swan Manor. That might have ignited envy in the workers, and Cornelius Swan wouldn't have approved of such sinful thoughts.

That's why he had a lengthy list of Village Rules. One of those rules prohibited more than eight villagers from forming a gathering. So I guess he feared regular exposure to Swan Manor's grandeur could have made civil unrest a distinct possibility.

I strolled into the park. The palm house was still the resplendent Victorian greenhouse of my childhood, only smaller than I remembered. Ah, the altered scale of youth. I would explore it and the aviary later, because for now, I wanted the comfort of the Tearooms.

I turned along the path to my right, which led to the ornate wrought iron and glass awning that covered the Tearooms' outside seating area. Several people sat outside in the morning sunshine, locals and visitors alike. I pushed open the wrought iron and glass door.

It was prettier than I remembered. Spruced up to cater for the tourist trade, I presumed. The essential *Victorianness* enhanced for their benefit... although, that wouldn't have been hard to achieve.

Pastel shades of gingham fabric covered each table, further graced by small potted parlour palms. The hard-backed chairs I'd suffered as a child now sported comfy cushions, speckled in a riot of polka-dots. Tea, sandwiches, and cakes were served on mismatched fine china with doilies, and novelty teapots added to the charm. I wondered if Mrs. B was still the manageress of the establishment.

"Jenny!" a familiar voice called, and I turned to see Hilda and her Clan seated near the serving counter.

"Oh no." I groaned and waved. I'd hoped the Tearoom would be a haven of food and solitude. But I had no choice; the group was already re-arranging their chairs.

Nelly Worsley had shifted closer to Hilda's seat to create space, and Peggy Plumpton pulled an empty chair from another table to insert me within the group.

"Such good timing," boomed Maud Higson as I settled myself at the table. "We were just about to order another pot."

She waved to a passing waitress, and an elderly woman dressed in a black dress and frilly apron acknowledged her. At once I recognised her as Mrs. B. She must be prehistoric, but her thin, slight frame was as agile as ever.

"Will be with you in a moment, ladies," Mrs. B called back to Maud, while she deftly delivered an armful of plates to another table.

"I need to order some food," I informed Maud, and

grabbed the menu to select something. "I missed breakfast."

The Tearooms were busy and seemed understaffed. Sitting with Hilda's Clan had its advantages. They always took priority over visitors.

"Oh, you shouldn't skip breakfast, dear," reprimanded Peggy Plumpton. "It's not good for you."

Peggy had a reputation for encouraging people to eat. No matter what life tossed at you, food was her resolution. If you were happy you should eat to celebrate. If you were sad, you should eat to lift your spirits. Peggy's visits to bestow a Hot Pot upon the infirm of the village were legendary. I'd always thought she liked to cook for others since her husband died many years ago, but those less kind put her motives down to an opportunity for gossip.

I devoured a ham and pickle sandwich, declined the offer of an Eccles cake to accompany my tea, and settled into the rhythm of Clan chatter.

"So weekend meetings are now on Saturday, not Sunday?" I asked Hilda.

"Oh, unique circumstances," Maud answered before Hilda could draw breath. "We had to meet today... You must have heard about Jack Nabb?"

I nodded.

"Terrible, simply terrible," muttered Nelly Worsley. "What's happened again?"

"Oh for heaven's sake, Nelly, pay attention," chided Hilda.

"Is Nelly okay? I mean mental health wise?" I asked Hilda in a hushed voice.

"Oh yes... she's been doodle-ally since she was a girl. Don't worry, she's not got Waltzheimers, as Nelly calls it," she added with a laugh.

"Jack Nabb... Nelly," re-iterated Maud loudly, as though Nelly was deaf, not daft. "Had his head smashed in at the allotments"

It seemed Maud was not into subtlety that's for sure.

"Although... somebody from that good-for-nothing Nabb family was bound to come to a sticky end," added Maud.

Mrs. B approached our table to clear away the debris of dishes and picked up on our conversation like an expert... as though she'd been there from the beginning.

"Alley cat morals, that's what I put it down to." Mrs. B compressed her lips while she gathered the cups and saucers into neat piles to fit them all onto a small tray. Then she continued. "Dolly Nabb had Jack when she was only fifteen years old and she didn't stop there—a different father for each of her six offspring. The old vicar before Reverend Horridge said he gave up trying to show her the error of her ways. And as for her family—well, need I say more?" She finished with an all knowing nod, to which the others nodded back.

It was like being party to the deliberations at a witches' jamboree. There was an unspoken agreement to the judgement handed down.

Maud and Hilda then entered into a conversational aside using the silent lip-reading of their youth at the mill.

Over the many decades since mechanisation of the factories, female mill workers had developed lip reading skills to enable them to talk over the ear shattering noise of the looms. It seems even the Factory Rules of no talking at work failed to impede the women from spreading gossip. Hilda had tried teaching me to lip read as a child, but I lost interest. I thought it far easier to talk. But when I saw the local women lapse into silent mouthing around their children or husbands, I understood the appeal.

With my limited skill, I tried to track what Maud and Hilda were saying. I think Maud mouthed something odd like, "Dolly Nabb was the village bike," but I wasn't sure.

At that moment an elderly gentleman came into the Tearooms and sauntered toward the counter by way of our table.

He had a full head of silver hair, a slim straight build and striking features. Years of laughter etched his tanned face and a twinkle in his eye showed mischief on his mind.

When I was an immature teenager I'd been aware of him as one of the older generation, but I'd never noticed his cheeky silver fox persona.

"Ah, I've hit upon a Merry Widows get together," he announced cheerfully, approaching our table. "And who are you dissecting with your tongues today, ladies?"

"Fred Entwistle, you reprobate. Stop calling us the Merry Widows!" Hilda scolded.

From the head shaking and narrowed lips displayed at our table, the women shared their disdain of Fred. But Nelly looked at him with a doe eyed expression.

Fred just grinned; aware his teasing banter pressed their buttons. Their reaction delighted him. He then ambled over to the counter where he proceeded to press Mrs. B's buttons too.

"Nelly Higson, stop day-dreaming over that man," warned Maud. "You know his reputation."

"But..." started Nelly.

"There are no *buts* about it, Nelly," cautioned Peggy. "I live next door to him and I've witnessed what he gets up to. That inflatable hot tub he has in the back yard has seen more action than the Playboy Mansion. Many's the time I've had cause to make a complaint about the nudity."

"He's not still nude bathing in the yard is he?" asked Hilda.

"Fred terms it 'skinny dipping,' saying it's how nature intended the human body to express itself," replied Peggy.

"The man's an old age hippy-turned-playboy," tutted Maud.

"The only thing he said he'd do to spare my blushes," continued Peggy, "was to string coloured lights around his yard. He'd turn them on when 'things were not for my eyes,' he said. And I should take it as a warning not to look out of my back bedroom window to see into his yard."

"Well, I never," whispered Nelly.

I glanced at Nelly's flushed face and somehow didn't think this convinced her Fred's carrying on was such a bad thing.

I now viewed the retired generation in Swansneck in a whole new light. There was more going on than I realised.

"That's the problem when men remain bachelors all their lives," commented Maud. "They never grow up. Left to their own devices they become deviants."

Heads nodded all around me.

"And Jack Nabb is part of that list," continued Maud. "Although deviant isn't quite the right word for him." She looked up to consider. "Ne'er-do-well," she concluded with a firm nod.

"And talking of bachelors..." began Peggy. "Mrs. Wilson, who lives next door to George Lees, was telling me..."

The heads around the table moved in closer, and I joined them. This was fascinating stuff, I considered it a completion of my education.

"She said she overheard a racket going on in George Lees' back yard." Peggy stopped to add dramatic effect. "It seems Jack Nabb attempted to break into George's shed, and George had caught him red-handed."

"Nooo..." breathed Hilda. "So what happened?"

"Well, George keeps his carpentry tools in the old converted privy, you know... storage for his joinery trade work, and they are very expensive tools." Peggy pushed her spectacles back up her nose. "The two men had *words* as Mrs. Wilson put it."

"And George Lees is such a well-built young man," added Nelly wistfully. "It must be all that time he spends at the gym."

All of the other women gaped at Nelly aghast, but chose to ignore her comment.

"Mrs. Wilson fully expected George to lay Jack Nabb out flat, but apparently their loud row suddenly changed to whispers." Peggy shook her head. "Mrs. Wilson told me she couldn't hear what was being said on the other side of the yard wall. But of course, if she'd been able to see their lips—well…"

Again, the others nodded in full understanding of Peggy's unfinished statement. I presumed she meant had Mrs. Wilson been able, she would have used the lip-reading trick to get a full bite of juicy gossip.

"So what happened?" I asked. "Did George call the police? Because he had caught Jack Nabb red-handed trying to steal his tools, as you said."

Peggy shook her head. "No, that's just it. He didn't call the police and Jack Nabb boldly left George's yard and strode down the back alley."

A communal "Hmmm," emanated from the group.

I checked the time. As much as this was fascinating stuff, I needed to go home and get ready for the wedding. I pushed back my chair.

"This has been lovely," I said, not sure what was so *'lovely'* about such salacious gossip, "but I need to go."

"Oh yes," said Hilda to the group. "Our Jen has been invited to the Yates' wedding."

"That'll be nice," said Peggy. "I know Sharon Yates has been going on about how her Amy has landed a prize fish of an accountant. She's over the moon about it."

This was news to me—that the wedding was also a target for tittle-tattle.

"Really?" I said, wondering if I should be aware of any gossip before I attended the event. Or was I only being nosy? Truly, I couldn't decide.

"Bit of a one, is young Amy," said Nelly vaguely.

I waited for her to say more, but nothing was forthcoming. I decided to quit; this stuff was addictive.

"Have a nice time, dear," said Maud.

"Why don't you come to Sunday lunch tomorrow, Jen, and tell me all about the wedding." Hilda smiled.

"That sounds good," I said, knowing my waistline disagreed with me. I had to join the hotel gym in double quick time if I was to continue to fit into my clothes.

I left the Tearooms and decided to skip the idea of going into the palm house. I'd save that for another day. However, I would walk the long way home to make a feeble start on my sudden figure concerns. Every bit helps I told myself.

So I took the path that led me to the aviary, and toward the main park gates to exit onto Church Road.

The aviary had changed somewhat since I was last here. It had been updated. No longer built in wood and mesh, the four walls were now wire grilling, coated in green plastic. It gave visitors a better view of the birds and was doubtless better for them too—more natural.

The aviary still housed an array of rare breeds. Bantam roosters with exotic plumage, pheasants and pea hens, ornamental ducks, budgies, and canaries. Plus the occasional exotic plumed parrot that needed re-housing when an owner lost patience with their incessant talking.

I smiled to myself as I walked toward the gate and spotted Derek strolling on the grass verge. His tail was up and fanned out in all its glory, causing passersby to bestow flattering comments upon him, which I guessed he relished.

But as I admired Derek, a wave of guilt about Bert came over me. The police were very interested in Bert's movements on Friday evening. And stupidly I confirmed Bert was headed toward the allotments. Had I told the police they were right to suspect Bert? That Bert was involved in Jack's murder?

I shook my head to dislodge the awful thought that I'd dropped Bert in it with the police, and marched through the main gate.

Faced with Swan Manor, I turned left toward the road bridge to get back into the village. This was the first time I'd walked on this section of Church Road for many years. If I had turned right, I'd be headed toward Upper Ribbly, the small market town some three miles away. I reached the other side of the bridge and saw the bus shelter, and memories of my school days came flooding back.

The old school hall of Swansneck was shut down way before I was born. Government policy had long ago elevated the village children's educational needs to more than a lone school mistress and hand-held chalkboards.

So every morning, Kim, Greg and I had waited at that bus shelter with the other kids of the village. The school bus would ferry us into Upper Ribbly and bring us back at the end of the school day.

That was as far as our adventure went. All our escapades took place in Swansneck and the park and therefore involved Bert. I flinched at the memory. Oh, how we tormented the poor man.

During the school summer holidays, we would visit the allotments to pull up random carrots from the plots. With great care, we'd press the soil back into place so nobody would notice the missing veg. Although it was stealing, we felt justified in our mission. Then we'd run to the far end of the allotments where a low timber fence marked the border of the Donkey Sanctuary. Happily, we'd feed the retired donkeys who had come to finish their days in that field edging Swansneck. After a lifetime of carrying rowdy children and overweight holiday makers to and fro on Blackpool sands, we considered the stolen carrots well deserved.

The three of us would then climb over the fences to access the river bank. The incline and drop at this section of the river wasn't steep, and the low summer water level would reveal a row of stepping stones enabling us to cross and reach the opposite bank. That river bank marked one perimeter of the park, and, scrambling up next to the boating lake inlet, we'd push through the shrubbery and plan our mayhem for the day.

I smirked. Greg's son would need to ramp up his misbehaving if he was ever to match our output.

Turning left into the top of Park Road, my thoughts drifted to the confrontation between Jack Nabb and George Lees. What had prevented George from calling the police? The Nabb family had such a bad reputation, a Swansneck resident should have jumped on the opportunity.

Passing the short row of almshouses, I crossed the road and tried to work out why George Lees had failed to bring a Nabb family member to book. Without a doubt, the police would know the Nabbs' reputation. The Nabbs must have enemies lining up to take revenge? Surely DI Kenon couldn't think mild mannered Bert had anything to do with Jack's death?

I pushed my key into the lock. I should focus on a nice long bath and prepare for the day ahead... and stop playing at amateur detective.

Besides, from what I'd gathered from Hilda's Clan, this wedding should prove to be very interesting.

CHAPTER TEN

I made a point of arriving at the church fifteen minutes early to meet Marilyn. I didn't want to walk inside on my own and have to seek her out among the other guests in the pews.

It was a good sign that she was already waiting for me at the church gate. She knew about time-keeping—a bonus to any employer.

I waved to her among the typical milling crowd that always gathers outside a church on these occasions until the final moment the ushers will allow.

Marilyn wore a yellow silk chiffon tea dress ruffled at the hem. She'd paired this with a coquettish straw brimmed hat delicately draped with a fine black dotted veil.

"You look amazing," I gushed. I had to give her credit, the girl had taste.

"And you too, Jenny," she answered. "And hey... we've both chosen 1930s style tea dresses. Great minds, and all that!"

"That's kind of you to say, Marilyn, but I haven't come anywhere near your classic inspiration."

I considered my simple lilac cotton tea dress with its lace peter-pan collar too casual for a wedding. Although, as insurance, I'd grabbed a dramatic wide-brimmed vintage hat before I'd left the shop last night. With its multitude of shimmering pastel shades, the hat lent my outfit the pizzazz it needed for the occasion.

I wanted to explain my limited wardrobe situation to her. "I've only got a few outfits with me. There's lots of stuff in storage back in London, but I've yet to transfer it to Swansneck."

I reflected on the mountains of beautiful vintage items I'd collected over the years while browsing markets and thrift shops on my rare time off work. Even though my hording had caused a storage issue, I'd never had the heart to discard anything I'd found. I loved each unique item. And when the things I adored no longer fitted me, or rather—despite the fact that they had never fitted me in the first place—but I'd purchased them anyway, I simply boxed them up and put them into storage.

I shrugged my shoulders at the cost of storing my vintage closet, and returned my attention to the wedding.

Reminiscent of a child's drawing, the church at Swansneck was traditional in design. A steeple housed the bells, and stained glass windows depicted saints or Bible scenes. It could either impress or frighten you if you looked at old religious buildings in that way.

A neat row of flowers edged the path that led from the quaint church gate, and I drifted along behind Marilyn. The church organ struck up a faltering rendition of *Ave Maria*, and the ushers tried their best to shepherd the excited guests toward the imposing black oak doors.

We chose a mid-way pew on the Yates' family side of the church. Then, to achieve the best possible view of the bride, we selected seats nearest the central aisle. Marilyn whispered and pointed out hats from our shop within the congregation, and a strange glow of pride swelled within me.

The groom and best man walked up the aisle to take their places. I'd read the groom's name on the invitation. Mark Drinkall. What a surname to take on. Amy would have her hands full with a surname like that. The lifetime of merciless jokes headed her way crowded my brain. I knew from experience how a surname could weigh you down—I'd married a Winterbottom—only to be ridiculed for eleven years. Regaining my independence and moving back to Swansneck provided the perfect opportunity to return to my maiden name of Bradshaw and drop my Winterbottom, so to speak.

I observed Mark Drinkall as he stood before the altar. He looked like a pleasant enough chap, but slightly overweight. The perils of an accountant's desk job, I figured. He appeared quite a bit older than Amy. Not the type of man I'd picture her falling in love with, but then, who was I to criticise? I'd hardly made the right choice when I married handsome, charming Paul Winterbottom.

The organist switched to a more practiced *Wedding March,* and the mounting anticipation peaked as Amy and Tim appeared at the doorway. We all turned to watch them glide down the aisle.

Amy looked angelic with the white lace of her bridal gown silhouetted by sunlight. Indeed, Tim had referred to Amy as "my angel." How fitting that phrase seemed today.

The pair approached our pew and Amy smiled ahead to Mark waiting for her at the altar. Tim looked anxious, but he conducted the pace exactly as he should. Few men could handle such pomp and ceremony, and Tim had obviously ramped up his own stress levels to make Amy's day special for her.

I turned to Marilyn, who grinned at Amy as she passed. Marilyn then redirected her grin to me and raised her shoulders in a cute little shrug. I could see the good wishes she held for her friend's happiness was genuine. Every emotion I'd witnessed from Marilyn so far was genuine. She was quite a rare being.

The ceremony ended without incident, and the organ cranked up again to give an odd interpretation of the classic, *Congratulations.*

Then the happy couple, the bridesmaids and the congregation poured out of the church into the sunshine. A peal of wedding bells filled the air, and Marilyn thrust a box of confetti into my hands.

"Is this stuff still allowed?" I questioned.

"It's bio-degradable." She giggled. "Reverend Horridge insists on that, saves on the brushing up."

We crowded the happy couple and threw confetti in their general direction, and Amy shrieked with joy at the mayhem. The couple attempted to escape the snowy onslaught to get into the waiting antique wedding car, embellished with ribbons and bows.

"See you all at the hotel," Mark called out as he helped his bride arrange her skirt and train to squeeze into the car.

Marilyn took the empty confetti carton from me and stuffed it into the small waste bin at the church door. "To think..." she said wistfully.

My curiosity piqued. "What?"

"Oh, it's just that only four months ago Amy had cold feet about marrying Mark. But they seem so happy together, don't you think? I believe she made the right choice."

"Choice?" I echoed. "She had a choice?"

"Well, not a choice as such, but she had a crush on Vinnie Nabb."

Surprised, I forced myself to keep a level tone. "Any relation to Jack Nabb?" I asked, aware there must only be one Nabb family in the village, but wanting to delve deeper.

"Yes, Vinnie is—was—Jack's younger brother. About ten years younger I'd say, although, age has never mattered to Amy. She's always had a thing for older men. Father figure syndrome maybe? Anyway, her dad has always worshipped the ground Amy walks on; so she probably wanted to have that in a husband too."

Marilyn strolled along the church path toward the gate and I followed, trying to process what she'd told me. This must be what Nelly hinted at earlier when I mentioned the wedding. *"Amy being a bit of a one,"* as she decorously phrased it.

It was hard to know what made people tick. Who'd have thought angelic Amy had a past?

At the gate, the vicar held the wedding guests captive. One-by-one he released them through the restricted space, but not before he had made a strident request for more regular church attendance.

By the time I reached her, Marilyn was in deep conversation with the vicar.

"And how is Mrs. Horridge managing with her broken arm, Reverend?"

She obviously knew him well, because they talked amiably about the wedding service and then, more about his wife.

Marilyn was becoming another mystery to me. Her Hollywood movie siren obsession seemed to be a shell, used to disguise her true self from the world. At that, I stopped myself short. Hadn't Greg said Marilyn reminded him of me? Was I like Marilyn? Did I hide my real self from the world?

Their conversation and light chatter floated by me, but then, hearing Marilyn call my name jolted me out of my trance.

"Jenny!" she repeated. "I was just telling Reverend Horridge how you're a computer whiz and that you'd be happy to run the Swansneck Messenger while Mrs. Horridge's broken arm heals."

She fixed her appealing child-like eyes on me again, and I didn't have the heart to refuse her. Dazed, I just nodded, not registering what she was talking about... and then, I realised.

The Swansneck Messenger, the village newspaper, or—if I remembered more accurately—a few stapled pages that announced upcoming community centre events along with appeals for lost pets.

"Oh, I err..." I quickly tried to backtrack my agreement. "But Marilyn, there's so much we need to do at the shop, and I don't think I'll..."

But the vicar shrewdly brushed off my concerns before I could voice them.

"Your professional input with the paper would be most helpful, Miss..."

"Jenny Bradshaw," added Marilyn. "Her dad's the baker."

"Oh, I see," said Reverend Horridge. "So you're back in the fold, how delightful, Miss Bradshaw."

"Jenny, please..." I said limply, knowing there was no way out. These two could convince Attila the Hun to don a tutu.

"Edwina... my dear wife, will gather the items she has ready to go to print. She'll be delighted to hear a professional will be creating the paper. It's all been getting too much for her lately, and then, breaking her arm in that nasty fall, well..."

He aimed a smarmy smile at me. You had to hand it to him—he was good. I didn't stand a chance. Although I'd no idea what all this 'professional' guff referred to. What on earth had Marilyn said to him while I was ruminating over Amy?

In the time Marilyn and I had monopolised the good vicar's attention, the remaining guests had managed to squeeze behind us and sneak through the gateway. So, for helping those people escape Reverend Horridge's overtures to attend Sunday service, I deserved a drink at the wedding reception.

CHAPTER ELEVEN

Now converted into a spacious function room for the hotel, the old cotton warehouse proved the perfect setting for the reception. While I waited to go to our table, I collected a complimentary glass of wine from a passing waiter and wandered around the room.

Wherever space allowed, enlarged sepia photographs clad the walls. Stark images of mill workers in a bygone era.

The striking photographs commemorating the lives of mill workers held me mesmerised. Women dressed in long skirts and shawls working at the looms. A group of men—no doubt over-lookers and mechanics—in white shirts, baggy woollen trousers, and wide leather belts. Scores of mill workers streaming out the factory gates. The images were so touching, so vivid, I could practically hear the wooden clogs clattering across the cobbles as the crowds walked home at the end of a long shift.

The austere imagery clashed with the modern sumptuous decor, and I considered how interior designers relished the opportunity to romanticise history. But perhaps we were all guilty of that. Didn't I wear vintage clothing in the belief the cut and quality were better in those days gone by? Maybe looking back through rose coloured glasses was the safest way to view the past.

Marilyn arrived alongside me, having dutifully studied the table seating plan.

"Come on, we're over there," she said, indicating a table in the middle of the room.

At this point in the proceedings, I simply did as instructed—and went with the flow. I followed her to a large round table that seated ten, with a tall flower arrangement dominating its centre. Artfully sculpted from colourful tiger lilies and trailing ivy, I wondered if this was a Flora Laura creation.

Waitresses distributed the starters of asparagus soup and a roll, and my taste-buds recognised the delicious bread as being from Dad's bakery. It seemed Swansneck businesses were getting a boost from the hotel's presence, just as Greg had said.

As people ate, the chatter of the room subsided. This gave me an opportunity to study the bride and groom seated at the long top table, bookended by their parents, bridesmaids and best man. Anxious expressions shadowed the faces of Tim and the best man, and I suspected it was because they had yet to make their speeches. I noticed Tim sank his glass of wine with speed and then waved to a passing waiter to refill his glass.

We devoured the delicious main course of *Chicken in a piquant white wine sauce served with seasonal, locally sourced vegetables*—as the ornate menu card had pompously described it. Waiters then presented every guest with a glass of champagne in preparation for the toasts.

A tapping noise on the microphone attracted our attention for Tim's speech. He pushed back his chair and stood up with a slight wobble. A low murmur plus a few giggles travelled about the room.

"This sort of thing isn't really in my comfort zone," he began, possibly to warn his audience not to expect a stand-up comedian. Amplified by the microphone, he cleared his throat then continued. "I just wanted to say my Amy looks beautiful today, a proper angel."

At this, the room echoed with words of agreement and Amy dropped her head in embarrassment. Mark, Tim, and Sharon beamed with pride.

"And I'd like to say thank you to my wife Sharon for giving me such a beautiful gift of a daughter."

A series of sentimental "Ahh's" crept around the room, along with the odd sniff into a handkerchief.

"Amy is precious to me, and it's been hard to accept that the time has come to give her away. But Mark is a man I know I can trust with my girl." Tim nodded to Mark, who returned a serious nod of acknowledgement.

It seemed these few words were all it took among men. They get it. No need to go on.

"So if you'd all raise your glasses..." Tim picked up his champagne glass, "I'd like to make a toast. To the bride and groom, I wish you a lifetime of happiness together."

"To the bride and groom..." echoed the room.

Tim's speech impressed me. He'd resisted the temptation to go down the *Drinkall* joke route. Then it occurred to me he'd left that honour to the best man. My suspicion soon proved correct.

Once the guests finished their pudding, an extroverted young man bounced up from his chair. He delivered the sometimes funny, more often dodgy messages from cards and texts that covered every connotation the Drinkall surname could provide.

I'd had enough. There was only so much romance and wedding night humour I could handle in one day.

Deciding my escape to the bar upstairs couldn't be considered desertion of the wedding, I pushed back my chair and muttered to Marilyn something about visiting the ladies room. She nodded and blushed at yet another earthy text message being read aloud and I made my getaway.

Safe and sound upstairs, I settled onto a bar stool then ordered a white wine spritzer from the young barman. I couldn't see Kim around, although, that wasn't surprising. She must be at home and in shock about Jack.

I relaxed and noticed I wasn't alone in my escape idea. Several people from the wedding reception were also at the bar—although it was their suits and flower filled buttonholes that gave them away. I still didn't know many people in Swansneck. Having been away for so long put me on the social periphery of the village. Characteristically, the group standing near to my seat was all men. From my experience they were always the first to evade formal gatherings, preferring their own company at the bar.

It came as no surprise that the hot topic of conversation was the mystery of Jack Nabb's death. Although one man seemed to believe it was all resolved.

"They reckon it was Bert Scrogham. He caught Jack trying to break into his shed," he announced. "The lock had been jemmied. Bert is nobody's fool... he'd stand up to Jack."

Another man questioned his reasoning. "But Jack Nabb could handle an old fella like Bert... no contest."

"Ah, but I heard Jack was found lying on that pile of old rockery stones Bert collects alongside his shed. All it would have taken is for Jack to lose his balance in a tussle and fall back to crack open his head."

"So when you say '*they reckon it was Bert Scrogham*', you really mean '*you*' think it was Bert..." corrected another voice.

"Well, it's not for me to say he did or he didn't." The man replied, becoming defensive. "But the questions the police have been asking around the village make it seem like they've declared Bert their prime suspect."

"You've been watching too much telly to use words like *prime suspect*." His friend snorted. "Who do you think you are?" The gathering howled with laughter and someone requested another round of drinks from the barman.

"They've also been looking for Vinnie Nabb," said another

man. "The police were asking about him down at The Flying Shuttle. The regulars said he hasn't been in there for a few days."

"Ha, I bet the takings are down in The Flying Shuttle then!"

More chuckles rippled around the group.

"Yeah, he told the copper to check with his employers, you know, that haulage firm he works for, Maloney's Transport."

The conversation then became fractured by an uproar of voices welcoming a new member into their group. I turned to see who warranted such a greeting. It was Tim.

"Hey, great day," each said, giving him a slap on the back.

"What'll you have, Tim?" said one man, pulling out his wallet, ready to get Tim's order at the bar.

"S'whiskey," slurred Tim.

"You sure?" the man asked. "On top of all that wine, you had downstairs?"

Tim nodded and moved away from a friend who had an arm about his shoulders. Except being released from that stabilising support caused Tim to stumble and he fell against a low table. He banged his leg hard against the solid edge, but showed no sign of pain, seemingly anaesthetised.

"Whoa!" said his friends, settling him down into a chair.

"There you go, mate," said another, presenting him with the requested whiskey. "But I think it should be your last."

"I'll decide that," snapped Tim. He took a swig of the amber liquid and winced as it went down, which made me suspect he wasn't a big drinker.

His friend held up his hands. "Hey, it's your decision mate, you can do what you want."

The group then collected more chairs to join Tim around his table and their conversation was now out of my earshot.

I stared down at the smooth marble topped bar, and the words *'Bert is the prime suspect'* echoed through my head.

Was I responsible for making Bert the prime suspect? How could I have been so flippant—telling the police that I'd seen him with Derek?

I looked up again to spot Kim behind the bar dealing with a drinks order. She was the last person I'd expected to see here. I studied her as she worked, noting she seemed composed. I didn't detect the slightest shake of her hands as she deftly placed several delicate brandy glasses onto a tray and carried them through to the restaurant.

She returned and then came over to greet me.

"Have you been to the wedding?" she asked. "It looked like a lovely event."

"Yes, yes it was," I stuttered. How was I to ask how she felt after the death of her boyfriend? It wasn't an enquiry I'd ever had to make. So I just jumped in and hoped for the best. "And you? How are you, Kim, after the news...?"

"I'm doing okay." She avoided my eyes by needlessly wiping the bar top. "It's all very sad, but you know... life goes on."

"You can always talk to me if you need to..."

She received my offer with a silent nod—not a promising response. I guessed we weren't as close as we once were. Actually, there was no guessing required. We were just old acquaintances now. I decided not to pursue the subject further.

Kim fiddled with a scarf draped around her throat. This was more my territory, so I used it to break the awkward silence.

"That's a lovely silk scarf." I smiled. "You should get Marilyn to show you the pussy cat bow she styled on a mannequin. It'd suit you."

Kim's lips twisted into a vague smile. "You know Marilyn?"

"Oh, yes—you wouldn't be aware. I've bought the Hat Shop. I guess we'll have more opportunity to meet up, now that I'm working downstairs in The Arches Arcade. Perhaps we could get together for coffee at Greg's?"

This was one more shot to re-kindle our friendship, but she didn't react to my shop news or my friendly suggestion of coffee.

"Yes... we should do that sometime." Her words were evasive, and I wondered why. "Oh well, I can't stop... We're so busy tonight." At that she turned away.

"Yes... hope to catch up..." I agreed, but she'd already gone into the restaurant and out of view.

I wasn't sure what was worse, putting up with the romance fest downstairs or sitting here alone at the bar. I twiddled with the straw in my glass, delaying my decision to go home by surveying the room. Then I spotted Greg coming through the balcony doorway. How long had he been out there? Did it matter?

He saw me and walked over.

"Drinking alone I see..." he said, pulling up a bar stool to join me. "That's a bad sign." His mocking tone suggested I'd become an alcoholic in the hours since my birthday.

"Danny," Greg called to the young barman further down the bar, and pointed to our depleted glasses. "We'll have another, thanks."

Danny nodded and set to work.

"You clean up well." Greg looked me up and down with admiration then settled his eyes on my hair. "You suit your hair swept off your face, you should wear it that way more often."

"Thanks," I said, stunned by his flattery.

"I'm glad you stayed a brunette. I always liked the coppery colours that appear in your hair during the summer."

He paid Danny, and I wondered how many Greg had drunk while sitting on the balcony.

A compliment from Greg made me feel uneasy. He was my best friend; although I was beginning to sense he wanted more. I needed to be careful not to give him false signals. Relationship wise, I wasn't in the same place. Greg was far more important to me as a friend. I didn't want—or need—a romance.

"I attended the wedding today... it was very nice but too gushy for my liking." Deliberately, I pulled a funny face, part of my ploy to dampen the romantic direction his conversation may take. "I'm totally over all that 'happy ever after' stuff."

Grabbing my drink I hoped my comment made my position clear—without it being a reference to his flirting. I kept going with the distraction.

"Mark Drinkall seems a bit old for Amy, but Marilyn tells me she has a thing for older guys."

Thankfully, Greg didn't seem to notice my switch of direction.

"Yeah, she's been involved with several older men. I've seen her out on dates, you know, having a meal in restaurants."

"Really?" I wondered who Greg had been dining with to see Amy on her dates. Not that it mattered who he had dated. I was just curious. "Marilyn said Amy had a thing for Vinnie Nabb that nearly made her call off the wedding."

Greg raised his eyebrows. "I think she's got the wrong brother there. I saw Jack and Vinnie having an enormous row over Amy some months back. They were outside The Flying Shuttle."

"Really!" I squawked in surprise, moving to the edge of my seat. I *really* had to find another word to use—I was becoming repetitive. "How do you know it was about Amy?"

"That family are not very subtle in their communications. As I passed the pub, I saw Jack push Vinnie against the wall. 'You go near Amy and I'll kill you,' he said." Greg shrugged. "Anyway, being told not to see Amy didn't seem to have bothered Vinnie. He moved on to another girl. I've seen him at The Flying Shuttle with several girls in recent months."

"But don't you think it strange? I mean, Jack is dead, and he'd threatened to kill his own brother?"

Greg shook his head. "Nah, I know there was no love lost between the brothers, but those two were always threatening each other—and anyone else. It was just the way the Nabbs talked. They act hard, trying to convince people they're tough guys."

"Yes, but even so..." I drifted off. We both picked up our drinks and fell into a contemplative silence.

Did Amy have a romantic connection with Jack Nabb during her dubious dating history? But then, Jack had moved on to Kim, so why would he threaten Vinnie? Was Jack Nabb a guy who still considered past girlfriends his property? I'd heard of men like that. The possessive, jealous type. Hadn't I witnessed Jack giving Greg and Kim the evil eye as he watched their dispute over the bar bill discrepancy? Or was there history between Greg and Kim to give him cause for suspicion?

Even though I barely knew anything about him, I suspected Jack Nabb had a short fuse.

I peeked at Greg and caught him staring a little further down the bar at Kim. She was a real head turner, and still as stunning as when we were teenagers. The black fitted dress she wore tonight certainly flattered her figure, and the multicoloured silk scarf about her throat cast a luminous light on her complexion. I halted my musing over how Kim had retained her slim figure long enough to notice that she looked stressed. A man this side of the bar had demanded her attention.

"What's going on?" I nudged Greg's elbow. "Who's that?"

"That," said Greg with taut lips "is our landlord, Oliver Swan." He picked up his drink again.

"Nooo," I breathed. "Really?"

I had to stop saying that. I was beginning to bore myself.

Oliver Swan was not what I expected. I had somehow pictured a balding, tweed clad figure. Not this smooth, sophisticated man in his early thirties, leaning over the bar to face up to Kim.

They were having *words*.

Greg put down his glass, and we both remained still to tune into what was being said.

"I was totally humiliated in front of the other club members," fumed Oliver Swan. "The club president complained of being charged for several bottles of wine they hadn't ordered when they dined here last week."

Kim looked ashen. Her eyes wide with fear, she didn't reply.

"How can we expect to get repeat customers from my golf club if we become known for billing errors?" He clenched his fists on top of the bar.

Following this reprimand, Kim regained her usual self-control and squared her shoulders.

"I understand how upsetting this is, sir," she said levelly. "But as I explained to the gentleman that evening, it was an innocent error. Both Danny and I had applied their wine order to the tab. Saturday was a very busy night, sir, we were rushed off our feet..."

I could tell by his expression that Oliver Swan was not an easy man to persuade. Kim had her hands full trying to explain herself.

"How dare you embarrass me!" He cursed. "People will think this hotel is run by a complete bunch of amateurs."

"But, as I've said before, sir, we are understaffed. Two people are not enough to cover the bar and the restaurant." Kim sounded exasperated.

"Don't give me that excuse," countered Oliver Swan. "Get your act together or you'll be out of a job!"

"Yes, Mr. Swan." Kim acknowledged his threat with admirable calm. "I'll speak to Danny to double check with me before ringing up any orders he hasn't delivered personally to a table. I can guarantee it won't happen again, sir."

"That's more like it," said Oliver Swan with a gratified smile. "You've just shown how capable you are of finding a solution to the understaffing problem."

Kim nodded but remained silent.

Without further comment, Oliver Swan spun on his heel and strode into the restaurant. Kim busied herself behind the bar once again.

Greg and I looked at each other.

"So..." Greg smirked at me. "That was our landlord."

"I've never met a member of the Swan family," I said. "Hilda and Dad used to speak of the older generation of Swans. And I knew there were two great-grandchildren of old Cornie's somewhere, but I've never paid much attention."

"Yeah, well he is one of them. Can you believe that cocky little sod is only thirty years old?" Greg shook his head. "He has a brother, Simon, a few years his senior. Simon is not so bad, but Oliver seems to rule the Swan roost now since their father died. Oliver's the one who had all the ideas to reinvent the Swan dynasty. I've heard him complain his father was too lax with the family's assets. It seems Oliver is the one who pushed for the mill conversion."

It was all becoming clear now. There had to be a powerhouse of a personality behind the resent changes in Swansneck. It was the only way to generate such a rapid and momentous turnaround of fortunes for the village. But was it necessary to be such a tyrant to get something done? Maybe it was.

CHAPTER TWELVE

The next morning, I lingered in bed for a while, so didn't get to the pigeon lofts as early as usual. My slovenly behaviour was not only due to a slight hangover from yesterday's indulgence, but another reason. I was beginning to resent the commitment the birds demanded. I should be using my valuable time to unpack the moving boxes and focus on the future of the business. Not to mention the Swansneck Messenger matter Marilyn had roped me into. I should have a word with Hilda later today, to see if she had any suggestions for off-loading Wilf's birds. Dad wouldn't object to the idea, I felt sure.

Strolling over to the lofts at the old bathhouse, I turned the corner and came upon Tim tending his birds. He looked as bad as I felt. It seemed neither of us was a seasoned drinker.

"Hey, Tim, thanks for inviting me to the wedding... such an amazing day."

"Yes, wasn't it?" Distracted, he continued to check a birds' wing.

"Are they okay?" I tilted my head toward his loft. "After the training event, I mean? Did they all return?"

"Oh yes, they did well." He entered his loft to put the bird back in its coop. While locking the door he turned to smile at me. "Yes, the wedding went without a hitch, didn't it?" He spoke with uncharacteristic vitality.

"You didn't expect it to?"

He guffawed. "Well, with the week I've had—I couldn't predict anything going without a hitch. Between the hectic organisation and rehearsals for the big day, then, just when I had an important business meeting on Friday I got stuck in traffic on the M6. A tanker had spilled its load causing miles of tailbacks. Eventually, they cleared one lane, and we crawled past the sludge to go on our way."

"Oh no..." I consoled, as you do when someone relates their boring tales of woe.

"Then, while trapped in that traffic jam, my client called to rant about my being late and then threatened to cancel if I didn't get there soon. I told him traffic jams are beyond my control, so he relented and pushed the appointment back to later in the afternoon. But he wasn't at all happy about it."

"So those extra drinks yesterday were for stress release?" I grinned to show understanding.

"I'll say." Tim winced. "Was it that obvious?"

"Let's say the father of the bride has every excuse and we'll leave it at that."

"And then, on top of the traffic jam, when I got home, I was removing my laptop and samples from my car." He shook his head. "You know—due to the recent thefts—and my damn car alarm went off and I couldn't shut it down!" He laughed at his own misfortune. "So, yes, all in all, I had the week from hell."

Chatty Tim was a surprise. A different person from the man I'd met days earlier.

"Well, after all of that, you had good reason to switch off at the wedding."

He cracked a relieved smile. "I appreciate your support, Jenny... Oh, and Sharon mentioned the office furniture you need. I'll check the stocks for you when I go to work tomorrow."

"That'd be great, thanks." Turning, I could see that Bert's

pigeons hadn't been fed today. I became concerned, for both them and him. "Any sign of Bert recently?"

Tim shook his head. "I've not seen him, and from what I've heard, it's not surprising."

I nodded. "I'll put food and water in for his birds then."

"Sorry I can't stay to help. Relatives travelled quite a way for the wedding, and I need to say goodbye."

I dismissed his concern. "Oh, don't you worry, I can do it. You say farewell to your guests."

"Thanks, Jen," he called over his shoulder as he hobbled around the corner of the bathhouse.

I finished up and checked the time. Another of my bed prone ponderings this morning had resulted in a decision. I should join the gym. The vast changes in my diet were now clear as the many dresses I tried on yesterday for the wedding no longer fitted me. It was imperative I nipped this waistline expansion in the bud. I could join the gym today and get a few miles done on the treadmill before I attended Sunday lunch with Dad and Hilda. Although called Sunday Lunch, it was generally eaten around three to four o'clock— due to people's habit of eating a full English breakfast on a Sunday morning. Why a tradition to over-eat on a Sunday had evolved was beyond me. But, now back in Swansneck, I resolved not to fall into bad habits. I had to keep an eye out for the slippery slope.

And joining the gym would be a start.

I returned home with a partial power-walk to my stride, washed up, and dug out my gym bag. After pulling on Lycra leggings, I viewed my reflection. My heart sank. A firm roll of overindulgence overflowed the broad waistband and there was no way my usual matching top could disguise the fact. So I donned a loose cotton shirt to hide the mound and prayed it wouldn't embarrass me during these early days of working out.

I headed along Queen Victoria Road and neared the

village green that backed onto The Flying Shuttle beer garden. On such a clear sunny day, parents relaxed with a cooling drink on the benches while their children ran around on the grass.

Passing the village green I considered I must be mad to enclose myself in a gym on a beautiful day like today. But unless I pounded away on the treadmill, I wouldn't make the progress needed. The alternative of strolling in the park and being tempted by the Tearooms just wouldn't cut it.

Inside the hotel, I crossed the lobby to reach the logo emblazoned doors that marked the gym and spa entrance. Approaching the small reception desk a young duo dressed in sporty uniforms greeted me with brilliant white smiles.

I instantly felt unfit and un-pampered. I would have to up my game.

The young lady guided me through the forms about my health history, and more importantly for them, my bank account details for the monthly payments. Then, the young male instructor led me into the facilities and introduced me to the gym.

Exasperated by his lengthy scripted spiel, I assured him I knew how the equipment worked. And yes, I would complete an introductory session on another occasion. But for today, please could I get on with the exercise? He agreed, and I found a treadmill that pointed toward the rest of the gym, so nobody could observe my rear while I jogged.

After only fifteen minutes, I was out of breath—so reduced the speed to a steady walk. This also gave me the opportunity to sneak a look at the other members.

Amongst the mix of ages, gender and physiques were a few girls dressed in the mandatory crop tops and shorts I'd seen in adverts. These girls hadn't yet reached full gym-bunny status, such as those in my London gym, but they were on the right track.

The strength training section had the obligatory range of

muscle-bound men. But they weren't all young studs. Weight training knew no bounds, no matter where you travelled in the country. My attention fixed on a twosome spotting a companion with a heavy barbell. He inclined himself on the training bench to prepare for another lift, and beads of sweat trickled down his forehead.

"Here you go, George," said one, as they hefted the barbell over him. "Nice and steady now."

George gripped the bar and pumped the iron. More sweat expelled itself from his body.

"That'll squeeze the beer out of your pores," laughed one of his comrades as they took away George's instrument of torture.

"What do you mean—you cheeky sod," warned George, getting to his feet. "I only have a couple when I finish work and then I go home. The Flying Shuttle wouldn't shut down if I stopped buying my two pints each evening that's for sure. Not like some I can mention."

I wondered if this was George Lees, the man Peggy had referred to at the Tearooms. My deduction was further confirmed when I remembered Nelly day-dreaming over his muscles. He was certainly well built.

As I marched on, I watched the trio move on to more equipment.

George wasn't a young man. I'd put him in his early fifties. I tried to visualise his confrontation with Jack Nabb in his yard. Even if George hadn't called the police why hadn't he thrown a well-deserved punch at Jack?

It didn't add up.

I hit the stop button on the treadmill, deciding I shouldn't over-exert myself on the first day. Well, that was my excuse. In all honesty, I wanted to consider this George Lees conundrum without bouncing my brain up and down in the process.

I ventured into the well-appointed locker rooms, had a

luxurious shower, and left for Sunday lunch at the Bake House.

Strolling along Mill Road, I turned into Cornelius Road and floundered over the notion that Bert could be a killer. In all my years of knowing him, Bert had always shown himself as a gentle soul. Although, one man at the bar last night said Bert was nobody's fool. So was he a different person in the company of men?

Still, pinning a violent act on Bert just didn't work for me. However, George Lees was a different kettle of fish. He looked like a man who wouldn't have a problem becoming aggressive if needed. Had the police heard of George's backyard confrontation with Jack Nabb. Had that juicy bit of village gossip reached DI Kenon's ears, I wondered?

When I entered the Bake House kitchen, the smell of the traditional Sunday roast was divine.

Busy at the oven, Hilda extracted a joint of beef and gave the roast potatoes a final basting. She'd also made Yorkshire puddings, and my favourite vegetables, honey glazed parsnips, and carrots.

This was not diet friendly, but hey, I could always run it off at the gym.

Dad sat and continued to read his paper while the radio chattered away in the background. The chirpy presenter interspersed his inane chat with songs dating back to the 1950s and 60s.

As I stood in the doorway to appraise the scene, Fat Cat meandered over and curled his body and tail around my legs in welcome. Cosy and mellow, it was as though I'd travelled back in a time machine. To an era when it had been four of us seated for Sunday lunch, not three.

Hilda strained and dished up the carrots. "It'll be ready soon, Jen, sit down"

I eased myself away from Fat Cat's affections and he returned to his usual station on the back door mat.

Before I sat at the table, I cautioned Hilda against her generous portions and explained about my limited wardrobe choices. She relented by removing two roast potatoes from my plate and gave me only one Yorkshire pudding—which I considered a small victory.

While we ate, I described Amy's wedding and the reception, remembering to pass on the favourable reviews Dad's bread rolls had received. Dad seemed gratified I'd bothered to mention it, and once we'd finished our meal, he announced he was going to the pub for a game of darts. I recognised this as his old routine. He usually only went to The Flying Shuttle for an hour or so before returning home for an early night. His habits were as regular as clockwork over the years. There were never any surprises from Dad in that department.

I helped Hilda with the dishes and decided it was an ideal opportunity to speak to her about George Lees.

"I don't believe Bert could harm a fly," I began, "and the police don't know half the scandal that goes on in the village."

"You should consider that to be a good thing, Jen," she cautioned me while drying her hands.

"But what Peggy disclosed in the Tearooms yesterday..." I said, ignoring her caustic comment. "About the argument George had with Jack Nabb. Don't you think it strange he didn't report Jack to the police? Isn't it more likely that George had something to do with the murder and not Bert?"

Hilda made us both a cup of tea and we sat at the table. Fat Cat meandered over and lay across my feet, effectively trapping me with his heavy ginger fur belly.

"Sometimes, there are things best left alone, Jen." Hilda tightened her lips. She only did that when she didn't want to be pushed any further on a subject. But this time, I felt justified to push.

"But why wouldn't George give Jack a thump for daring to rob his expensive joinery equipment? I've been to the gym today, and I saw George for myself. He doesn't look like he'd hesitate in putting a member of the Nabb family in their place."

Hilda blinked at me for a moment then let out a deep sigh. "George Lees isn't that kind of man. He's not as tough as you may think."

"What do you mean by that?" Why was she being so mysterious? She must know I wasn't about to let this drop.

"Because George likes to dress up in women's clothes," she said softly.

I gasped. "You are kidding me, right?" All those muscles stuffed into a dress proved way too much for my brain to compute. "And how do you know this exactly?"

"A few of us have seen him washing dresses at the launderette. He tries to disguise them amongst his normal wash loads."

"Us?" I asked with wide eyes. "You said *a few of us.*"

"Maud, Peggy and myself. We didn't mention it to Nelly in case she got mixed up and said something."

"Never mind Nelly, you should be more concerned about Peggy blabbing it around the village."

"No, she wouldn't do that. We think the poor boy just misses his mum, that's all. Josie Lees was a lovely lady. She and George were very close; we believe that's why George never married."

"But the cross-dressing... How can you be so sure?"

"Why else would he be washing his mother's clothes five years after her passing? Josie was a well-built woman. George could fit into them easily."

Hilda's logic dumbfounded me, but I understood her point. If it were any other son, the clothes would have been donated to charity by now. And why would they need washing if they hadn't been worn?

I raised my eyebrows. "Does he know you're all aware of his propensity for women's clothing?"

"Oh no!" She looked shocked at the suggestion. "We wouldn't embarrass him, and we certainly wouldn't tell anyone else in the village. Some people wouldn't understand, and they'd taunt him. Oh no, no..." Fervently she shook her head.

I drained my tea cup. If ever I considered this village as boring, I only needed to remind myself of this moment.

I shuffled my feet and Fat Cat took the hint. He stretched then wandered to the cat flap and squeezed himself with great care through the restrictive gap.

Hilda stood up and took our cups to the sink.

I sighed. The thought of seeing to the pigeons again in the morning hovered over me like a cloud, I had to broach the subject.

"Would you have a word with Dad about the birds, please? Now I have the Hat Shop to deal with, I have little time... so I was thinking..."

She turned to me with her familiar open expression. Although a sharp, reprimanding tongue can often accompany her disarming grandmother persona. "Hmm?" She waited for me to continue.

"I was thinking... as Dad is short of time too, and Bert reported that Carl was useless with the birds..." I became lost on how to express my need to abandon the pigeons, so I blurted it out. "Hilda, would you allow Wilf's pigeon legacy to be passed on to someone else, please?"

I'd just announced her brother's precious birds were an inconvenience to everyone involved. I lowered my eyes and stared at the floor.

"Hmm..." she reiterated, although the tone of her hmm had altered. "Yes, I see what you mean. Leave it with me; I'll have a word with Peggy. She has a grandson, Billy, who might want to take them over."

"Oh, that's wonderful!" I jumped up and gave her an excited peck on the cheek.

It was such a relief to hear I could soon be free from the torment of pigeon muck under my fingernails!

CHAPTER THIRTEEN

Once home, I opened the mini-towers of packing boxes stacked in the front living room. If I unearthed the contents and piled them on the floor, I could then sort items onto the sideboard and consider where I should store them permanently. That would be a start.

After thirty minutes of this exercise in futility, all I had was a room more messed up than when I started. Although, from this chaos, I had extracted the laptop and power cable to take to the shop. But there still wasn't a decent desk in the office on which to use it. I groaned. This was all too much, so I abandoned the room and went upstairs to lie on the bed—the only place free of clutter.

I stared up at the ceiling and considered the strength and unity of the Swansneck villagers. As a returning member of this tight-knit community, why did I feel surprised by Hilda's refusal to disclose George Lees' cross-dressing to the police? The Clan's loyalty to their old friend's son was commendable, for sure.

Her comment that George tried his best to hide the clothing among his own washing was interesting. He evidently knew what others may think or say about him, otherwise, he wouldn't care who spotted the clothes at the launderette. But what if Hilda's Clan were not the only people aware of George's covert habit? How far might he go to keep his secret?

I sat bolt upright on the bed. Jack Nabb was a window cleaner... and not only that; I had seen his slow, nosy technique while he cleaned the windows. Had he seen the clothes hanging in George's house? Or, had he in fact witnessed George wearing them?

Yes, I told myself. That was more than likely the reason George hadn't shopped Jack Nabb to the police when he had the opportunity. This answer seemed blindingly obvious.

I scampered downstairs and flicked on the kettle. Caffeine would sharpen my thinking. Strong coffee prepared, I sat on one of the round padded stools that belonged to the Formica kitchen table set. Its yellow and black 50s retro pattern dazzling my eyes as I stared down into my mug.

I put things into the order of events.

George had caught Jack Nabb trying to steal tools from his yard. They'd had a loud argument, verified by Mrs.Whatever-her-name-was, who lived next door to George.

George threatened to call the police... and then the decibels of their conversation dropped, so Mrs.Whatever-her-name-was could no longer gather the gossip.

So, at that moment, what had the two men discussed?

Had Jack countered George's police threat by spilling his knowledge of the cross-dressing secret? Did Jack threaten to share this information at The Flying Shuttle?

Could George have lived that down? I doubt it, not judging by the strong man persona he so carefully upheld at the gym.

George couldn't risk antagonising Jack after he'd threatened to air his dirty laundry at the pub. I chuckled at my errant pun and glugged my coffee.

That would explain why Jack was free to walk away from George's yard that day.

Although, Jack was now dead.

Did that mean Jack continued to exert his power over George?

Had Jack demanded something in return for keeping his mouth shut?

I jumped up and ran into the living room and searched among the clutter on the sideboard for DI Kenon's card. Finally, I found it—it was a bit bent, but I found it.

This information was too important to keep to myself. I grabbed my phone and dialled the number.

It connected to the station call centre, and I asked for DI Kenon, but he was off duty.

"Could another detective be of help?" the officer queried.

I stressed I wanted to speak with DI Kenon only, so the officer said he'd relay the message and DI Kenon would return my call as soon as possible.

I rang off with a rising sense of dread. Could I contain my treacherous actions in the way I hoped? Hilda would go berserk if she found out I'd betrayed her confidence.

But deep in my heart, I knew it was the right thing to do. I would tell the police my suspicions about George, to save Bert.

However, Bert wouldn't be in this mess if I hadn't told the police I'd seen him on Friday evening walking to the allotments. If I'd stayed silent, the police would have conducted a far more thorough investigation without my input making Bert their main suspect.

That was it. I needed to retract my statement; then the police would consider alternative suspects and ask deeper questions around the village. Someone to whom Peggy had blabbed about the George Lees vs. Jack Nabb yard spat, would be more than happy to pass on the scandal. That way, the police would make progress in the correct direction, and I wouldn't be in the dog house with Hilda.

Perish the thought.

The shrill ring tone of my phone pierced the silence, shattering what remained of my nerves.

It was DI Kenon. Quick service.

"The station said you wanted to speak with me, Miss Bradshaw." He sounded officious.

"Yes... yes... I... err..." I took a deep breath. I'd gone too far to back out now. "I've been thinking carefully about Friday evening, just as you asked, and I err..."

"Would you like to meet? It's not a problem. Why don't you pop over to see me now?"

"At the police station?" I squeaked, the suggestion filling me with dismay. What if someone saw me enter? They might think I was snitching about something or other and I'd be ostracised by the entire village.

"No, that's not what I meant," he said lightly. "I live across the road from you, in an almshouse—the one on the end—next to the car park."

"Oh!" I sounded shocked because I was. "I, err..."

Did this make it any better than the police station?

"Don't worry." He seemed to read my hesitation. "Just walk into the car park, I have a side entrance through the shrubbery that leads to my door, nobody will notice."

"Okay," I relented. "I'll be there in five minutes."

After combing my hair so I didn't appear to have spent all day in bed, I left.

I didn't cross Park Road until I'd reached the low shrubs that bordered the small car park. This parking area served the almshouses and the residents of Park Road, me included. Although, since returning to the village I hadn't needed my car—because everywhere was within walking distance.

Each of the four single story almshouses was beautifully renovated. It was strange that in all the years I'd lived in Swansneck, I'd never been inside an almshouse. Although, I'd always had an amused fascination with the original list of Almshouse Rules posted on a board outside. The board was still there, with its paint and lettering now refreshed, probably to entertain the tourists.

Rules for living in the Swansneck Almshouses. 1855
By order of Cornelius Swan

1. Only persons of 'good moral character', who are deemed either too old or unable to labour, will be admitted.
2. Inmates must be destitute and have nowhere else to live.
3. Occupants will receive free accommodation and a weekly pension, 7/6d for a single person and 10/- for a married couple.
4. Each house is to be kept clean by, or at the expense of the occupant.
5. Any damage to any of the houses, fixtures or furniture, must be made good by the occupant, or otherwise, the cost thereof will be deducted from the weekly allowance.
6. The founder will make a periodical inspection of the Almshouses.
7. No clothes are to be hung out to dry in front of any of the houses.
8. Nor shall any inmate take in washing, or carry on trade or business of any kind.
9. None of the inmates... shall underlet the tenement assigned to him... or take any person to lodge or reside therein, without the written permission of the founder.
10. No inmate shall absent themselves from the Almshouses for a period exceeding 48 hours, without the express written consent of the founder.

I wondered if DI Kenon was a member of the enforcement committee. And if so what punishment he would administer if someone broke the rules? Like for like perhaps? Hang the resident who hangs out washing in front of the property?

My brain had now rambled into obscure territory as

always when stressed.

From the car park, I spotted the entrance to the end almshouse, obscured by shrubbery as he'd said. Stealthily, I headed for the open door.

DI Kenon stood in the doorway. He was taller than your average man on the street, most likely one of the requirements to join the police force.

He closed the door behind me and showed me into the living room. Springy underfoot, the deep pile cream carpet complemented the striped soft furnishings and light oak furniture. The room had a modern, manly appeal. It struck me as more of a sumptuous apartment than an almshouse cottage.

"Coffee?" he enquired.

I thought better of it, any more caffeine and I suspected I'd confess to the Great Train Robbery—just to get it off my chest.

"Oh, a glass of water would be fine, thanks."

I hovered around the room while he fetched the water and a coffee for himself. We then sat; me on the overstuffed sofa and him on the masculine striped armchair. The chair suited him somehow. It was lean and efficient, like him.

He was cleanly shaven, and I guessed he'd just showered due to the lingering scent of pine in the room.

"So, you wanted to speak to me about something?"

"Err... yes, I have been going over Friday evening in my mind, and I'm sure I gave you wrong information about my seeing Bert. So I'd like to retract my statement please," I said, topped off with an added innocent smile for good measure.

"Hmm, I see."

"I was mistaken. I saw Bert and Derek on Thursday evening, not Friday, as I'd said. Sorry about that. I've no doubt delayed your investigations by misdirecting you. Sorry," I repeated, trying to look forlorn. "So you can concentrate on finding the real killer now."

He studied me for a moment, then rose from his chair.

"Thank you for coming, Miss Bradshaw."

"Call me, Jenny, please. Now we're neighbours, it should be Jenny." I smiled. "How long have you lived here?" Judging by the newness of everything I guessed it wasn't long.

"I moved in a few weeks ago. There are still a few jobs to do..."

I scanned the room, which was impeccable. In my eyes, no outstanding jobs remained. I felt a pang of guilt over the mess I'd made in Wilf's. I hadn't so much moved in as detonated an explosion of feminine tat inside the place.

DI Kenon attempted to usher me toward the exit.

"So yes, sorry to have wasted your time," I prattled on as I walked. "You know how it is when you're so busy-busy-busy; events merge in your mind."

But DI Kenon shook his head at me.

I frowned. Perhaps I hadn't cleared up the matter after all.

"Oh no, your previous statement was correct," he said. "You did see him on Friday evening."

I gawped. "But how can you be so sure?"

"Because I saw him too, as he walked past the almshouses."

You could have knocked me down with a pigeon feather. All this time I'd stressed over pointing the finger of guilt at Bert.

DI Kenon continued to explain. "To me, it was only a man wearing a shabby tweed jacket with his cap pulled down, but you put a name to him. Gaining such information only saves us time, that's all. We weren't misdirected as you assumed..."

"But you were surprised when I told you about seeing Bert," I said, trying to cover my confusion.

"My surprise came from your report that Bert was accompanied by someone named Derek... until you explained that Derek was a peacock." He raised one eyebrow. "I hadn't been aware of the peacock. It was too low to the ground for me to see him, hidden by the shrubs."

Shaken, I wanted to understand why the police had Bert so keenly in their sights.

"How can you be sure Jack wasn't already dead when Bert arrived at the allotments?"

"Because other gardeners worked at their plots until 4.30 and then left for home. The body was discovered by an evening gardener, at 6.15. So the murder took place within that time frame. The only person seen headed for the allotments was Bert Scrogham. And we both saw him at approximately 5.15."

"But that doesn't necessarily mean Bert did it..." I blustered. "Jack could have already been dead when Bert got there..."

"So can you explain why Bert was at his allotment shed but didn't call the police about the dead body that was lying alongside? Jack Nabb's legs were clearly visible. Bert couldn't have failed to see him."

I swallowed—I couldn't explain that point at all.

"So that's your reasoning for his guilt?" I ventured. "That if Bert had found the body he would have been the one to call the police and not another allotment holder?"

He nodded.

"I see," I muttered. "And what has Agnes told you? I presume you've questioned his wife?"

"Of course."

He took my question as an insult, but I didn't care. I felt irritated because my plan wasn't going to plan.

"And..?" I wanted more... but would he tell me?

He sighed. "She said Bert was at home, *in bed with a bad chest* as she termed it. Agnes Scrogham seems like a genuine woman, although, a devoted wife will always be protective of her husband. She overly stressed that she remembered Bert was home on Friday evening because she'd given him his favourite cheese and onion pie for tea." He shrugged, expressing his distrust of such a wifely alibi.

My eyebrows shot up in horror when it occurred to me that I had sold Agnes the cheese and onion pie she referred to—but on Thursday—not Friday. Was Agnes covering for Bert, or was she simply confused while under questioning? This whole experience must have affected both Bert and Agnes terribly. How could they stay an integral part of the village community after such allegations?

"Inspector, I realise it's not for me to ask, but you will be discreet with your enquiries into Bert won't you? Until you discover everything, that is."

By *everything,* I meant—*until you discover Bert didn't do it and George Lees is exposed as the killer.*

"Of course." He nodded. "The 'D' in CID stands for discretion, you know that don't you?"

I tried to remember what CID stood for and came up with Criminal Investigation Department. I shot him a cautionary glance.

"Don't worry." He smirked. And at that, he showed me to the side door and back to the car park.

I made a play of locking my car doors before heading out. Trying to convince myself that I'd done the right thing in speaking to DI Kenon—although frankly—I had accomplished nothing.

My attempt to retract my statement had been a waste of time. All I had done was make myself look like an idiot who didn't know what day it was.

The only way to prove Bert's innocence was to reveal the real killer. As a 'village insider,' I had knowledge about George Lees the police didn't have. Information that may take them weeks to uncover—if they uncovered it at all.

But I had to be one hundred percent sure before I disclosed my theory to the police. I daren't risk breaking

Hilda's confidence on guesswork alone. I had to prove it. Then, and only then, could I justify involving the police. After all, murder is murder, and Hilda couldn't oppose the severity of that fact.

Then, once George Lees was behind bars, Hilda would praise me for getting a murderer out of Swansneck.

All I had to do now was prove George to be the killer.

Hmm...

CHAPTER FOURTEEN

I took immediate action. At home, I changed into jeans and t-shirt—so I didn't look too conspicuous—and tramped off to The Flying Shuttle.

George Lees drank at the pub; this I'd overheard via his comment in the gym. Although he said he only stopped there briefly after work and today was Sunday, I still thought it worth a shot.

I pushed open the heavy oak door and entered the low-ceilinged bar. It'd been many years since I'd been in this room, but by the looks of it, little had changed. The layout was still the same, with the long carved oak bar to one side of the room, plus a handful of bar stools. The room still had a long run of bench seating positioned around the walls, fronted by sturdy tables that could also double up for a game of dominoes when required.

Set high around the walls a picture rail shelf still displayed a centuries old collection of Flying Shuttles. The infamous invention of 1733 after which the pub was named.

I looked up at the dusty collection of shuttles, still holding their original weft threads. I recalled part of an essay I'd done for school homework. *The Fly Shuttle, invented by John Kay, a local man to Swansneck. It was one of the greatest innovations in the history of textile production. The speed at which the device worked was described at the time as 'unimaginable.'*

In today's fast-paced world, it seemed funny to think a small wooden bullet shaped device for speeding up loom production had caused such a fury. People rioted in the streets as they fought to protect their jobs from this early sign of mill mechanisation.

The heavy aroma of old wood and ale still hung in the air, firing memories of misspent evenings with Greg and Kim after we'd turned eighteen and could legally drink. The fleeting few months before I left them—and Swansneck—to attend University.

I was relieved the place hadn't become a restaurant thinly disguised as a pub. No, The Flying Shuttle was still very much a working man's bar—despite a prominent snack menu chalked up on a blackboard.

I decided I could live with that development as I made for the bar and ordered a bitter shandy—the final drink I'd bought when I was eighteen. This was proving to be a trip down memory lane and a murder investigation combined.

Strategically, I chose an empty table not too far from the bar. I sat on the banquet bench with my back to the wall, a key position to listen into bar conversations and scope out the whole room.

Given it was now past seven o'clock on a Sunday evening, there weren't many customers. The throng of locals and tourists I'd seen outside earlier must have drifted home.

Other than a few random couples at the tables, there was only a group of three middle-aged men standing at the bar. They drank pints of real ale and discussed the merits of different micro-breweries. Someone suggested to the pub landlord he should stock an exclusive Swansneck brew on the pumps. To which the landlord told him he'd consider it so long as they came in to drink twice as often.

From his side of the bar, the landlord seemed content to join in with the group and their chat, as business was slow.

He was a short, bulldog of a man, and I gathered he would take no nonsense from customers who might have 'one too many'. I wondered if he'd had any run-ins with the Nabb family and guessed he had. Over the years, it seemed everybody had.

My ears pricked up when I heard the conversation switch subjects.

"So what are we going to do about the darts tournament arrangements, now that Vinnie's gone AWOL?"

"Has anyone seen him of late?" queried the landlord. "He's cutting it a bit fine if he's on a long-haul run."

"Nope... although there was word that the police had asked Maloney's boss where Vinnie was on Friday... you know, the night they found Jack."

"And?" prompted another. "Did Maloney's boss say where he was at the time of the murder?"

"Yeah, Vinnie was on a run for the pigeon racing association—an overnighter, a hundred miles away. It was all confirmed, so the police have cleared him."

"So why isn't Vinnie back to organise this bloody darts tournament then, like he always does?" moaned the landlord as he polished a beer glass.

"Yeah," chorused two more.

"Ever thought Vinnie's staying away for a reason?" said the third man suggestively. "Maybe it's self-preservation..."

"Do you think?" someone said, sniffing a hint of speculation.

"Well..." continued the third. "You know what the Nabbs are like, always into something. One of them was bound to come to a sticky end."

"Vinnie seems like an all right kind of lad though, eh?" ventured one.

"Ha! Don't be fooled. He's a Nabb—end of story!" was the curt reply.

The conversation lulled, and I turned to study the group.

They had all picked up their pint of beer and were now in contemplative mode.

Suddenly one chuckled. "He'd better get back in time to write up the names for the darts league on the notice board—because your handwriting's crap, Frank."

The pub landlord sent the man a narrow-eyed glare. "I'll have you know I could have been a doctor with handwriting like that. It's the main requirement to pass the exam."

The group howled with laughter at his good-natured quip. Frank, the landlord, moved away from them with a look of contentment. He'd successfully entertained his loyal customers once more.

I sipped my cold drink and considered what they'd said about Vinnie.

So, he didn't kill his brother, and that was official. But why was he staying away from Swansneck? From what I'd heard from Greg, Vinnie wasn't the best of pals with Jack. But wouldn't he have wanted to be with his family at a time like this? The Nabbs were a close-knit gang; they must mourn Jack's loss.

It made little sense... unless, as one man at the bar had phrased it, Vinnie was staying away for self-preservation. Was Vinnie avoiding Swansneck to stay clear of George Lees? Had George killed Jack and threatened Vinnie too? It would make sense.

I picked up my drink and sauntered over to the far side of the pub, with its well-worn dart board and league notices alongside. The dates listed were of past games, so the players must await the new schedule of matches against other pubs in the region.

I read the list of surnames, neatly written in capital letters, and wondered if I might see BRADSHAW. I didn't. Dad must still be a hobby player. Since my childhood, he'd always resisted the pressure to join the team. He said he wasn't able to attend the evening trips to another pub when he had to be up so early in the morning. As an adult, I guessed such restrictions on his social life must have been tough for him, and Mum. Such was his commitment to the bakery. Nevertheless, I knew he was a respected player when anyone wanted a quick game late in an afternoon, and that he'd been in here earlier today. I hoped he'd won if he found a worthy opponent.

On my way out, I deposited my empty glass on the bar, and Frank nodded in appreciation for my kindness. It seemed being short staffed behind the bar was the norm in all the Swansneck drinking establishments.

As I walked back toward home along Cornelius Road, I had a desire to call in and see Dad before he went to bed.

I knocked on the door, and he opened it with his reading glasses propped up on his forehead. A clever trick, I'd always thought.

"Hey, Dad, just wanted to stop by and say goodnight."

His startled expression softened within a second.

"Come in, Jen." I followed him to the kitchen. "Hilda's out. She's gone to play bingo at the community centre with her Clan."

"That's nice," I said and noticed he'd been reading a book. He never liked interruptions when engrossed in a good story.

Fat Cat came over and circled my legs, somehow wrapping his long tail all the way around me like an escape artist's rope.

I wondered what I could talk about, what might be a topic of mutual interest that didn't come to an abrupt halt after two sentences. In view of my problem with George Lees, I decided Dad might know something relevant.

"I've just been to the pub, and thought I might have met you there," I said, fully aware he never stayed all evening.

"That would have been nice," he said, much to my surprise.

"Did you get a game with anyone?"

"No, there weren't any players about, but I managed a spot of practice."

"So who are your regular early evening competitors then—if you're lucky enough to catch someone after work?" I was only trying to extract information about George, but at least it kept us talking, a rare event in itself.

"Oh, you know, just the old crew..." He evaded my question, not helping me to continue the conversation. Characteristically he began to shut down again.

"Like George Lees?"

"George? No, he's not much of a player. He's more into body building than pub games."

"Don't you chat with him though?" I pushed, ever hopeful.

This was like trying to crack walnuts with a pillow.

"Not really. George pretty much keeps to himself. He comes into the pub after work every evening, but he tends to sit outside on nice days like we're having right now. He enjoys watching the dogs being walked on the green, he once told me."

I was stunned; I'd actually got Dad talking. I had to keep this going.

"So he's a dog fancier?"

"Not sure..."

I feared that was all he would say, but then he added, "His father was a Whippet breeder back in the day. I remember Wilf talking about him. He used to breed prize winning dogs."

"Really?" I said vaguely, not sure where this was headed. But I waffled on. "That's probably why he likes watching the dogs; it reminds him of his dad. I've heard he misses his mum." I could have bit off my tongue, but luckily Dad registered nothing from it. Hilda's secret was still safe.

"Yeah... George is not as hard as he looks. Got a heart has

George, under all those silly muscles."

He became quiet, and I lost him to contemplative mode again, having hit his word limit for the day.

"So I'll let you get off to bed then, Dad. Tell Hilda I called."

"Okay, Luv. You can see yourself out, can't you?" With a brief distracted smile, he settled into his book once more.

"Sure, Dad. Goodnight."

I left the Bake House and felt a pang of guilt. Both Hilda and Dad seemed to have a high regard for George Lees. It seems the man had a sensitive soul—but wasn't that exactly the type weakness Jack Nabb would exploit?

Despite the input from my family, I still regarded George as the prime suspect. I just had to prove it, but couldn't fathom how.

CHAPTER FIFTEEN

I tramped to the pigeon lofts with heavy feet. The overcast sky threatened rain at some point this morning. I didn't need this. Thank heavens for the possibility of young Billy taking the birds off my hands. With the digital distraction of modern life, few were prepared to accept the commitment, so I hoped he wouldn't balk at the prospect. The life of a pigeon fancier was not as easy as caring for a cat or a hamster at home; you had to show up at the lofts come rain or shine.

I turned the corner of the bathhouse to see Nick attending to Bert's loft.

"Hi, Nick. Have you seen Bert? Is he okay?"

"I didn't get to see Bert, but Agnes said he's not at all well," replied Nick, scooping bird seed into a tray. "Terrible chest infection, she told me."

"I'm sorry to hear that." Poor Bert.

"And the police badgering him with questions can't be helping either," added Nick. "Agnes looked stressed. She said she's feeding the birds at the park aviary, so I suggested I'd take over the pigeons—until Bert's better."

"That's kind of you, Nick. Bert will appreciate it."

I refreshed the water and feed for my birds, then checked the coop and heaved a sigh. Could a cleanout wait until another day? Despite the likelihood of stern criticism from Bert, I decided it could.

Nick finished his tasks and waved goodbye. He seemed like a decent guy although I didn't know him well. Sometimes you sense things, like a friendly, easygoing manner.

Once again I headed off toward the hotel to wash up before going to the shop, my shop. I had to adjust to being the proprietor of a shop. It felt strange, not having a boss breathing down my neck anymore, being ordered here, there and everywhere. No matter how much my boss had yelled at me over the phone, sometimes his demands were a physical impossibility. The stress suspended me from a mental trapeze every day.

Yes, being my own boss was a great relief. I just had to make a success of it now.

I pushed open the door of *my shop*. It was a haven of feminine ideals. Colour, style, and fashion oozed from its displays. I had Marilyn to thank for that. She certainly had the touch. I found her cleaning and checking a hat returned yesterday.

She brandished one of her wide smiles. "Morning!" she chimed.

"Sorry I'm late." Although I was the boss, I considered it impolite not to apologise and acknowledge my tardiness. "It should only happen till I'm free from caring for Great Uncle Wilf's pigeons." I raised my hands to show they were clean. "Pigeons and hats don't go together..."

"Natural enemies if you ask me!" Marilyn laughed. "But you needn't explain why you're late. You're the boss; you can do what you like. I'm okay dealing with things here."

"Thanks," I said, apologetic again. I had to get into this *boss* mentality soon or I'd appear woolly headed, which wasn't the real me. I was just disorientated, that's all.

Marilyn came out from behind the counter, and I had to gasp in awe.

"Oh wow! Who are you today?" It seemed a daft thing to

say, but I guessed she had some starlet or other in mind when she created her vision.

"Oh, thanks." She gave a twirl of satisfaction. "I saw an old Liz Taylor photo online, and decided on the 'Cat on a Hot Tin Roof,' look. What do you think?"

I gazed in awe from her head to her toes. She'd tucked a fitted white shirt with wing collar into a full cotton skirt. A broad belt nipped in her waist, and about her neck was a brightly coloured neckerchief. Earrings and bracelet finished the effect.

I had a flash of inspiration.

"Marilyn, how would you feel about adding to the shop collection?"

She stared at me, waiting for more. I had her hooked.

"I have lots of vintage clothing stored in London. Some items I bought purely because I loved them so much. I have to admit I purchased them with my heart, not my head. I'll never fit into most of them."

Her eyes widened. "Oh, tell me more..."

"It's ready stock," I said. "We could relaunch the shop as a vintage clothes shop and expand our reach to customers. It would enhance sales in our vintage millinery too."

Marilyn quickly surveyed the shop. "We'll need racking..." she said. "But there's space if we reorganise the layout." She looked me in the eye and grinned. "Oh Jenny, it would be fabulous."

"I'll build a website, and that, along with the social media promotion you mentioned, could lead us to customers from all over."

As I spoke my ideas aloud, I found myself building on my concept. It was like a soufflé, growing before my very eyes. I just hoped it wouldn't deflate when I took it out of the oven and presented it to the real world. But there was little financial risk involved as I already had boxes and boxes of items for our stock. Although, what then—when we had eventually sold those items?

"What would we do when we run out of the stock I have collected?" I asked her, pinching my lower lip in concern.

"We could advertise," suggested Marilyn. "Offer to buy vintage period items; I'm sure many people have something they've saved that belonged to their grandmother or their mother. A honeymoon outfit, or say, the dress they wore to their first dance."

She gave a little jive twist to illustrate her theory, and we both laughed with excitement. The idea was contagious.

Then she stopped mid-swing as something occurred to her.

"Oh... we could advertise for more stock in the Swansneck Messenger!" She shrieked. "That'd get people talking. I bet there are lots of little treasures in the wardrobes around the village."

I winced at the suggestion. "Mostly old pinafores, I'd guess."

"I think you underestimate the women of Swansneck, Jenny," Marilyn said with a meaningful gesture toward her outfit.

"But you're the exception to the rule..."

"Oh, you'd be amazed, I'm sure. Anyway, it would be a start. And you're going to be the editor of the Messenger, so you can put in as many adverts as you like. We could advertise the hats and the vintage clothes too."

"I don't think that's in the true spirit of the community paper..." I cautioned. "It's not for us to fill it with adverts to our benefit. Besides, I'm only doing it for a couple of weeks, until Mrs. Horridge recovers."

Marilyn stared down at her feet and fidgeted. "Well, it may be for a while longer than a few weeks—" she mumbled.

"What do you mean?"

"Mrs. Horridge has decided she doesn't want to continue as editor, and I said you'd take over." She looked up at me. "I'm sorry; it sort of came out like that when the vicar asked for help. I said you were looking to become part of Swansneck again, and he said he had just the thing..."

"Oh Marilyn, don't say you committed me to the paper permanently?"

"Well, I... err... I'm happy to help out. It'll be fun. And besides, the vicar said the parish fund would still pay for the printing. So we would be able to advertise for free."

She was now grasping at straws to justify her actions.

"We can't do that! What would people say if we commandeered the Messenger for our own gain and had the parish pay for it? No, there's no alternative, the business will have to pay for the printing."

Marilyn hung her head. "Sorry..." she murmured. "I didn't think."

I would have to keep an eye on Marilyn; her enthusiasm was commendable but dangerous.

"Okay," I said, not wanting to crush her spirit. "Don't worry, we'll figure that out when we come to it. Right now, I think we need two of Greg's coffees. Why don't you go along to the coffee shop and get them as take-out? Tell Greg I need to start a tab and will pay him at the end of every week. I'm sure he'll agree to that."

She smiled at me with relief. "Okay, how do you like your coffee?"

"Greg knows," I said as she sashayed out of the shop like a Hollywood starlet leaving her film set.

Going into the small office, I winced. It required serious organisation if I had any hope of running the shop... and the Swansneck Messenger efficiently.

I found a box into which I stacked all the loose paperwork that comprised the shop accounts. Then I attempted to rearrange the shelf-come-desk to make better use of the space. There, that was a start. After the coffee, I'd head home to collect my laptop.

Marilyn returned with our drinks. Having forgotten my

reprimand she eagerly chattered about the shop conversion.

"I'll get my computer," I told her, "and then we can take a look for some second-hand retail racking."

"We should ask George Lees to fit it," said Marilyn as she examined a corner space. "He's a terrific joiner, and I'm sure he'd give you a good rate, being a local."

My mouth gaped open in shock. George Lees! How could I possibly employ him when I was busy trying to pin a murder on him?

I quickly altered my cod fish expression.

"We'll see," I evaded. Now it was my turn to look down at my feet and fidget.

In that instant, the doorbell tinkled. I had literally been saved by the bell.

It was Sharon Yates, carrying a candy-striped hat box.

"Hello, I've come to return the hat." She plopped the large box onto the counter. "I had so many compliments on my hat at the wedding." She smiled at me. "Thanks for taking the time to help me with the choice, Jenny. It truly made the day for me."

A blush stained my cheeks. Having someone appreciate my input on an important personal style decision proved very satisfying—although, I wouldn't react so well to negative feedback. Best not go there. I thanked Sharon while Marilyn sought the invoice book to calculate the outstanding bill.

"Did Amy and Mark get away on honeymoon okay?" Marilyn asked. "Amy was so stressed about making the flight. She must have been exhausted dashing off to the airport like that after the wedding party..."

"Oh yes, she sent me a text, they arrived at the airport on time. They had plenty of time to relax on that long flight to Dubai."

"Oh Dubai, how exotic!" said Marilyn. "Amy is so lucky."

"Marilyn, what Amy has now is not down to luck," said Sharon.

I hovered near the office doorway, shifting small boxes of labels and such while considering where we could fit racking. My ears pricked up as I overheard Sharon giving Marilyn some life advice.

"You have to be careful about the man you choose to spend the rest of your life with," added Sharon. "I encouraged Amy to choose a stable man with a good job, and she found the ideal man in Mark."

I turned to look at her. Sharon sounded earnest, her voice was not strident or dictatorial.

"Be alert to the decision you make," she continued to Marilyn. "Passion comes and goes—but friendship and reliability are constant."

Although I wasn't part of their conversation, I considered what she said. Wise words. They lacked any prospect of excitement, but they were wise. I doubted my mother would have agreed with her. My dad was reliable, and they were good friends, but she craved passion and adventure, not stability. Was it possible that the grass was always greener on the other side of the fence? As for me, I was naïve when I fell for Paul. I mistook his passion for life as a passion that would include me. So I hadn't consciously chosen him for friendship and reliability either. It simply became a convenient living arrangement, that's all.

Sharon had a stable man in Tim, I presumed, with his steady job at an office furniture company. Was that all she wanted from life? No passion?

Sharon paid Marilyn and departed.

"I'm going home to get the computer," I said. "I'll be back after lunch, and we'll check out the shop fittings."

"Okay, no problem," Marilyn replied, although she also seemed distracted, thoughtful about Sharon's words.

I wondered what effect they may have on a twenty-two-year-old girl who hadn't been down the same roads of marriage and romance as Sharon and I. My sudden decision to marry Paul was based on fleeting passion, and I'd paid the price.

Was Sharon's insight into such an important life choice correct? Should we avoid the danger of passion at all costs?

Did it always lead to disaster?

CHAPTER SIXTEEN

Next morning, I dashed into the hotel washroom and frothed the sweet smelling soap onto my hands. Oh, the pleasure of it. I hadn't noticed I'd become a sanitization freak in the years since my childhood fondling the pigeons. But now, I'd become somewhat paranoid. I couldn't handle many more days of this. I must chase down Hilda to ask if there'd been any progress with Billy. A final hand-over day had to be on the horizon.

The mind-numbing or, depending on your point of view, soothing, music floated through the air. Having entered a toilet stall, I decided it was mind-numbing.

Hearing someone enter the ladies room, I headed to the basin once more to wash my hands, only to realise the newcomer was Kim.

She stood at the mirror, re-arranging the scarf about her neck. She hurried her movements as I approached, but in her haste, the scarf slipped through her fingers and unravelled.

Her appearance shocked me. Her throat was a mass of purple bruises.

"Kim!" I exclaimed, whirling to face her. "What on earth happened to you?"

She attempted once more to re-tie the scarf but became flustered and fretful. Tears welled up in her eyes. In exasperation, she dropped the ends of the scarf.

"Oh Jenny," she sobbed, "I can't go on like this."

She turned away from the wash basins and collapsed onto one of the padded chairs near the makeup mirrors.

"What is it?" I pleaded, never having seen her in such a state.

I reached for the complimentary tissues and pushed them into her hand. After a few more deep sobs she dabbed at her eyes and blew her nose.

"I can't keep this up," she said with a heavy sigh. "I have to tell someone, and I can't tell the police."

"What on earth is wrong, and who did this?" I edged the scarf away from the side of her neck. The bruising was awful. She'd done an amazing job of hiding it so far—there'd been no clue.

"Jack did it," she whispered, taking a deep breath, aware she'd have to tell me more after dropping a bombshell like that.

"It was Jack? But how... when?" Her disclosure was such a surprise that I asked stupid questions, pointless because he was dead—so it had to be before Friday evening. But frankly, I was just making noises while my mind caught up with my voice.

Kim sniffed into the tissue once more, and I grabbed a replacement for her. She calmed down and regained her self-control, then swivelled in her seat. I recognised her earnest expression from our youth when we had a secret to share.

"Jenny, you don't understand what I've been going through," she began, taking another steadying breath. "Jack has been... was," she corrected, "demanding things of me." She looked down and picked at her fingernails. "He threatened me..."

"To do what? Why would he hurt you like this? He was your boyfriend!"

"Early in our relationship, we were fine. But then he had

money problems—and he came up with an idea." She met my gaze. "You must believe me, Jen, he made me do it." Her eyes pleaded with me to accept her words. "I love this job."

Then I realised. "Jack made you steal from the hotel, didn't he?"

Her eyes flew open. "How do you know?"

"I didn't, not until now... but..."

"Has anyone else guessed?" Concern etched her face, and she sat forward on the chair.

"No, not that I'm aware of," I said. "But what did Jack want you to do?"

"In the beginning, he told me to take money from the till and slip it to him at the bar pretending it was his change. But I told him, as bar manager I couldn't sustain a discrepancy in the takings, it would raise questions."

"So he had another idea?"

"Yes, he suggested I add drinks to bar tabs and restaurant orders. That way I could take the surplus money from the till without the stock being reduced."

"Clever," I conceded.

"Jack would sit at the bar every night. He'd watch for groups of customers who may be oblivious to the number of drinks they'd ordered, or bottles of wine consumed with their meal. Then, he'd insist I ramp up their bill." Kim grabbed my hand and squeezed it. "I wanted no part of it, Jenny, you have to believe me. He had me trapped." She let go of my hand and sagged into the chair.

"But why didn't you go to the police if he was threatening you?"

"I begged him to end the pressure on me to steal, but you didn't know Jack. He wasn't an easy man to refuse."

"I'm certainly getting to know the man of late, I can assure you," I muttered. "Is that when he did this to you?" I pointed to her neck marks.

"Yes, he wouldn't let me stop the fraud. I told him it was

becoming too obvious and that somebody would surely catch me. I thought my time was up when Greg argued about the bill on the night of your birthday, and then Oliver Swan complained about his golf club cronies. People were becoming suspicious."

"But Jack is dead now..." I groaned. Her story was a complication to my earlier clear cut thinking about Jack's murder.

"Yes!" she said, a little too gaily for my liking. "It was such a relief to hear Jack was dead."

She looked positively elated.

I became positively worried by her elation.

"Don't you see?" she said. "Now that Jack is dead I needn't falsify the bar bills anymore! I can go back to being a good bar manager—because I am a good bar manager."

She appeared relieved to have this confession off her chest, but the weight of it now pressed heavily on mine.

"You haven't answered my question, Kim. Why didn't you tell the police how Jack had been pressuring you to steal—and that he did this to you?" I pointed to her throat.

"But that's precisely why I can't tell the police. It has to stay a secret, Jen, between you and me..." With determination, she shook her head. "If the police knew about the stealing—they'd tell Oliver Swan and I'd lose my job. I've worked long and hard to reach this position in my career. I'd never get another managerial post ever again. No!" she finished firmly. "And you must promise you'll not tell the police."

She stared at me, awaiting my reply.

What else could I do? I promised. I squirmed in my seat, but I promised.

Kim then jumped up and checked herself in the mirror. After a few judicious swipes at her mascara and an expert manoeuvre to recreate the bruise coverage of her scarf, she was ready to go again.

"I must get back... Doing a stock take this morning and restocking the bar. Then everything will be in order and ship shape once more. No more lies and deceit. It's over, thank heavens. The nightmare is over. I now have my life back."

I sat there, dumbfounded by her fast recovery and carefree smile.

She swooped down to give me a bear hug then stood before me. "Thanks, Jen. I needed a friend to offload on. You've always been a good listener."

"Of schoolboy crushes and erotic pop-star dreams maybe..." I muttered. "Not of fraud, attempted strangulation and dead boyfriends."

But she didn't catch my sarcasm, she just laughed, as though I'd made a joke.

"Oh Jen, everything's fine now. Jack can't threaten me or hurt me anymore. It's over. Relax."

At that breezy instruction, she headed out the door and left me sitting there, dazed and bewildered.

This news had blown my certain belief that George Lees had the biggest motive for wanting to see Jack Nabb dead. Now, he was not the only one who had a vested interest in silencing Jack. Kim, my oldest friend, may have killed him. I shuddered at the thought. Could she kill somebody? I suppose, given enough motivation, anyone might be driven to murder to protect something they considered worth the risk.

I went back to the wash basin and washed my hands, yet again. Did I have OCD? I dismissed the vague thought as I smothered on hand cream.

What was I to do?

I dare not go to DI Kenon with Kim's information, or relate my knowledge about George. Even if I convinced myself the disclosure of a murder suspect trumped a promise to Hilda—or an old friend—I'd look crazy. To the police, I'd be the mad woman of Swansneck who accused everyone in the village of being a killer. DI Kenon couldn't possibly take anything I said seriously, and it was imperative he believed me when I eventually uncovered the murderer and proved Bert's innocence.

Until this moment, I had been sure it was George Lees, but now?

I sat in the low chair that Kim had occupied only moments ago and realised it was solely my duty to discover the truth about Kim.

Did she kill Jack?

How could I prove that she did, or she didn't? She certainly had the motive, but did she have the opportunity? I wasn't sure. Did she have the means to kill Jack? Was she strong enough? Well, on that point, the police considered Bert capable, and he wasn't strong either. Strength must not be a decisive factor in the situation of Jack's demise, but opportunity and motive were.

As for motive, Kim was a prime suspect. Now I had to find out if she had the opportunity.

CHAPTER SEVENTEEN

I practically ran to The Arches Coffee Shop. I needed a java hit, and I needed it fast. But reaching for the door handle, I stopped. If Greg saw me flustered like this, he'd know something was wrong. What could I say to him? Kim's fraud secret was out of bounds, and therefore my fear she had murdered Jack.

I turned away. Marilyn would have to make another coffee run.

Still in shock, I stumbled into the Hat Shop. Fortunately, she was busy attending to a customer, so I said "Hello" as I passed and hid in the office.

I opened the laptop now installed on the shelf and made a mock show of being engrossed in a new accounting system. Marilyn popped her head in, and I requested the coffee. She sensed not to interrupt my feigned concentration with idle chat and left to collect the coffee. I wasn't sure how long I'd be able to keep up this subterfuge, but for now, it suited my purpose.

I needed time to think, to collect my thoughts and create a plan.

How would I prove guilt lay with George or Kim? Or even Bert, I cautioned myself. I should evaluate everything and everyone, just like a detective. I should stay unbiased in my thought processes. Blinkered thinking had led me to jump to the wrong conclusion—like my certainty it was George. Now I had Kim thrown into the mix.

Feeling more at home with a keyboard beneath my fingertips, I opened a fresh file and entered my thoughts at random:

MOTIVES:

Why did George want Jack dead?

Answer: to keep his cross-dressing secret. A strong motive.

Why did Kim want Jack dead?

Answer: to keep her fraud secret and stop further pressure to continue. A strong motive.

Why did Bert want Jack dead?

Answer: Jack attempted to steal tools from his shed. A weak motive.

Unless Jack's death was an accident—or something else was in the shed, of which I am unaware.

Why did Vinnie want Jack dead?

I discounted my earlier motive to link Vinnie with his brother's death. The "Keep your hands off Amy," warning was now only tough talk as Greg had said. Plus Vinnie had been busy dating other girls since Jack's threat.

I moved on...

ALIBIS:

Where was George at the time of Jack's death?

Answer: I don't know.

Where was Kim at the time of Jack's death?

Answer: I don't know.

Where was Vinnie at the time of Jack's death?

Answer: a hundred miles away. The police had confirmed this.

Where was Bert at the time of Jack's death?

Answer: At the allotments. Both the police and I saw him, although anxious Agnes stated otherwise.

Oh dear, it was looking obvious. Unless I found out where

George and Kim were on Friday evening, I was up the creek without a paddle.

Or rather, Bert was.

The shop doorbell warned me of Marilyn's return, and I switched files.

In a theatrical manner, Marilyn tip-toed into the office like a comedic cat burglar, placed the coffee cup on the edge of the shelf-turned-desk and crept out again. She perceived my accounting work as difficult, but that perception suited my frame of mind right now. I wasn't in the mood for casual banter or a discussion on who we should use to fit the racking ordered yesterday.

Although... Having George Lees come here might not be such a bad idea. It would give me an opportunity to find out his whereabouts on Friday evening. But I'd have to be careful how I phrased such a question. Even if he were guilty, it was unlikely he'd thrust his hands in the air and shout, "All right, you've caught me, Jenny, take me away."

Then there was Kim. I needed to check out her movements too.

I sipped the coffee while analysing my motive and alibi list and groaned. My hiding in this office wouldn't offer the missing answers demanded by the alibi list. Answers would only come from making enquiries and asking questions. But why would anyone be willing to answer my questions? I'm not the police; people have no reason to tell me anything they know.

I took another sip. This coffee was good... too good. I could become addicted to this stuff. I should switch back to tea... take a walk to the Tearooms more often. Though I'd bump into Hilda's Clan, and they'd entrap me into gossip. Even if I avoided their usual gathering times, Peggy, Nelly, Maud and Hilda often called by on their own to chat with Mrs. B.

Then it hit me—gossip. That's the reason people want to

talk. They love to gossip. But I risked being labelled a village gossip monger if I indulged in non-stop probing.

A gentle rap on the office door frame alerted me to swap files. An apologetic smile touched Marilyn's lips.

"It's the vicar," she whispered. "Reverend Horridge is here to see you."

I must have been so deep in thought I hadn't heard the tinkle of the doorbell. I resigned myself to the inevitable.

"Okay, ask him to come into the office, would you?"

I dragged another folding chair into position next to my '*desk*'. The vicar loomed into the doorway. He was a rotund man, and I doubted the plastic folding chair would hold his weight. This was tricky. I pointed for him to sit, but thankfully he declined my offer. Disaster averted. An uncontrollable giggle rose in my throat as I pictured a flattened mass of plastic shards and a floundering, flapping vicar on the floor. My crazy overactive brain had kicked in again.

Reverend Horridge held a sheaf of loose papers, which, I mused, he could lose if not kept in a folder. Why was I being so finicky? OCD rearing its head again, perhaps?

"Good morning, Miss Bradshaw," he boomed.

I considered he must have a volume dial that was stuck in pulpit mode. In the confined space of my office, it was most disconcerting. I fully expected him to damn me to hell. Not sure why he would—but he gave out that impression. That I'd sinned mightily and he knew all about it.

I swallowed.

Was it a mortal sin to suspect people of murder? Would the vicar sense my guilty consternation and condemn me on the spot?

My feet felt hot. Were my toes already dipped into Satan's flames?

"Hello," I said shakily.

He waved the papers in my direction. "Mrs. Horridge...

Edwina," he corrected with affection, "has asked me to deliver the details she's gathered for this month's Swansneck Messenger."

He gave a wide smile of uneven yellow teeth that conveyed nothing pleasant despite his intention.

"Oh, oh, yes..." I mumbled jumping up to receive the offering. A few loose tatty pages floated to the floor, and I scrambled to retrieve them. I then surveyed my overloaded '*desk*'. With nowhere to set down the sheaf of papers, I plopped them onto the empty chair before me.

"I said to Edwina on Sunday, after service..."

Did he stress his last words for my benefit as I hadn't attended? Or was that just my guilty conscience?

"I said, Edwina dear... I know it is a hard thing for you to do, but it's time to hand over the reins of the Messenger to the younger generation. And who better than a signet who has returned to Swansneck?"

He seemed to think his swan analogy warranted another yellow grimace that passed for a smile in his book, and I felt compelled to give him a smile in return. He continued.

"And not only that, but she is a member of one of the founding families of our community. Edwina, I said, your little newsletter is going into safe hands... someone who respects its history and its indispensable function within our village."

His tone altered to show he'd finished, like at the end of a sermon. The point when you instinctively know it's time to get on your knees for the next segment of worship. I resisted the impulse to drop to the floor in front of him.

"It's rather embarrassing that you think so highly of me," I began. He'd put me on a pedestal to Edwina like I was the second coming or something. What did he expect me to do? The Swansneck Messenger was six sides of A4 paper stapled together in the corner. Bundles were usually deposited around pre-arranged hot spots in the village, the post office and launderette being the main distribution centres if I remembered correctly. It was hardly the Sunday Times.

I lightened the tenor of responsibility. "Well, I guess I'm now the editor-in-chief of a major publication," I quipped, raising my right hand as an oath. "I hereby affirm my dedication to its readership and expansion thereof."

I heard the echo of my words. What was I saying? Was I mad? I had recently dropped myself into caring for Wilf's, Dad's, or were they now *my* pigeons? And now, here I was approving my takeover of the community scandal sheet. Well, not so much a scandal sheet, unless you count a change in the percussion section of the local brass band...

"Well, I can see you are a busy young lady." He cast his eyes around the still chaotic office and let them rest on the computer screen. "And I presume you will take the Messenger into the digital age. Such is the march of progress, and our part is to be one of the foot soldiers on the journey."

Did this man never give up on his analogies? The perils of many years spent writing sermons I guessed.

"So, you wouldn't frown upon change?" I enquired, as in the back of my mind lurked the certain knowledge I could speed up producing this darn thing if allowed to use suitable software. But I wouldn't want to give dear Edwina the vapours. I'd never met the woman, but I envisioned a delicate blossom of a lady in a flowing floral Edwardian dress—sniffing a handkerchief laced with smelling salts.

"Not at all," he said jovially, turning to leave the office. "Not at all."

I followed him to the shop door and opened it for him.

"Please tell Edwina thank you," I said. Not sure why I was thanking her, but it seemed the polite thing to say, under the circumstances. It wasn't Edwina's fault that Marilyn was as dizzy as a dot and landed me with yet another thing to stress over. But, hey...

"And anytime she needs a hat, she knows where to come."
A sales pitch to someone who spends her entire life
attending church services never went amiss.

"I will indeed, I will indeed," said Reverend Horridge as
he passed through the portal.

I spun around to glare at Marilyn, but she had chosen this
convenient moment to stoop behind the counter.

So I stomped back into the office and closed the partial
glass door with a thud. Taking care not to slam it so hard it
shattered the glass—thereby adding more expense to our
already stretched budget.

So... where was I before being accosted by the clergy?

Irritated, I gathered up the loose papers he'd delivered
and attempted to stuff them into an empty file. All the
papers—or should I say scribbled notes—were in varied
handwriting. I presumed people must drop their notices into
the vicarage for Edwina to compile for the next issue. A bit
of a hit and miss approach to gathering news of interest if
you ask me. All you'd end up with is a diary of upcoming
events at the community hall or missing pet notices.
Precisely what I held in my hands right now to create the
next publication.

Perhaps Marilyn had the right idea to introduce our
adverts? And not only that, wouldn't other businesses be
willing to advertise... and pay to advertise? If I produced it
with a more professional layout, the Swansneck Messenger
could expand its reach to the tourists who visited the village.
And, charging for advertising would cover the printing cost.
Profits may well go to a fund of sorts, for the church, or
community centre.

I downed the last of my now cold coffee. Marilyn had got
me into this, but she may not be the dangerous loose cannon
I'd previously thought.

In her innocence, she said editing the Messenger would
be a way to reintroduce me to the village, and she was right.

But not for the purpose she proposed. This could be the cover I needed to visit strangers and businesses and ask questions, under the guise of launching a new style Swansneck Messenger. This could work. It's no longer viewed as gossip if a journalist poses the questions. I pictured myself strolling around the village wearing a trilby with a press ticket stuck in the hat band. I chuckled. No, I'd only be gathering suitable news and information— information I specifically required to solve this crime. I wouldn't be printing anything I found out.

It was to confirm my theory about George Lees... and to find out the truth behind Kim's inferred innocence—and Bert's—of course. I'd done it again, my thoughts had failed to stay unbiased. Must try harder.

I checked the time. Buying a notepad was my first necessity, then a call inviting Hilda to meet me at the Park Tearooms after the bakery closed.

This investigation was about to hit the road.

CHAPTER EIGHTEEN

Feeling officious with a notepad and pen in my hand, I entered the Park Tearooms to see Hilda seated at her favourite table near the counter. She chatted with Mrs. B, who had already delivered a teapot to the table, along with china cups and saucers plus two Eccles cakes.

I sat down, accepting the tea and cake. I'd skipped lunch, and this current filled, buttery pastry melted in my mouth.

"Have you heard anything more from Peggy?" I asked. "About Billy taking over the pigeons?"

Despite her nod, I wanted to expand on my many reasons for abandoning her brother's legacy.

"You see... I'm the editor of the Swansneck Messenger now." I pointed to my notepad and pen. "So between that, and running the Hat Shop, plus adding vintage clothing to the range..."

Hilda lifted her hand to stop my torrent of excuses. "It's okay, Jen, I understand. Don't worry. I've spoken to Peggy, and she said the responsibility of caring for something will do Billy good." She dropped her voice. "Don't tell Peggy I said so, but between you and me, Billy is a penny short of a pound, if you know what I mean? He's slow on the uptake."

I nodded in understanding. "But caring for the birds isn't complicated. Consistency is all that's needed."

"Yes, I realise that, but Billy wants to learn how to enter

the birds into races. He's a typical teenager. Just owning the pigeons isn't exciting enough for him—he wants to have them dashing about—racing all over the place." She heaved an exasperated sigh, which condemned every speed obsessed teenager, not only Billy.

"Well, I'll show him the ropes on how to care for them. But I know nothing about becoming a member of the racing club, or clocking procedures." I finished my tea. "I could ask someone to help him in that respect." My immediate response was to ask Bert, but I dismissed it. Trouble was, I didn't want to delay off-loading the birds until Bert felt better.

I had a brain wave. "Yes, I know just the man." I smiled. "Tell Peggy to have Billy meet me at the pigeon loft on Friday after school. Say 4.30?"

Hilda agreed to pass on the message, and I grinned. An end was in sight for my pigeon fancying career.

Time to raise something more pressing. On my walk to the park, I had decided to practice my questioning technique on Hilda before letting myself loose on George Lees or the public.

I flipped open my notepad, pen at the ready. I needed to tread carefully, so she didn't guess what I was up to. Hilda was the ultimate test. If I foiled this wily old bird, I could sail through an interrogation from the Secret Service.

"I want to change the Swansneck Messenger. It needs updating, to appeal to a broader audience. Along with adding adverts, I plan to include village news or even profiles on local characters." That last I invented on the hop. Maybe I was good at this? Hilda didn't seem fazed in the least. I continued. "So, because I'm out of touch with the locals, I hoped you would bring me up to speed. A who's who, or 'who's connected to whom', with background information."

"Jenny, girl. We'd need a month of Sundays to accomplish that! It'd be quicker for me to tell you who isn't connected." She laughed.

Hmm. I chewed the inside of my cheek.

"Well... what if I ask you specific questions? Would that be easier?"

Hilda's brows knitted together. "Jenny Bradshaw, what are you up to?"

"Nothing," I said, trying to emulate Kim's breeziness from this morning's confession. "I want to understand more about the village residents, so I'll be successful in relaunching the Messenger. I don't want to fill it with knitting tips if the locals would prefer celebrity gossip..." I made a grab for the teapot and poured another cup. My hand shook ever so slightly.

Hilda looked at me with a confused expression. Confusion was good. It meant she hadn't suspected me of anything... yet.

"For example, would people want to read about Jack Nabb's murder at the allotments—or would they prefer I wrote about the history of the park?"

"And what on earth qualifies you to write about a murder?" barked Hilda. "Only the police are familiar with such matters..."

Drat, I'd made the wrong move introducing Jack Nabb into the conversation too soon. I had better revise my methodology. I should declare her reply was astute. That might be a clever journalistic approach, a way to extract information without raising suspicion.

"Well yes, that's part of my point." I strongly agreed with her. "Do we, the locals, have any information that would help the police to find the killer?"

"They're saying it was Bert..." Hilda shook her head in disbelief. "But Bert wouldn't hurt a fly, let alone kill a man."

"Yes, I couldn't agree more with you, but perhaps Bert has a secret that Jack threatened to reveal... had you considered that?" I was hinting at my thought processes here, balancing on a knife edge. Would she suspect the true motive behind my seemingly innocent questions?

"Bert! A secret? Like what? That he planned to elope with Derek!" She howled with laughter. "The only secret Bert has is a passion for our cheese and onion pies!"

She poured herself another cup of tea, still chuckling.

"So, there's nothing from Bert's past you have ever heard on the grapevine? Something Jack may have used for blackmail?"

Hilda's eagle eyes darted toward mine, trying to fathom my innocent expression. She held my gaze for a moment.

"Ah, I see," she said. "You want to discover if there's any truth to Bert being the murderer." She patted my hand maternally. "You shouldn't get involved, Jen. Yes, Bert has been a part of your life for many years, but you must leave this to the police. You can't do anything to save him."

Oh, if she only knew...

Despite the lack of facts from Hilda, our conversation had been helpful. I'd asked questions without raising her suspicion as to my purpose. That was enough for me.

"Don't worry," I told her. "They were just example questions; I'm not really getting involved in the murder." Oh, my feet were on fire now, I could feel the Devil pulling me downward.

Convinced by my act, Hilda rummaged in her handbag for her mobile phone. "I'll contact Peggy," she said, beginning to text.

I smiled. How times had changed from the Clan using lip reading at the mill.

The vacant chair beside me suddenly lurched back from the table, and Maud Higson deposited her not inconsiderable weight.

"Hoped I might catch some of you in here." She picked up the menu to fan herself. "Coo-ee Mrs. B," she trilled, eyeing her behind the counter.

Mrs. B didn't glance up from her task, but called out, "I'll be right with you, Maud."

Maud frowned at my doily topped plate with telltale flakes of buttery pastry scattered upon it. "Are the Eccles cakes fresh?"

"Yes—yes they are..." I replied.

Maud was observant, either that or a real pastry flake connoisseur. I bet she could give Hilda a run for her money in that competition.

Now that Maud had arrived, I couldn't leave straight away without appearing rude. Besides, her arrival gave me another guinea pig for interview testing.

"So how are things with you?" I smiled.

Maud dropped the menu on the table, an action that declared it useless for the job of cooling her ample bosom.

"I could do without this heat," she complained as Mrs. B approached to take her order.

"Another pot of tea for three and one of your delicious Eccles cakes if you please, Mrs. Bivins," Maud said without a hint of sarcasm.

Mrs. B jotted down her order and departed.

I noted Maud was aware she'd irritate Mrs. B with a question such as "Are the Eccles cakes fresh?" Asking that of Mrs. B would mean Maud would never receive prompt service in the Tearooms ever again.

I mused at the delicate social balance in the village. Sometimes, what people said to your face, and what they thought, could be poles apart.

"I hear you attended the Yates' wedding?" said Maud.

Hilda had now finished her lengthy task of sending a text message to Peggy, in which time she could have typed out *War and Peace*.

"Yes, it was quite the occasion," I said, "Tim and Sharon didn't skimp on any of the arrangements."

"Pure foolery if you ask me," grumbled Maud, lifting the newly arrived teapot to pour our tea. "Why waste all that money on one day, when the *'happy couple'*..." she intoned wryly, "has a lifetime of bills ahead of them. That's if the marriage lasts that long." She plonked the delicate teapot down with a thud. "Besides, most of the guests on those occasions are free-loaders."

I winced, hoping I wasn't included in that remark. But Maud had a point, and it reminded me of Sharon's effort to life-coach Marilyn.

"Sharon said Tim insisted on giving Amy her dream wedding," I countered, in a half-hearted effort to decrease Maud's pessimism about weddings and celebrations. Besides, most of my trade at the Hat Shop now depended upon such lavish gatherings. "Tim adores Amy," I added defensively. "So why shouldn't he give her a beautiful day if he can afford to?"

I sipped my tea.

Hilda said nothing.

"Besides," I continued, irritated by Maud's condemnation. "Sharon came into the Hat Shop yesterday and gave Marilyn sound advice. She said how important it is to choose the right man to spend the rest of your life with. She said you shouldn't let passion cloud your judgement. So it seems Amy made her choice of Mark Drinkall using her mother's advice. She doesn't expect to be looking for husband number two in a few years' time."

Maud made a grunting noise. "Well, Sharon would say that, wouldn't she?"

"And by that, you mean...?"

"In her youth, Sharon used to go out with many good-for-nothing men from the village. She was gaining a reputation. Until she met Tim Yates—and realised she'd found a solid chap. Married faster than you can get served in The Flying Shuttle, they were."

Hilda sniggered.

"Well, yes, that's my point. She recognised a good man, and now, it seems, with Sharon's advice, so has Amy. So why not have a beautiful wedding if you want... and can afford it?"

"A waste of hard earned money, if you ask me," Maud huffed.

I sighed. Who had the energy to change her point of view? Besides, she wasn't a lady who would alter her pre-conceived opinions, no matter how convincing the argument. I had other things to attend to.

Hilda's phone chimed to signal a text message, and she checked the screen. She must have sensed the tense atmosphere at our table because she readily relayed the message.

"Oh, Peggy has confirmed Billy will see you at the lofts on Friday. At four-thirty, as you suggested."

She gave me a knowing smile. She'd grown up with Maud and had negotiated her strong opinionated views for a lifetime.

Hilda checked the time on her phone. "Didn't you say I should alert you when it's time to leave for your meeting, Jen?" A twinkle glinted in her eye.

"Oh yes!" I grabbed the escape route she kindly provided.. "Thanks for the reminder, Hilda." I pushed back my chair. "Sorry to have to go, but business calls, you know how it is."

Maud nodded and smiled up at me.

"You have a nice day, Jenny," she said, and I sensed she had already moved on from our little disagreement.

It seemed she was so used to opposing views it was all water off a duck's back for her.

Reconciled by Maud's well-meaning parting comment, I headed for the door. Ruminating over people's spending habits in the Tearooms would get me nowhere.

CHAPTER NINETEEN

Once outside I walked down toward the aviary to exit the park via the main gate.

I neared the large bird enclosure with its wire mesh frontage then stopped. I could see Agnes inside, wearing Bert's old tweed jacket, the pockets bulging with seed. From a distance, I watched her behind the wire mesh. She meandered between the eager birds while they pecked at the seed she had strewn about the floor.

I could only imagine the stress she must be under about Bert. She was a simple soul, and her whole life revolved around 'her Bert'. If he was convicted, how on earth would she cope?

Once Agnes had fed the captive birds, she came out the side door and slowly traversed the path that led toward the palm house. The larger, free roaming birds gathered about her: swans, ducks and as expected, the peafowl. Once she had distributed all the seed from her pockets, the birds ignored her presence, and squabbled among themselves, competing for the remaining grains.

All that is, except one.

Derek.

As Agnes walked away from the squabbling crowd, Derek followed her. She wasn't giving him any food I noticed; he simply wanted to follow her. I watched and shook my head in bemusement. Derek must miss Bert so much he was following his jacket... how sad.

I decided not to stop and talk to Agnes since I couldn't offer her any hope about Bert's predicament. So I waited to see her remove the jacket and hook it within the palm house doorway where Bert always stored it. While she was pre-occupied I slipped out of the main gate and headed home.

I pondered what I'd just seen. Derek's loyalty to Bert was truly amazing to behold. Who'd have thought our feathered friends may not be bird-brained after all?

Fishing my front door key from my bag, I knew I needed a clear idea on who to approach first with my new line of questioning. Once inside, I headed to the small kitchen and made a sandwich, then pulled out one of the dazzling yellow and black padded stools stored snugly beneath the matching table.

I'd pretty much ignored Great Uncle Wilf's decor when I was a teenager. It'd never occurred to me that one day it would be mine. My initial shock at seeing this riot of 50s kitsch again had mellowed into an appreciation of its charm. It suited the tiny kitchen well.

I munched my sandwich and considered redecorating the blue kitchen colour scheme to the palest primrose on the walls. And I'd replace the tatty outdated kitchen cabinets with hygienic white units, to enhance the bright yellow table set.

This brief mental diversion came to an end as I flipped open my notepad and skimmed the scribbled distracted words I'd scrawled in the Tearooms.

Jack Nabb found dead at allotments. Police suspect Bert.

Although I fully believed in Bert's innocence, it haunted me that the police hadn't cleared him of any involvement. I needed proof of my beliefs, not just speculation. But where did I start?

"At the beginning, stupid," my mind shouted. *"Go to the*

allotments and see the scene of the crime for yourself."

With a new sense of purpose, I grabbed the pad and left for the scene of the crime.

Situated at the bottom of Park Road, the allotments were close to the bakery. I'd spent much of my childhood sitting on the large wooden eight-bar gate at the entrance. It had been a good a spot as any to hang out with Kim and Greg, plotting our mischief.

I pushed open the gate and closed the latch behind me. I knew how paranoid the gardeners were about that.

The allotments looked very much as I remembered. Wooden planks demarked planting areas, and each plot possessed a wooden shed for tool storage. Jokey signs hung from the shed rafters.

A few men and one lady were busy weeding plots and cropping sections of their harvest. I smiled and greeted them before walking down the narrow pathway toward Bert's plot and shed.

The police cordons were no longer evident. I imagined the important facts from the horrific scene had been duly gathered. Now, it was just an allotment plot again, with a shed... although it would also be a local talking point.

I studied the shed, a typical apex-roofed garden shed with a door in the centre. The base of the hasp and staple lock were damaged. This was the aforementioned attempted theft, I supposed.

The side of the shed still bordered an untidy mound of old limestone rockery stones that Bert had collected over the years. There were no gnomes balancing amid the rocks, as there had been in my day, and I wondered why Bert had got rid of them. They used to be a comical sight, some faded, others missing a hat or an arm, as though they'd seen battle.

I noticed the police had removed stones that had blood on them. I inspected the soil. If they had tried to take moulds of footprints, like they do in the TV crime thrillers, they wouldn't have had much luck. The dry weather of the last month would have made imprints from the compacted soil impossible.

The side of the shed had a window frame without glass, long ago boarded up for extra security. So whoever planned the theft must have known what tools Bert owned.

"Can I help you?"

I spun around to see the lady who'd been diligently weeding. She was short in stature and peered up at me with curiosity. Her curly salt and pepper hair and weathered face revealed a steadfast gardener who tended her plot in all seasons.

Her gardening clothes were dusty, and although she was standing, the knees of her corduroy trousers had formed a permanent dome from years of kneeling.

"Hello," I said.

"Are you from the papers? I thought we'd had all the reporters we would get..." She nodded toward my notepad.

I felt quite gratified to be regarded as a reporter at first glance. There was hope for me yet.

"Ah, no, I'm not..." I contradicted her, but then thought better of it, so rephrased myself. "I'm not from a national newspaper—it's a local paper—the Swansneck Messenger."

She burst out laughing, a real belly laugh that caused the other men to turn their heads from their labour.

I rapidly needed to clarify before I lost all credibility. "It's under new ownership. There will be a new version published, with more local news." My explanation seemed feeble. I'd have to improve on it for my next foray. People were bound to think it funny when I admitted to representing the Messenger.

"Oh, all right..." She fought to contain her laughter as she studied my solemn expression. "What do you want to know?"

That was more like it.

"Do you know what Bert—Mr. Scrogham—stores inside his shed? Anything of value?"

"Nah, Bert's only got the basics; he's always stood by the old fashioned way to tend a plot. Good hard graft and grunt work. He's not got any of those new-fangled ploughing contraptions, not like some of the young holders here." She jerked her head, in vague reference to the younger generation who greeted the twenty-first-century advances in horticulture with gusto.

I nodded, relieved she wanted to continue talking without a further prompt.

"Unless someone's into nicking vintage tools, like an old oak-handled spade and a hoe, I can't see any reason why they'd try to get in there."

She smiled up at me with an expectant look, ready and willing to tell me anything I needed to know. The influence you had by saying you were a reporter while holding a notebook and pen was truly amazing. The power was going to my head already. Only, I wasn't sure what to ask next. I made something up, so she wouldn't return to her work.

"And did anyone witness the event?"

"No, we all go home to eat at half past four. What's the point in growing all this produce if you don't go home and cook yourself a decent meal?"

"Indeed," I hedged, making a squiggle on my pad, confirming her input was important. "But did you or any other plot holders notice anything strange when you returned to the allotments... which I would presume was Saturday morning?"

My pen hovered over my pad.

"Well the police had trampled all over our produce," she tutted. "I know it was a murder scene and all that, but still, they showed no respect for our efforts. Luckily the hotel chef had been down earlier on Friday to collect what he wanted for the wedding function, or we'd have been seriously out of pocket."

She then looked toward another man who was busy creating a drill for seeding. "But Arthur there, he was most put out." She yelled across the allotments, "Weren't you, Arthur?"

"What's that?" Arthur shouted back.

"Most put out—I said you were most put out by how the police had trampled over everything."

"Oh yes..." he yelled. "Most put out. Destroyed my marrows. Pecked to unusable they were. Police had left the gate open, you see..." He bent his head once more and continued his work.

"Arthur was hopping mad about it, he was. Can grow prize marrows can Arthur, real beauties, but that darn pheasant got in and pecked them all to destruction."

"Pheasant... You mean Derek?"

She eyed me with suspicion.

"I grew up in Swansneck," I informed her. "I know the Derek tradition."

She seemed gratified by that. "Oh well then, you'll know, Bert never let Derek into the allotments, always kept him on the other side of the gate until he was ready to leave. Then he'd lead him safely back to the park before he went home to Agnes."

"I see," I said, writing as fast as I could. Having never learned shorthand, I could now appreciate the appeal for reporters. I hoped I'd be able to decipher my squiggles later.

No further questions came to mind, but I wanted her to feel she'd played an important part in my report.

"Thank you for your assistance, Mrs...?"

"Lilly Halliwell," she offered, leaning over my pad to check my writing. "With seven L's," she corrected.

I added more L's as instructed.

"You've been most helpful." I smiled.

She returned to her plot, with what I sensed was great satisfaction.

People actually wanted to help, or rather, offer their point of view on anything and everything. It must be human nature. I hoped everyone I interviewed would prove so communicative... although, I somehow doubted it.

I walked to the far end of the allotments to reach the fence of the Donkey Sanctuary. It was still there. Different donkeys obviously, but it still provided a retirement home for the worn out bearers of burden. Three of them drifted over to meet me at the fence. I apologised for not having any carrots with me but guessed they'd had a right old treat last weekend with all the spoiled produce.

I glanced over to the far fence that protected the donkeys from straying onto the river bank. It was all exactly as I remembered, even the stepping stones that always poked their heads above the water line in summer. Those stones couldn't help but become tomfoolery for naughty children. Who could resist? Now my adult brain screamed how hazardous such enticements were, but back then, we were brave—or stupid.

I preferred to think of us as brave.

Was I still brave? Or was I just stupid?

CHAPTER TWENTY

Instead of going back to the shop so late in the afternoon, I called Marilyn. Rather than ask for the rest of the afternoon off work, I showed my managerial confidence and informed her I wouldn't be returning this afternoon. Without missing a beat, she said she'd lock up and would see me in the morning.

With the shop issue resolved, I determined my next port of call should be the florists. Only a short walk from the allotments and on the opposite corner of Cornelius Road, it was the obvious follow-up to my investigation. I recalled how I'd said hello as I passed the lady locking the florist shop that evening—on my way to Dad and Hilda to confess my purchase of the Hat Shop. Which turned out to be the evening of my being sacked... but let's not go there.

Although she'd had *Flora Laura* written across her back, I wasn't sure if she was the owner. I was about to find out.

I pushed open the shop door and stepped inside, setting off a buzzer concealed beneath the rubber entrance mat. The shop was ablaze with colour and perfume, and I made a mental note to become a regular customer. How glorious it must be to arrive home to beautiful blooms.

Summoned by the buzzer, a lady—the one I had passed on Friday—appeared at a wide archway that led through to her work space.

"Hi, can I help you?" She smiled.

An attractive, trim young woman around my age, she wore a smile that emitted a sunny disposition. Perhaps from soaking up nature's beauty all day. She approached me from her work room.

I'd needed to switch tactics here. This was probably the business owner, so would draw the line at gossip. It would not be as easy as talking to Lilly Halliwell with seven L's.

"Hi... yes, I'm here to introduce myself. I'm Jenny Bradshaw, from..."

"From across the road? The bakery?"

"Well yes, that's true, I am one of those Bradshaws, but that's not exactly why I'm here." I licked my lower lip; she'd thrown me off balance. "I'm the new editor of the Swansneck Messenger."

"Oh wow," she said.

"And you are?"

"Laura... Laura Patten." She offered her hand for me to shake. "Of Flora Laura fame." At that, she twisted her torso to point out the logo on the back of her pink polo shirt and laughed at her antics. "It's good to meet you, Jenny. I didn't think the Messenger would ever creep out of its Victorian beginnings. It's a bit of a local joke. You are brave taking it on," she said with feeling.

I thanked her, appreciating the reference to my bravery, not stupidity.

"I wanted to talk to local business owners to get feedback," I said. "About the possible introduction of paid advertisements. It would enable me to revamp the paper with modern design and printing, and any profits would go back into the community. Would you be interested in taking part?"

"Oh yes—that sounds like a great idea, Jenny."

She seemed on board with the notion and I glowed with pride. Encouraging local businesses to advertise was actually a good idea. I warmed to my scheme.

"I'm also aware of the growing numbers of visitors to Swansneck. If the Messenger was more professional—with perhaps articles on village history—visitors may pick up a copy to take home. As a result, businesses would expand their advertising reach, so it's not purely village locals."

As I spoke, I increased the advertising rates in my mind. Local businesses would get a good deal, and my shop would get a super advertising opportunity too. Oh—the Hat Shop, I'd forgotten to mention it.

"You see, since my return to Swansneck a week ago, I've become a small business owner. I've taken over the Hat Shop in The Arches."

"Wow, you have been a busy bee." She grinned. "It's no wonder I've not seen you before—you're too busy taking over Swansneck! At this rate, you'll be buying out the Swan family by the end of the month!" She poked her thumb up to point toward her work room. "Do you fancy a quick cuppa? I can pop the kettle on."

We entered the back room, an organised space of steel work tables and racking that housed the essentials of her trade; secateurs, wire, cellophane and a multitude of ribbon reels.

She returned with two mugs of tea.

"Sugar?" Laura dangled a sachet she'd retained from a café visit. I declined. "No, me neither, but I keep a few of these things for customer emergencies."

She propped herself against the solid work table and regarded me. "Somehow you seem familiar... But I don't believe we've met."

"Oh, I said hello as I passed by on Friday evening. You were busy locking the shop."

"Ah yes! That's it; didn't I see you go into the Bake House?"

"Yes, that's right. How observant of you."

I made a mental note that she may have seen something at the allotments. But I had to steer this conversation with care, so I didn't raise suspicion.

"I was going to eat with my dad and Hilda. She's my grandmother."

"So you have no plans to become a baker? Along with the Bradshaw name, I'd presume you get the baker's gene."

I laughed. "Afraid not... well not according to my dad, anyway."

With good intention, she was trying to get to know me, but she was controlling this conversation, and I wasn't gaining the information I needed. I tried again.

"I heard you did the flowers for Amy and Mark's wedding last Saturday. They were very impressive, well done."

"Thanks... you attended the wedding?"

"Yes, it was a lovely event, the ceremony, and the reception. Were you not invited?"

I presumed she would be since she'd made the floral arrangements and this was a small community.

"Yes, but I rarely accept invitations to the weddings I'm commissioned. I'd spend the whole day fussing over what I should have altered, or fretting if someone pulled a flower from my painfully considered design to pop behind their ear. I'd be a nightmare of a guest!"

That I could understand. I liked Flora Laura; talking to her was easy.

"Well, I can tell you everyone admired your table centre pieces. It was a clever idea to make them tall, so they didn't block conversation with guests around the table."

"Ah, you noticed that trick, eh?" She grinned. "Not everyone does—it makes them a real pain to transport though, that's the trouble. They're tall and fragile, so I have a hell of a time getting them into my small van and travelling to a venue. Thank heavens, on this occasion Kim came up with the transport to help."

Laura turned to put her mug down on the table, so didn't spot my surprised expression.

"Kim?" I squeaked and then cleared my throat. Why I should feel so startled, I wasn't sure. After all, Swansneck was a small place. "You know Kim Renshaw?"

"Is that her surname? I only know her as Kim. Yes, she commandeered the hotel van on Friday evening to transport the tall arrangements. She was a great help, bless her."

I tilted my head. Why add 'bless her'? You wouldn't expect anyone to use such a phrase when speaking of Kim. How odd.

"Yes, she can be most helpful... at times," I hedged, and then it clicked. "Oh, so that's why I saw the hotel van parked outside the Bake House that evening. My dad was none too pleased."

Laura looked shocked, as though I was complaining, so I quickly explained.

"Oh, don't worry; it's just that he gets his flour deliveries late in the evening. So he stresses if the parking space is occupied. It isn't a problem during the day, only in the evening." At this, she visibly relaxed.

"Please pass on my apologies to him," she said. "When Kim asked if it was okay to leave the van there for a while, before going back to the hotel with the flowers, I said 'sure'. I had no idea about your father's deliveries." She shrugged. "I've never stayed in my shop past five-thirty, you see, so I've never seen your father taking his deliveries."

At this point, I wished I could flip open my notepad and make more hurried squiggles. This was vital information. I'd plainly have to keep a calm head and try to remember everything she was telling me.

"So Kim didn't take the arrangements back to the hotel straight away?"

"No, poor dear..."

Again, 'poor dear'. Were we talking about the same Kim

here? I mustn't get distracted. I must concentrate, Laura was still talking.

"Apparently Kim was on the work rota for another double shift. They work that girl like a dog, judging by what she's told me. She said she desperately wanted to nip home for a quick shower and change of clothes before her evening shift. So when she suggested leaving the van here and picking it up half an hour later, I agreed." Laura gave me a conspiratorial wink. "I offered to tell the hotel she was still here helping me with the arrangements if they should call. But in reality, I locked up and went home. I didn't think they'd check up on her, anyway. Kim worries too much about job security."

I nodded in silence. Thirty minutes was ample time for Kim to meet Jack at the allotments, kill him, then reclaim the van and return to the hotel.

I paled at the thought but had to push this conversation onward.

"Have the police been in to question you?" I ventured.

I'd informed DI Kenon that I'd seen Flora Laura, so wondered what she may have told them. Were the police aware of Kim's movements that evening and checking up on her as we speak?

"Yes, they came to see me. Oh, that detective, have you met him?" She gave me another wink. "Talk about a hunk!"

"Can't say I noticed," I said, evading distraction at this vital moment. "Did you tell him about Kim being here that afternoon?"

"Yes, of course, I said she came for the flower arrangements for the wedding reception."

"But that's all?" I didn't want to push my curiosity and make it obvious, so casually fiddled with an off cut of ribbon lying on the table.

"The police are busy enough finding a murderer. I didn't want to bog them down with tales of tyrannical bosses not giving staff time to take a shower." She gave me a knowing look. "We've all been there, haven't we? Well, I have. That's why I bought this place—to get a man off my back," she concluded, her words loaded with meaning.

I had to agree. Hadn't I put up with a tyrant of a boss too? It was no joke.

Laura was a true pal to support Kim like that.

But did she know what she was helping Kim to do?

As I placed my empty mug on the table beside Laura's, she commented it was time to tidy up and close shop.

I announced I had to leave now anyway, saying how pleased I was to meet her. I urgently wanted to escape and make notes.

In one afternoon I had discovered a multitude of jigsaw puzzle pieces. But my problem was the pieces belonged to different jigsaw puzzles. They were now all mixed up in a sack inside my brain. And as I pulled out a piece and tried to slot it into place, I had no clue which puzzle I was trying to complete.

CHAPTER TWENTY-ONE

I stepped out of the florist's somewhat dazed and confused. As I was close to the Bake House, I considered visiting Dad and Hilda but thought better of it. Hilda might guess I was up to something. So I retreated home.

While the visit was clear in my mind, this would be the best time to make notes on the facts Laura had provided. After that, with no logic at all, I decided I should unpack the rest of my possessions.

In the last day or two something had become clear. My subconscious had railed against unpacking, as the deed would mean acceptance of my return to Swansneck. But since buying the shop my anxiety and internal battle had ceased. I was staying, for a few years at least, so I would feel much better if my home was organised the way I preferred. I couldn't think when surrounded by chaos, always a matter of tension between me and Paul. But now that I lived alone, I could be as tidy as I pleased, without receiving snide comments on Obsessive Compulsive Disorder.

Having noted down Laura's information I entered the downstairs front room to survey the mess. It was a small room with one front bay window that looked onto the road. I told myself not to get bogged down with thoughts of decorating or replacing furniture at this moment—there would be plenty of time for that.

For now, I had to acknowledge the lack of storage space as the main challenge. It was a clear indictment of how much stuff we accumulate these days. When the Victorians built these homes, they were considered big enough to meet the needs of two adults, plus two or three children. But now, I'd be hard pressed to get only my belongings into here.

I tried not to panic and checked inside the cabinets and drawers of the side board. It brimmed with Great Uncle Wilf's possessions.

I sat down in the winged back chair for a moment and had a brain wave. I could transfer all Wilf's possessions in the cabinets and drawers into my packing boxes, enabling me to refill the space I'd created with my stuff.

That was the answer. Then, on another occasion, I would go through Wilf's stuff with Hilda. That way I wouldn't accidentally discard anything precious to the family archives.

I set to work, aware I was delaying my pursuit of justice. But the only way to clear up the mess in my mind was to clear up the mess in my house.

It was nearing eleven o'clock by the time I'd completed the task. To achieve this in such a short space of time, I'd refused to become curious while placing Wilf's lifetime of acquisitions into the boxes. If I'd lapsed into that, I would have been here for a month of Sundays, as Hilda phrased it.

I went upstairs, showered, and climbed into bed. The evening of methodical packing and unpacking made me aware of something playing on my mind. The nagging notion there may be more of a connection between Kim and Laura than floral arrangements.

Why had Laura not told the police that Kim had nipped home?

Her excuse of feminist solidarity and not wanting to bother the police with such matters didn't convince me. Was she truly the open, friendly person I'd judged her to be?

Laura was a newcomer to the village, not part of my childhood circle. Maybe I should make more enquiries about her?

I hoped that after a good nights' sleep I'd have a clear idea of who I should speak to next.

As I drifted into slumber, another concern crossed my mind. Was my questioning only creating more suspects, instead of eliminating them?

Full of purpose, I got up early, determined to deal with the pigeons. I also hoped to run into Nick at the lofts so I could ask him to mentor Billy and explain the wonderful world of pigeon racing. I didn't want Billy to catch my apathy about the birds. He needed to view ownership as exciting, not a tiresome commitment. So my early bird attendance at the loft was to kill two birds with one stone. I smiled wryly at that thought, although I felt guilty considering such a cliché funny.

I turned the corner of the old bathhouse, disappointed Nick was not there. Drat. I didn't know his phone number or where he lived.

Irritated by the inconvenience of Nick not being where I expected him to be, I chewed on my bottom lip and set to sorting out my birds.

Pigeon wings flapped in the next door coop when Tim arrived behind me.

"Hello," he said, gathering all he needed to set up his birds for the day.

"Hi." My voice sounded flat and hollow, failing to disguise the grumpiness that lurked within me.

"Are you okay? Do you have a problem?"

I huffed. Yes, it was churlish of me, but my irritation about Nick gnawed at me. I took a leaf from Kim's book and 'off loaded' to Tim.

"Caring for these pigeons every day is getting me down."
I sighed. "I've bought the shop, as you know, and I'm
expanding its range and there's so much I need to do. And
on top of that, I'm now editor of the Swansneck Messenger,
and I'm still not settled in my house…"

He shook his head. "And I thought I was under pressure."

"It's just that I'd hoped to catch Nick here this morning.
You see… Peggy Plumpton's grandson, Billy, has said he'll
take over my birds. I can show him the basics, but he's only
interested in ownership if he can race them. I know nothing
about racing, so I'd hoped Nick would be his mentor and
show him the ropes. It seems the lad's a 'bit slow on the
uptake' so I thought Nick might have the patience to deal
with him."

Tim raised his eyebrows and nodded. "I see your point…
but I'd be willing to do it if you like? I could explain to young
Billy what he needs to do to get the birds up to racing
standard and how we arrange the races."

"But you're so busy, Tim, with your job and travelling
around the country for meetings…" I hadn't considered him
for the task because he already seemed stressed enough.

"I've got more time on my hands now the wedding's over.
Pressure has eased right off me, so I'd be happy to mentor
Billy." His expression changed, and his grey bagged eyes
gained a tinge of sadness. "It'd give me another young
person in my life now that Amy's moved out…"

I hadn't thought about that aspect. Both Tim's and
Sharon's world had revolved around Amy, so maybe time
spent with Billy would benefit everyone involved?

"That would be fantastic. Thank you so much. But oh, I've
already agreed to meet Billy here after school on Friday,
about 4.30. You'll still be at work…"

"Oh, that's not a problem. Friday afternoon's fine by me.
Clients are never really interested in a sales pitch before the
weekend. They're not in the right mindset to give me a good

order. More focused on the prospect of golf on Saturday," he explained with a laugh.

An enormous sense of relief surged over me. This was killing three birds with one stone. I'd be free of the pigeons, Billy would gain a healthy hobby, and Tim would have someone to distract him from missing Amy.

"Although..." Tim's face twisted in thought. "Sharon and I are going away this weekend for a break—over to Belgium for a few days. I thought it'd be a nice treat for us. We need to leave Swansneck by five on Friday, to catch the ferry at Hull." He looked thoughtful then smiled as though he'd reviewed his travel schedule in his head. "Nope, it'll be fine, I can be here at four thirty, meet young Billy, and still be ready to leave home at five."

"Okay, it's a date," I said before he found any other excuse not to keep the deal.

"Terrific." He turned to his birds. "Okay my little beauties, you need more flying practice." We both laughed as he opened the coop and set them free.

I reached the shop as Marilyn was unlocking the door.

I'd washed my hands in the hotel ladies room as fast as possible, not wanting to risk bumping into Kim. Although convinced she wouldn't be at the hotel at 9 a.m., I couldn't take it for granted.

The shelves in the shop had now been re-stocked with all the returned hats. The earlier bald heads of the display dummies now sported a good cross section of styles that would appeal to all tastes. From dramatic wide-brimmed picture hats to cloches, pill boxes, and subtle feathered fascinators. I delighted in the knowledge this hat stock would combine well with vintage clothing. The two would meld beautifully.

Marilyn slipped off an embroidered bolero jacket to

reveal another of her creative outfits. She was wearing tight cropped pants and a fitted cotton shirt tied at her waist.

I considered the vision for a moment. "Gina Lollobrigida on her day off from filming?" I suggested with a raised eyebrow.

"Ooh, I'll take that! You're really good at this game!"

"Ah, you say that now, but wait until I tell you one day that your outfit resembles Nellie the Elephant!"

She shook her head with mock concern. "Jenny, if I ever fashion myself after a cartoon, you have my permission to shoot me!"

We both laughed. She would be a fun work mate.

We'd no sooner opened the shop when the phone rang. Marilyn answered the call while I went into the office. I planned to sort out the scraps of Messenger notes, to see if there was even a hint of anything decent to use in my revamped first edition. It would also give me an excuse to question more people.

I groaned as I split the notes into four piles.

Church and charity events.

Village social and community centre notices.

Lost and Found.

Food recipes and knitting patterns.

Oh wow, this was hot stuff! How would I generate interest from advertisers if this was the level of the news content? I'd have to come up with something more exciting. The Messenger still had to incorporate these important notices for the locals, but not as its primary focus.

Disappointed, I clipped each stack together, and the bold handwriting style of the darts tournament notice for The Flying Shuttle caught my eye. It seemed familiar. Then I remembered, it was the same capital letter printing as the paper scraps I'd found on the ground at the pigeon lofts.

I compressed my lips in thought. I didn't have those cryptic messages with me—they were at home in my jacket pocket. But I felt sure they were written by the same hand. And if I was correct, I now knew Vinnie had written the notes I'd found at the pigeon loft.

Not sure what this might prove, I folded the pub notice and pushed it into my pocket. I'd never seen Vinnie near the lofts, but I must pursue every path to be a thorough detective.

I considered morning time might be best to visit Greg at the coffee shop. He shouldn't be too busy to sit and chat, and perhaps he could shed more light on Flora Laura.

"I won't be long," I said, passing Marilyn at the counter, but she only grunted an acknowledgment. She'd lost her earlier sparkle and looked forlorn. I stopped in my tracks. "What's wrong... has something upset you?"

"That stupid phone call was from the customer from Bristol. She rang to complain about the hat she ordered. It wasn't delivered on the day she expected." Marilyn picked up the stapler on the counter and thumped it down again. "I told her, it wasn't our fault the courier collected it so late on Friday."

I shook my head. "Oh don't worry about her... it's all part of being in business. There'll always somebody moaning about something we have no control over. Please, don't let it get you down. Look, I need to speak to Greg and also pay his bill." I gave a slight laugh as I'd nearly forgotten about the bill. "How about I bring you back a muffin and a coffee?"

Her tense shoulders relaxed, and she mellowed. "That's kind of you. I'd like that."

"Okay, I won't be long." I headed out the door.

Thankfully I was right about The Arches Coffee Shop not being too busy at this point in the day. Visitors and hotel guests were more likely to discover this hidden gem from around eleven onwards.

I approached the counter, and Greg grinned at me.

"Have you got time for a break?" I asked, waving my

credit card at him. "My treat and I'll settle up the tab too."

"Sure, sit down, I'll bring it over."

I perched on a high stool positioned next to one of the tall tables. I hadn't brought my notepad as Greg would have laughed me out of the coffee shop. Besides, I guessed any answers he gave would be easy to remember. Although, I should be subtle in my phrasing. I couldn't sucker Greg into anything. He knew me too well.

"Here you go." He lowered the cups of frothy coffee and propped himself on the other high stool. "It's good to see you."

"Sorry, there's been so much going on I've barely caught my breath. You'll never guess what's happened..." I picked up my coffee.

He raised his eyebrows. "What are you up to now?"

"I am officially the new editor-in-chief of the Swansneck Messenger!"

He almost fell off his stool. "You are kidding me? Why on earth would you take that on?"

"It wasn't my choice... Marilyn volunteered my permanent services to the vicar... Mrs. Horridge had an accident and, well..."

Greg hooted with laughter "Well, you've got more than a turkey dinner on your plate now. Every crank and matron in the village will have you in their sights. They'll want to wine and dine you to ensure their recipes get printed. No, scratch the wine and dine, they'll stuff you full of homemade cake like they did with Mrs. Horridge!"

I groaned. "It can't be that bad... can it?" He had me worried. "Besides, I plan to change the format, bring it up to date, you know."

"With what?" Greg said, intrigued.

"Well, adverts for a start, and you can be one of my first advertisers. I'll give you a good rate." I winked.

"Hmm," he said, sipping his coffee.

"And there's Flora Laura. She will advertise too."

His eyebrows twitched. "Will she? Have you met her?"

"Yes, I was in the florist's for a chat yesterday. She seems nice. Although she's not from around here, is she?" I probed.

"No, Laura originates from Harrogate. She lives in Upper Ribbly now."

"How do you know where she lives?" I concealed my surprise as best as possible.

"Oh, we used to have a thing... you know, dated for a while."

I hadn't expected that piece of information. Although he was a single man in Swansneck, a rare eligible fish in this little pond.

"So what happened? She seems like a nice person from what I can tell." I chuckled. "Or did she turn into a bunny boiler?" My sense of humour didn't seem to impress him.

"You know how these things go... it dwindled." He shrugged.

"Oh, I'm sorry Greg, I didn't mean to..." I drifted off, feeling awkward.

He attempted to brush off my comments. "It's okay, Jen, it's history."

I leaned in closer to him. "And why would she leave a handsome hunk like you, eh?" I said, trying to bolster his obvious sagging spirits.

But he didn't answer me. Just picked up his empty cup and said, "Sorry, Jen, we're getting busy. I'd better help out at the counter."

"Yes... Yes... go ahead," I stuttered.

I'd hit a nerve and didn't want to prevent him escaping to his work.

"I've got to get back too, so I'll drop by again soon."

As soon as I pushed open the door to the Hat Shop, I realised I failed to collect a muffin and coffee for Marilyn. But I didn't want to go back now. I couldn't stand at the counter and place an order with Greg after he'd admitted having a *thing* with Flora Laura. I wasn't sure why that bolt from the blue made me uncomfortable. Greg was my best friend, not my boyfriend. His revelation embarrassed me, that's all.

"Oh, I'm sorry..." I apologised to Marilyn holding up my empty hands. "Honestly, if my head was loose...!"

"That's okay, I'll nip in and get one later," she said, seemingly back to her chirpy self. "Sorry about my rant earlier after the Bristol woman's phone call. I think it upset me because it was our first online order, and I want it to be a success."

"These things happen... you have to let them go."

She put down the netting she was arranging for the new window dressing. "I remember how the courier driver was beside himself that his whole delivery and collection schedule had been scrapped." Manipulating the netting again, she tried to work it into pleats. "That traffic jam on the M6 had a lot to answer for if you ask me. It was on the telly, the teatime news. Reeked chaos it did, but why they had to close *all* the lanes of the motorway for a tanker spill is beyond me. Why couldn't they simply drive through it?"

"Skid risk?" I replied. "I've really no idea..."

She continued to chatter away, but I had other things on my mind.

"Well, I was only trying to be helpful to him. When I saw the next address on his list was Kim's, I told him, she's here at the hotel more than she is at home. So he'd best leave the parcel with me to save him time."

My brain snapped into focus at the mention of Kim. "So what did he say? Did he leave the parcel here?"

"Oh no, you know what they're like..." She tone switched to imitate a grumpy male voice. "I can't do that, it'd be more than my job's worth. Got to go to the address and try to deliver, and if she's not in, leave a failed delivery notice."

"So I told him, don't get stroppy with me mate, I'm only trying to help you out. Forget it." She pushed the tangle of net into a pretty hat box to create a display platform. "I think we'll find another company to handle our online orders from now on. What do you think?"

"Oh yes, don't reward grumpiness, that's my motto." I pulled out my credit card. "Here, get your coffee and anything else you fancy. And pay the tab too please, I forgot."

"Okay!" She plucked the card from my hand and gave it a little tap with her red-taloned finger. "Thanks!"

CHAPTER TWENTY-TWO

During the afternoon, I looked up George Lees' trade contact number on the internet. He had a social media page showing photos of his earlier work and had built up a good reputation as a joiner. With such favourable reviews, it was understandable I'd contact him for a quote.

I sent him a brief text, requesting a visit to the shop, and he replied to say he would call in later today when he'd finished his current job.

This would give me an opportunity to question him about last Friday under the cover of refurbishing the shop. I could even, if needed, ask him to advertise in the Messenger. That should confuse the conversation to some extent, so he shouldn't suspect a thing.

For the next few hours, I attempted to reconcile the accounts, with the occasional amusement break to read the tatty notes related to the Messenger. Without a clear idea what would make it more interesting, I hoped something would come to mind, as it sometimes did.

The end of the working day neared, and the doorbell tinkled. I jumped up to see if it was George, but it wasn't. It was a late customer wanting to browse.

I wasn't aware I been on tenterhooks until I'd heard the bell. I resolved to calm myself down, or I'd blow this major opportunity to ask probing questions.

Marilyn dispatched the late customer and then popped her head into the office.

"Would it be okay for me to leave?" she asked. "Unless there's anything you'd like me to stay for?"

I couldn't hold her back, despite my jumpiness about George arriving—or being here alone with him. Besides, Marilyn might distract me, so it was best she went home.

"No, you get along, I'll lock up." I picked up my set of shop keys and jangled them for her. "See you in the morning—all being well."

At that, she regarded me with puzzlement, but just said, "Okay, goodnight."

I returned my concentration to the laptop screen and heard the doorbell tinkle as she left. Absorbed by the numbers it came as a major shock when a man's voice spoke from the office doorway.

"Jenny, is it?"

I spun around in my seat. It was George Lees.

"Oh! I didn't know you'd arrived."

"The girl showed me in as she was leaving," he explained. "It's a nice little shop you have here."

To my relief he turned his muscle bound bulk away from the office doorway, allowing me the chance to escape its confined space and follow him into the shop.

"Thanks," I squeaked, then cleared my throat. I had to get a grip on myself. "Thanks," I repeated. "I've only just taken over, so can't take the credit."

My tight smile went unnoticed as George walked up and down the length of the shop, studying the layout. I watched with nervous anticipation, wondering if he might want to try on a hat.

"I plan to expand into vintage clothing so will need clothes rails," I chattered.

He nodded.

"I've already purchased what we need online." I nipped

into the office to retrieve the sheets I'd printed out and thrust them into his hands. "What do you think?"

"Yeah, they look ideal for what you need." He glanced up and down between the sheet of paper and the walls. "I think putting them on that wall will be your best bet. They'd be secure there and not disrupt your current layout."

"Yes," I agreed. He knew his job although I had to remind myself this racking quote ploy was not to test his joinery aptitude. "So if you can give me a price for fitting, that would be great."

"No problem," he said, withdrawing a shabby notebook and pencil from his back pocket and making a crude sketch.

"Sorry I can't offer you a cup of tea, but we're out of milk," I lied. "At times like this, we're at the mercy of the coffee shop next door—or The Flying Shuttle." I wondered if that was a subtle enough lead-in to my next question. "Do you ever go to the pub?" I asked casually.

"Oh yeah," said George. "I'm a regular. Just a couple of pints after work to wind down, you understand," he quickly rectified, so I didn't get the impression he'd roll up drunk on the job one day and chop off his fingers.

"Oh totally." I agreed. "When you work for yourself you need a little time to gather your thoughts."

"Exactly, that's what I do, mull things over."

He looked up from his notebook with a warm smile. I could see why my dad would like him. Dad! Remembering that connection I used it.

"You may know my dad? Bob Bradshaw?"

"Oh, Bob, yeah, I've met him. He's not much of a talker is he, your dad, so I don't know him well, but a nice man, a very nice man. So he's your dad, eh?"

He finished his note taking and pushed the pad back into his pocket.

This chat was all very well, but I was floundering. How could I get more information about Friday? I had to keep on and hope for inspiration.

"Yes, I seem to remember my Great Uncle Wilf saying your dad was a dog breeder? Nice things, dogs." I frowned at my stupid remark.

But George perked up and became animated. "Yes. My father was a breeder. I still have a passion for dogs but no time to own one myself. An owner at work all day isn't fair on the animal. But I get great pleasure watching them run around on the village green, chasing balls with such excitement. It's a lovely sight."

"And you do that a lot? I saw a few dogs on the green last Friday as I passed by." Lying was becoming easier, I noticed. "Around tea time I think it was, can't remember what breeds though."

"Ah, that will have been Sandy, with two Whippets and a neighbour's Jack Russell. Takes it for exercise, as a favour. Nice thing to do."

"Yes," I confirmed, feeling bad about trapping him like this, but it had to be done. "I've never met Sandy, is he Scottish?"

"Oh no, Sandy is a lady!" George laughed. "She owns a couple of Whippets... but doesn't breed them. Actually, she was asking me for a few tips on Friday. She wants to become a breeder. We had a good old chin wag about my dad and his success at the dog shows. I enjoyed that, talking about my dad."

A chill ran down my spine. My line of questioning had successfully resulted in him disclosing what he was doing late on Friday afternoon. But had he been talking to Sandy at the time Jack was murdered, or later? Had he killed Jack then returned to sit outside The Flying Shuttle and chat with Sandy as an alibi? How on earth would I get that level of detail?

"So, if that's everything..." He wrapped up the meeting by walking toward the door.

"Yes," I said, "But if I need to ask you anything further, maybe I could catch you at the pub?"

He nodded. "Yeah, sure."

"What time do you normally land there?" I asked as nonchalantly as possible.

"Oh, about five. I park my van in the residents' car park by the almshouses and walk down to the pub. So usually five'ish, give or take."

I swallowed and felt my face draining.

But he didn't notice my reaction as he pulled open the door.

"Thanks for the offer of this work," he said, "and I'll pop a quote to you soon."

"Okay, thanks. Bye." My voice cracked with nerves.

He'd no sooner stepped outside the door when I slammed it shut and clicked the latch to lock it. I may be overreacting but I couldn't take any chances.

I ran into the office and shut the door behind me.

George's admission of his schedule dove-tailed perfectly with the timing of Jack's murder... It proved he had the opportunity.

I grabbed my notepad and wrote everything he'd said then tried to calm myself so I could think.

If he'd walked down Park Road around five o'clock on Friday why hadn't I spotted him? Logic then answered that question. Because he may have walked on my side of the road and I would not see him from my upstairs window. I can only see what happens opposite my house. Okay, but this wasn't enough to take to the police. I would have to confirm what he'd said. How he'd met and talked with Sandy at length.

I picked up my bag and made for the door. If I was quick, I might just catch Sandy with her dogs on the village green.

I was in luck. As I hurried along Queen Victoria Road, I saw a woman with three dogs walking toward me. I was too late to catch them on the green, but that didn't matter. I made a beeline for her, ready to fuss over her dogs and entice her to stop and chat.

Calm on their leash after exercising, the Whippets stayed at Sandy's side. In contrast, the Jack Russell bounded about like it was on a spring. Even a trip to the green hadn't exhausted him. I'd concentrate on the Whippets, as they were my link to George.

"Oh, what adorable dogs," I cooed. "I love Whippets." I deliberately stood next to one fawn coloured dog and slid my hand along its soft short fur.

I looked up at Sandy to see a maternal smile.

"Well, isn't that strange, only a few minutes ago I was talking with George Lees about his father's Whippets," I said.

Sandy grinned. "You were? Wow, what a coincidence; I was chatting to George only the other day about breeding them." She stooped to stroke the other calm dog.

I kept the former close by my leg. "George is a nice guy," I said. "Always ready to be helpful."

"Oh yes," Sandy agreed. "He said he'd check his bookshelves for the breeding manuals his dad owned. He said I could have them. How kind is that?"

It seemed accusing George Lees of murder was akin to trying to drown a puppy. But I had to keep my resolve. George had a major motive, and people did terrible things out of character when provoked.

Sandy was still nattering on. I tuned in again.

"I'm so excited about getting the books his father used. Did you know he was quite the legend in the Whippet breeding world?"

"Yes, I'd heard." I wanted to keep her talking. "So you meet George at the village green regularly? He told me he drinks at the pub after work."

"Yes, that's right. To be honest, I've never spoken to him

much, only passed the time of day, as you do when people make a fuss of your dogs." Then she chuckled. "Or when they crash into someone while mindlessly chasing their ball..."

Sandy bent to ruffle the fur of her dog as if reprimanding its past behaviour. The poor dog didn't have a clue. Then she looked up at me. "But, it was only last Friday that he had the time to listen to my dreams of becoming a Whippet breeder."

"Oh, how amazing it would be to breed these beauties," I gushed, giving the dog another stroke. Hmm, I must beware of overkill. "So you were talking with George on Friday." I backtracked for her. "It's a shame I couldn't have joined you. I passed the village green at about five o'clock..."

Sandy cut in. "Oh no, by then you'd have missed the main part of George's funny tales about his dad's glory days at the shows."

I frowned. This wasn't right. "I thought George only got to the pub by five?"

"Oh, last Friday he finished the job he was on a little earlier. He was sitting outside The Flying Shuttle by four-thirty. I know because I arrive at the Green to walk the dogs every day at the same time, and he was already there. That's probably why he could chat at length with me. He said he usually leaves around six'ish to go home and make himself a healthy meal. Said he doesn't want to fall into bad ways and end up buying one of those pies from the bakery." She wrinkled her nose at the very thought of a Bradshaw's pie.

I considered giving her a slap on Hilda's behalf but thought better of it.

I must concentrate on memorizing the pertinent details she was providing. But I had to admit—it was looking bad for my conviction rate—but promising for the potential puppy drowning.

The dog at my side squirmed from my persistent fondling, so I relented and concluded all was lost. George Lees was indeed deep in conversation with Sandy during the whole timeframe of Jack's murder. There were no two ways about it. The man was a nice guy, just as Hilda and my father had told me.

As I waved goodbye to Sandy and her dogs, my stomach churned at my next thought.

Kim was now my prime suspect.

CHAPTER TWENTY-THREE

I tossed and turned all night.

My concerns about Bert being found guilty were now over-ridden with Kim being the murderer. Obsessed by the knowledge that either of my childhood friends were involved, I threw off my bed covers in despair.

The fact that I couldn't go to the police with Kim's fraud confession was torturing me.

Had she deliberately told me her secret? Aware the longer I held it, the more involved I would be? Would the police view me as an accomplice?

I finally exhausted myself with what ifs and fell asleep, only to wake with a start as daylight crept through the curtains.

I got out of bed, relieved that today would be the last I'd spend with the pigeons. Tomorrow I'd leave them until the afternoon, to show Billy how to clean the coop and how the birds reacted when fed.

I took a long, long shower to re-humanise myself, then ate breakfast. I needed to be in top form today to decide how I should handle my Kim secret. The longer I left it, the more implicated I'd be.

This morning, I changed my route to reach the pigeon lofts at the old bathhouse. I strode down Queen Victoria Road and veered right to walk up Princess Helena Street. As

I was passing the side of the village church, the early morning sun picked out the stained glass windows depicting the crucifixion—scene by unsettling scene. I opened the loft, in no mood to fuss over the birds, and quickly dispatched my duty of leaving food and water.

Having reached the hotel ladies room, I washed my hands, then walked through the elaborate double doors from the reception area that led into The Arches Arcade.

On entering the silent space, I realised I was the first to open for business this morning. Even the exterior doors remained locked to the public. Alone in The Arches for the first time, I felt the history of the building steeped within its walls. People often said, on TV documentaries about such matters, how they believed brickwork can hold the emotional energy of earlier occupants. Unlocking the door to the Hat Shop, I wondered if that was the case here in the mill. Were the emotions of long gone mill workers still held by these walls? Were these walls now absorbing my emotions? And if so, what were they getting from me?

Thirsty after the morning activities, I entered the office and fired up my laptop, then checked yesterday's milk in the vain hope it wasn't stale. I wanted a cup of tea, but the sour stench told me all I needed to know. In desperation, I hunted down the bottle of fruity mineral water I'd stashed on a shelf for emergencies. I classed this as an emergency.

With my thirst eased, I sat down and opened the file I'd created only days before and reviewed what I'd written.

Now, with the knowledge of hindsight, it was clear I'd swayed in favour of George being the killer.

Just because I'd forced the pieces of circumstantial evidence from George's jigsaw into position, I shouldn't have concluded that I knew what the end picture was.

My final investigation of his alibi confirmed my mistake.

I highlighted George's name in green to check him off my list.

That left Kim, Vinnie, and Bert.

As for Vinnie, he had a solid, police proven alibi... so he wasn't the killer. I highlighted his name too.

Kim and Bert remained. I gulped a long drink of water and asked myself in my heart of hearts, could I ever picture Bert as a killer? Then I stopped myself from answering. I must stay impartial.

Since Kim and Jack were involved in bar fraud, I should obviously pursue my exploration of her movements on Friday.

I opened another file and then flipped open my notepad to the page where I'd jotted down notes from Flora Laura.

I typed up my squiggled words to absorb their implications...

As Kim and Laura had agreed, Kim arrived at the florist in the hotel van to collect the arrangements for the wedding reception at five o'clock.

According to Laura, they'd carefully loaded the van with the delicate creations, a task I guessed would take around twenty minutes. I typed 5.20 onto the page.

Laura said she'd locked the shop when Kim left. At that point, I'd passed Laura on my way to the Bake House to eat with Dad and Hilda.

Hilda always placed dinner on the table at five-thirty. It was a habit of a lifetime. So I could state with certainty it was 5.25 when I passed Laura because I was right on time for dinner.

I typed that time onto my chart.

I knew the hotel van was parked in the Bake House parking space, with no sign of the driver. So Kim had left it there to go home and change, just as Laura had reported.

Or had she?

There was a time slot between her leaving the florist and retrieving the van to return for her shift. Although, I wasn't aware of the time she actually moved the van... only that it was gone when I came out of the Bake House—having just been sacked.

I took another sip of water, surprised by how irate that episode with Dad and Hilda still made me. I shook my head, telling my brain to let the matter go, and resumed my deliberations.

From the florist shop, Kim was ideally placed, only metres away from the allotment main gate. She could have slipped across the road to meet Jack and kill him. Laura wouldn't have noticed her, while occupied with clearing her workroom and getting ready to leave.

I shifted in my uncomfortable plastic chair and it creaked in complaint.

DI Kenon told me Jack's body was found at 6.15 and the police arrived within ten minutes.

For Kim that left an unaccounted time span from 5.20 until 6.15.

I stroked my bottom lip and recalled my movements. The van was gone when I left the Bake House, and I saw the police car at the allotment gate. So that must have been around six-thirty.

Given that the murder had already taken place when the allotment holder found Jack I could probably knock off another five minutes from Kim's timings.

5.20 until 6.10.

I typed **50 Minutes** in bold onto the chart. Was that enough time? I'm no expert in such matters, but I'd say it was ample time to get in, kill and get out again.

Downing another mouthful of water I nodded to myself. I liked the clarity. My focus would now be on those fifty minutes.

Okay, so what next?

I was about to deliberate my next move when I heard the shop doorbell. I glanced at the time on the corner of my screen. It was nine o'clock already. I'd been so absorbed by my plotting I hadn't noticed that Marilyn would be due at any minute.

Before I had a moment to hide the document I'd been working on from the laptop screen, a male voice broke the silence.

"I've got the quote for you, Jenny." I spun around to see George Lees smiling and standing in the doorway waving a small envelope.

Caught red-handed, I considered how fast that smile would disappear if he knew what terrible deed I'd suspected of him. Then a shocking realisation hit me. His name was on the crime chart I was working on, and not only that, highlighted in neon green. In the off chance that his eyesight was failing, I'd made it nice and clear to read from a distance!

I jumped up and hastened over to him, hoping to distract his attention from my laptop. If I'd tried to shut the file down, it would have seemed obvious I was concealing something. Getting him away from the office doorway was my main consideration.

My behaviour may have appeared odd to him as I walked over to block his broad muscular body from the screen and deliberately stood a little too close for comfort; both his and mine.

"Thanks, George," I said airily. "Let's go into the shop so you can show me what the job would entail."

This seemed a valid excuse to draw him away from the office. Fortunately, he turned and made for the wall where he'd suggested we fit the racking.

For several minutes he explained his quote, but to be honest I absorbed none of it.

He then handed me the envelope and I said I'd be in touch. My stomach was doing somersaults as he walked toward the door at the same moment Marilyn was entering.

I breathed a huge sigh of relief as one person replaced the

other but still knew my scandalous file was open on the laptop. Before Marilyn had even taken off her cardigan, I asked her to get us coffee. That would give me the time I needed.

Dutifully, she went on the errand.

I had to be more careful, I told myself, as I wrote the pertinent timing from my laptop deliberations onto my notepad and closed the file.

I scrutinised what I'd written: **5.20 to 6.10**. Confident that such a dull nondescript note wouldn't arouse suspicion if seen. While Marilyn was out, I took the precaution of opening the shop accounts file, so she wouldn't disturb me. Of late, she had shown great reverence for all accountancy related work, so for now, at least, I wanted to keep it that way.

Marilyn returned from her coffee run. The caffeine invigorated my brain and the sense of focus it gave helped my resolve to dig deeper into Kim's movements.

Kim had told Laura she was going home to shower and change before returning to her shift, but I had no proof she'd actually done this. So, it seemed this was the place I had to start.

The one thing that foxed me was how to prove she had showered and changed as she'd said. I tapped my fingers on the shelf-turned-desk and mulled it over for a moment. For now, I didn't have to prove those points, I simply needed to know if she could achieve the tasks in the time she had available.

So, I estimated the walk from the florist to where she lived in Prince Leopold Street would have taken her roughly five minutes. That would make it 5.25.

Then, when she returned she'd have to leave home at least five minutes before she planned to be in the van to drive back to the hotel. This made the opposing time 6.05.

Could she have showered and changed during the remaining time? Absolutely.

Okay, so how did I prove it?

I drained the last of my coffee. Perhaps I should try the same tactic I'd used on George... just ask. Although, Kim would be alert, knowing full well her confession to me put her in the frame for murder. She'd suspect the motives behind my questions.

Unless... it wasn't me who asked the questions.

To say Marilyn was taken aback by my offer to buy her a light lunch in the hotel bar was an understatement. Although I had to warn this would not be a regular occurrence—it was just an opportunity to get to know each other better.

I'm not sure why she took this to be a major event. But with great excitement, she insisted she go to the ladies restroom in the hotel reception to freshen up her makeup and check that she was presentable.

Way too jittery to take part in such feminine frippery, I told her I'd go upstairs and meet her there.

Entering the lounge I spotted Kim behind the bar polishing long stemmed wine glasses. I hesitated at the doorway; the prospect of talking to her alone was not what I wanted. As luck would have it, someone called out her name to summon her into the restaurant.

I made a quick march across the room to reach the balcony. I thought I'd give it five minutes before peeping into the lounge to see if Marilyn had arrived.

Once outside, I wandered over to the far glass rail. There was something about this balcony I found hypnotic. Whether it was the sheer drop to the river and the exposed rocky bank below or the vista that stretched for miles beyond, I wasn't sure.

I turned and repositioned myself nearer the mill's solid wall to lessen my unease, but the move didn't improve things much as I now overlooked the massive waterwheel. Despite the wheel no longer being in use it still possessed a disturbing menace.

I stared at the jutting iron blades, powerful fins devised to slice through the river's flow. Suddenly my head jerked forward and I swayed—then realised, I wasn't falling—I was being pushed.

CHAPTER TWENTY-FOUR

From behind, two hands gripped my shoulders and gave me a quick thrust forward, only to pull me swiftly back again.

"Tell your mother I saved you!" announced the cheerful voice.

My heart pounded and as soon as the infuriating grip from the hands had released me I spun around to face Kim.

"Don't be so stupid!" I yelled, venting my anger. "What is it with you and Greg? Why do you do that?"

She displayed a wide grin. "Aw, come on, Jen, it's funny... we used to do it as kids, don't you remember?"

"Of course I remember, but we were young and stupid then. It's dangerous for heaven's sake."

"I wouldn't let you fall, Jen." Kim gazed at me with what appeared to be genuine remorse. "I came out here to say thanks..." She stopped and glanced around to check we were alone. "For not saying anything about *you know what.*"

I shook my head to express disbelief over her immature playfulness, but she misread its meaning.

"No, really, Jenny, don't dismiss what you've done for me. I appreciate it. You're a good friend."

I swallowed hard.

"So are you here alone?" she asked.

I shook my head again and took a deep breath to steady my nerves. "No... I'm here for a quick lunch with Marilyn. A sandwich or something..."

"Oh all right, come on, let's go inside," she said, leading the way. "I'll make you my priority... take a seat at the end of the bar."

As we entered the room, Marilyn appeared at the doorway and Kim waved her over to our bar stools. Still disturbed, I noticed our location at the end of the bar had previously been Jack Nabb's post.

Kim returned to her position behind the bar.

"And what can I get you ladies?" she said with a smile.

"I'll have a tomato juice with ice and Tabasco sauce, please," I said, although I secretly wished I could add a large vodka to calm myself.

"That sounds nice," Marilyn said. "The same for me please."

"And can we see the bar snack menu," I added. Nodding, Kim set about our order.

I tried to get my act together. This was a vital opportunity to ferret out the information I needed to check Kim's alibi. I mustn't let the chance slide. Earlier I'd considered priming Marilyn with the questions I needed answering. But aware of Marilyn's innocent free-wheeling ways, I couldn't risk it. I would steer her conversation with Kim and hope she'd take the direction I intended.

Kim delivered our drinks, took our sandwich order then left us alone.

Distracted by my mission and how to bring it about, I wasn't the best dining companion. I left Marilyn to rattle on about how she would have chosen a different outfit for today had she known we were coming upstairs. She'd seen *Roman Holiday* on an old movie channel and had devised an outfit that was a fabulous take on Audrey Hepburn's style in the film. Had she known, she would have worn it today.

While I was apologizing for not forewarning her, Kim reappeared with our sandwiches. Then the idea struck me.

"Thanks, Kim." Marilyn twisted the plate of finger

sandwiches and salad titbits before her.

I had to seize my chance before Kim hurried away again.

"Kim... Marilyn was saying said she had a '*set to*' with the parcel delivery driver on your behalf the other day."

"Did you? What on earth was it about?" asked Kim.

"Oh, honestly." Marilyn sighed. "I tried to do the driver a favour, as he was moaning and groaning about running late on his route due to that traffic jam on the M6."

Marilyn picked up a slice of cucumber that adorned the side of the plate and popped it into her mouth before continuing.

"And when I spotted your home address as the next drop on his list I told him you worked long hours here so would probably not be at home. I suggested he should leave your parcel with me."

"And what did he say?" I asked innocently.

Marilyn sent me a confused look, aware she'd already told me, but repeated it for Kim's benefit, anyway.

She imitated the driver's grumpy attitude again.

"I can't do that, my boss would go nuts. Got to attempt the delivery myself..." She shook her head in dismay. "You know what it's like, Kim, there's no helping some people."

"So did you get your parcel?" I gave Kim my best guileless smile and hoped she'd come across with a clear reply.

"As luck would have it, yes I did..." she answered. "I'd ordered a dress online to wear for the Saturday evening of the wedding reception. All the black outfits I own have washed themselves grey..."

"Oh, don't you hate it when that happens?" consoled Marilyn. "I must tell you about the great laundry detergent I found that..."

Impulsively I knocked the paper serviette off Marilyn's lap to prevent her from wandering into laundry talk.

As Marilyn jumped off the stool to retrieve the serviette, I ensured that Kim stayed on track.

"You were saying…"

"Yes, so I was in when he called, purely fate…"

But much to my dismay, Marilyn climbed back on her perch and changed the subject again for Kim.

"Oh! Was that the stunning black fitted dress I saw you wearing on Saturday evening? Wow, you picked a winner there Kim. You looked terrific. You must tell me where you found it."

"Sure, I'll note down the website for you…" Kim grabbed her pen and order pad.

Short of knocking Marilyn's serviette back to the floor— or, better still, Marilyn herself—I wondered how to recover the conversation that had been going so smoothly.

"Fate's a funny thing," I said with a hint of mysticism. "How it can direct your life…"

Pushing the slip marked with the website toward Marilyn, Kim stared at me as though I was crazy. I quickly clarified what I meant by my airhead comment.

"As you said Kim, it was pure fate that led you to be at home to receive the parcel…"

"Oh yes… that's right…" Realising what I was getting at, she smiled. "If I hadn't suggested to Laura, the florist, that I could get the hotel van to transport her arrangements." She directed her next words to Marilyn. "You know—those tall table centres she created for the wedding reception…"

When Marilyn took a deep breath, ready to extol her thoughts on the fabulous Flora Laura creations, I knew I had to pre-empt her. Subtly I slipped my hand onto the edge of her handbag strap, encouraging it to slide from the back of her stool onto the floor. It did so with a clatter. Marilyn jumped down to retrieve it, muttering something about having butter fingers today.

"How kind of you, Kim," I said, to keep her on track. "I bet Laura was grateful for the help…"

"Yes, but as it turned out, it gave me a good excuse to

leave here and change for my evening shift." She dropped her voice to a whisper. "Oliver Swan expects double shifts back to back from me without a break." Her face expressed loathing for the man.

"And so..." I prodded, not wanting this to end.

"And so... Usually, I'd never have been at home to receive the parcel, as Marilyn rightly said to the driver. But as fate would have it I was just headed back out the door to return for the six o'clock shift when the driver caught me." She lowered her voice again. "If the driver had been ten minutes earlier I'd have answered the door with a towel around me. Not recommended!" She laughed. "So it worked out well, and I got to wear that dress on Saturday night. And I'm glad you liked it, Marilyn, as you have super taste in clothes."

Two hotel guests approached the bar, and Kim glanced their way. "Sorry, have to go. Nice chatting... see you soon."

At that, she went about her job, and Marilyn and I tucked into our sandwiches. I felt appeased that my ploy had worked.

Despite telling Marilyn this lunch was an opportunity to get acquainted with one another, I quickly finished the snack and said we should get back to the shop. I used the lengthy conversation we'd had with Kim as an excuse. We'd run out of time... customers may be standing at the shop door.

Marilyn would never retaliate against that logic. She had shown herself to be a stickler for customer service in the short time I'd known her, so we left the bar.

Once back in my little office, I reviewed my progress. There was enough to confirm Kim's alibi, but every piece of information was given by Kim herself—and that was a problem. I needed proof before trusting her. Even the story about being at home to receive the parcel could be false. What if she'd simply worn a dress she'd never used for work before and said she received it on Friday?

Corroboration of the parcel delivery was my first task, but how did I do that? I should ask the delivery company, I decided.

Riffling through the paperwork of the shop accounts I retrieved the invoice for the Bristol hat order. Written in the dispatch section was the name of the courier service Marilyn had chosen. After finding the office number on their website, I gave the company a call.

A young male voice answered. "Hiya, First Fast Couriers."

It was a most casual approach to customer services.

"Hello. I hope you can help me. I received a parcel last Friday, delivered by your company, and I just need verification of the exact time of delivery please."

"What? Why? You got it didn't you, so what's the problem?"

"Well, I..." He had a point, but his aggressive attitude annoyed me. "I need to know, and you don't need to know why I need know." I hoped that would confuse the few brain cells he was using today.

"Yeah, but it's not that simple, lady..." he grumbled. "Besides, we can't give out information to just anyone. Who's to say you are who you say you are? You could be anybody."

It seemed he was trying my confusion ploy right back at me... and it was working. I was losing track of my goal.

"It's just the time..." I groaned. His rudeness only confirmed an earlier decision. There was no way we'd use this company in the future.

"Nope, no can do... it's all about data protection ye see... And how customers' empty houses could be tracked for burglaries and their signatures used for fraud. All that legal stuff... nope, no can do."

I resigned myself to the impregnability of the brick wall I'd been banging my head against for the last few minutes.

"Okay, okay, I see your point. Thanks for your help," I said sarcastically.

"Thank you for using First Fast Couriers," he chirruped and hung up.

I had to think again. Then realised I had attempted to tackle this from the wrong angle. I called out to Marilyn in the shop.

"Do you have the name of the website Kim purchased her dress from?"

Within seconds she handed me the slip of paper.

"Thanks," I said, jotting down the website and giving the paper back to her. She returned to the shop.

I typed in the details and found the company phone number. I had to give this a try.

A polite young lady answered my call. I created my story for her—which was how I preferred to think of it—rather than calling it a lie.

"I ordered a dress from you a little while ago and haven't received it. Would you check your system please?"

She asked for my name and address, and I gave her Kim's details. I apologised for not having the order number, but she dismissed that problem by finding it on her computer. Yes, she assured me, it was dispatched from their warehouse... and not only that it showed receipt by me.

"Really?" I made a play of sounding shocked. "What day was it delivered?"

"Friday, Miss Renshaw. Just a moment..."

There was a lull in the phone call during which I was subjected to an abysmal promotional jingle until she returned.

"I've checked our access to the courier delivery note, and I can assure you it was delivered on Friday the 18th, at 5.46. We have your signature on record; K Renshaw. It's digitally captured and the time logged." She droned on about the proof of delivery they held, so I couldn't demand a refund.

"Oh!" I exclaimed, thinking fast. "My sister must have signed for the delivery. Karen, with a K... same initials.

Thanks for your help, I'll speak to her. Little minx probably planned to wear the dress first!"

The girl laughed with relief at my explanation, and I finished the call.

5.46.

It looked like Kim was telling the truth; she had been at home getting changed.

She'd also said at lunch her evening shift started at six. Given this ever shrinking time frame, I couldn't see how she could have killed Jack Nabb.

She'd have had to leave the florist, walk home, shower and change. Then sign for the parcel, walk back to the Bake House to pick up the van, and get to the hotel for six o'clock. It wasn't possible to fit a murder in there too.

I had corroborated my old friend's alibi without bringing the police into it. That accomplishment pleased me. Although... I sighed with mixed emotions.

I had cleared Kim from my list, so now the only name that remained was Bert. My heart was heavy with fear for him. I couldn't conceive him capable of murder.

But if Bert wasn't capable, who was?

CHAPTER TWENTY-FIVE

I needed a drink, but not at the hotel bar. The only other option was The Flying Shuttle, but I didn't want to go there alone, so I called Greg to tempt him into a little get together.

During the popular after-work hours, locals frequented the pub for a quick pint or two before going home for a meal. Greg had taken little convincing to meet me and waved as he entered the crowded room.

I'd managed to get a good table not far from the bar and had already purchased his drink. He sat down with a weary grunt.

"Oh, it's been a busy one today," he said, taking a long draw from the chestnut-coloured pint of real ale. "Ah... that's better."

He looked at me with expectation. "So? What's brought this on?"

I could hardly admit I'd cleared Kim and George of being rampant murderers—without revealing the secrets I held about both.

Oh, this was all so very stressful, it was no wonder I craved alcohol. I covered my agitation by chugging a big gulp of my gin and tonic, the ice clattering against the side of the glass.

"There's no real reason," I hedged because I wasn't sure why I wanted to see him. Other than having a companion in the pub so I didn't give the locals a chance to label me a lonely lush.

"You're downing that drink at a rate of knots, so I don't believe you."

I shook my head, on the verge of tears, but choked them back. It was the gin doing its famed depression thing, I told myself.

"So you've heard the news then..." Greg studied me intently.

"What news?" I croaked then cleared my voice.

"Bert. He's been arrested."

"What!" Despite my efforts, a tear escaped from one eye and trickled down the little nook around my nose. I rubbed it away.

"Sorry, I thought you'd heard it on the grapevine and that's why you wanted to have a drink together."

I recovered from the shocking revelation. "It's just not right, Greg. Bert couldn't do such a thing... he's not the type."

"Who's said murderers have a type? Anyone can be pushed to the brink."

I sighed.

"You've got to let it go, Jen. I know Bert was kind to us as kids, but the past is the past, and people can change. Who's to say what might have driven him to kill?"

I nodded. He was right, although I had a problem accepting it.

"The police must have enough evidence to arrest him..." he added.

With that, a man strode through the door and a group clustered at the bar hailed him.

"Vinnie!" they called out. "Come over here, son, good to see you back."

My jaw dropped open. Not only had Vinnie returned to the village, but his cronies bestowed a warm welcome. Mind you, he wasn't guilty of anything other than being a Nabb, and the rest of his family had been lying low.

Several men in the pub shook his hand and offered sincere condolences for his loss. Although, nobody said Jack would be deeply missed.

It was the first time I'd seen Vinnie, which felt strange because I knew a great deal about him and his family, in a roundabout way. His heavy eyebrows and deep set eyes lacked the black brooding expression of his elder brother, and his dark wavy hair was fastened into a ponytail at the nape of his neck. He looked drawn and pale as though he'd slept little of late.

I considered my laptop file. How I'd listed him among my suspects, and the overheard comment suggesting he stayed away from Swansneck for self-preservation. Did his return prove that wrong? Well, it seemed so, he was here in the pub telling everyone he was back. Or was Vinnie's return prompted by Bert's arrest and he now considered it safe?

Half-heartedly I made small talk with Greg but my mind was in overdrive, unable to focus on our conversation. No matter how I tried, I didn't accept Bert being a convicted murderer.

I finished my drink, as did Greg, and he proposed ordering another. I declined his offer, saying I should go home. It'd been a long day, and I didn't sleep much last night. Realising his news had shaken me, he didn't put up an argument, so we parted.

I strolled toward home feeling sick to my stomach, a sensation I couldn't put down to the gin. It was because none of this made any sense. There were so many people in Swansneck who had serious reasons to want Jack Nabb dead, and yet they had solid alibis. Poor Bert's alibi was his scatterbrained wife, and the police must have discounted what she said. They, in all probability, believed she had lied. She had a vested interest to protect him.

It all seemed so unfair. How could Agnes exist without Bert at her side?

How could the birds of Swansneck thrive without Bert's tender loving care? Would Derek pine away without him?

I knew Swansneck would never be the same without Bert.

Another rogue tear escaped from my eye, and I angrily jabbed it away.

CHAPTER TWENTY-SIX

Since my arrival this morning, I'd spent four hours sitting in the office and made no progress at all. This was pointless. Unable to concentrate on the accounts or the new Swansneck Messenger layout, I had to get out.

With a vague excuse to Marilyn, I left.

My intention was to go home and go to bed. The prospect of hiding under the covers felt very appealing right now. Not being in the mood to witness the bustle of the local shops along Cornelius Road I walked along the quieter Queen Victoria Road. But passing the village green with its sweet smell of freshly mown grass, I freely accepted a stroll in the park would give balm to my sad soul.

On entering the park, the first structure to welcome visitors was the aviary sign board, displaying species names of the various fowl with an explanation their origins. I stood before the sign and browsed the images and descriptions. Beyond the more ordinary birds, I mulled over the list of parrots from distant lands: the African Grey and the Eastern Rosella native to Australia. I wondered what the birds thought of their life in Lancashire. Did they now talk with a Lancashire accent?

Inside each of the aviary sections, sturdy tree branches provided perches for the birds. The angled branch within the Canary section bustled with over twenty neon yellow examples; they were feisty and fit as Bert used to say.

I strolled along to the next compartment to scrutinise the red, yellow and blue plumage of an Eastern Rosella parrot. He'd positioned himself at the front of the aviary by attaching his sharp claws around the green mesh. While he dangled in this precarious pose, he'd decided it was time to take a nap. Why he didn't fall off while he slept was a mystery.

Birds were a mystery, I mused. And there was such an affinity with birds in Swansneck. Did it all stem from Cornelius Swan perhaps, or was Lancashire already a hotbed of bird fanciers?

I strolled away from the other aviary sections and headed toward the palm house. As I pulled open the glass panelled door to the huge greenhouse structure, the humidity struck me. I couldn't handle it, not on a warm day like today, so I closed the door again—another time, perhaps.

While fearful I might run into Hilda, I toyed with going into the Tearooms. Would she chastise me for feeling upset about Bert? I glanced at my watch, it was nearing one o'clock. There was maybe an hour before she or her Clan swooped down for a gossip summit.

I made my way to the Tearooms.

Cautiously, I peered through the window before entering but spotted no familiar faces other than Mrs. B. I ventured inside and found a quiet corner table.

Mrs. B promptly came over to take my order.

I requested a sandwich and a pot of tea for one then sat back and tried to relax. The lyrical flow of visitor chit-chat floated to my ears. Broken conversations and voices of strangers enthralled by the traditional Victorian Tearooms.

Mrs. B arrived with my perfectly presented sandwich and pot of tea. Because I was eating alone, she'd chosen to give me a novelty teapot. I'd seen nothing like it before. The charming pot was designed as an old style treadle sewing machine, complete with spools of thread and fabric under the needle. I had to smile.

"Mrs. B, that is delightful…"

"You looked a bit down as you came in, Jen, and I thought a little treat was in order to cheer you up." She nodded her grandmotherly bespectacled head, without a single movement from her tightly curled grey locks.

"I appreciate your kindness," I said truthfully. For as long as I'd known her, which was forever, Mrs. B had never fussed over anyone. I'd always thought she was more like a sergeant major in a frilly apron. "Yes, I am a little down…" I admitted. "I guess you've heard the terrible news about Bert's arrest?"

She nodded again and pursed her lips.

"Have you seen Agnes?" I asked.

"She came in about half an hour ago; she was in a state… said she was on her way to deal with the aviary birds."

I shook my head. "I don't know why the police don't believe Bert was with her all Friday afternoon."

Upon hearing my words, Mrs. B took the unprecedented action of sitting down in the chair beside me then glanced about to check that nobody was eavesdropping.

"That'll be because of Mrs. Quinn at number one." She spoke in a low conspiratorial voice. "She saw Bert going up Park Road at the time the police say the murder took place."

My heart did a double flip.

"Don't you mean going down Park Road? Down toward the allotments?"

"Oh no dear, she was quite clear when she told me what she'd seen. She saw Bert strolling *up* Park Road with Derek, at 5.45, she said it was. She was sure about that because she had a cake in the oven. It was due to be removed at 5.45, and that's when she saw him pass by her kitchen window."

"Did Mrs. Quinn tell the police she saw Bert?"

"Oh, no, no… She wouldn't say anything that might introduce suspicion to one of our own dear… oh, no, no."

I felt awful. Mrs. Quinn hadn't relayed Bert's movements to the police, but I had—with gusto.

Mrs. B stood up abruptly, aware of incoming customers, but leaned closer. "So it seems Bert was the only person who could have done it," she whispered, her brow knitted into a frown. "Terrible business—simply terrible."

At that, she hurried off to the new arrivals.

I poured my tea from the little sewing machine teapot.

These timings didn't tally. Both DI Kenon and I had seen Bert walking down Park Road at about 5.15. If he'd then reached the allotment gate, he certainly wouldn't have allowed Derek in to devastate the plots. And if he'd walked toward his shed, and come across Jack then killed him, it was baffling to think Bert would then hang around for a further thirty minutes.

I quickly finished my sandwich and tea, paid the bill and left.

My mind was now in more turmoil than ever.

I glanced around the park and wondered where I could go to fathom these contradictions. I spotted the band stand further along the path to my right. There I could sit unnoticed under the shade of its cherry red roof. Such solitude appealed right now.

I climbed the three steps and sat under the awning, trying to rationalise the tumble of thoughts that wrestled for prime position in my brain. Until I reasoned them out they would continue to mess with my head.

I began with Jack Nabb.

Information only I knew plagued me. Why had Jack gone to steal basic tools from Bert's shed when he already had Kim providing him with money from the hotel? It seemed a rather *low* thing to do—even by Nabb family standards. And why choose to rob Bert around five o'clock in the afternoon when the locals knew he went to his allotment after finishing work in the park? If Jack had planned on stealing from Bert's shed, he'd have checked that fact out ahead of time, surely?

I stroked my index finger along my lip... the questions were valid, but knowing they were valid questions didn't answer them.

I tried a totally different angle, this time leaving money out of the equation. Had Jack dated Amy and was still in love with her? Had she ditched him because he wasn't a good provider—the all-important quality her mother hammered home. Was Jack bitter about being dumped? That was possible, as from what I now know of him, he was a man capable of bearing grudges.

I stood up and gazed from my elevated position across to the park lake. A flotilla of swans drifted gracefully across the glassy surface. There wasn't even a gentle breeze today. This August drought was becoming prolonged.

I opted to stroll down toward the lake. It looked so beautiful, so serene, and I needed serenity. Taking the shortcut across the grass I hoped a park gardener wouldn't reprimand me.

I crept across the manicured lawn to reach a bench by the small jetty, overlooking the water. It appeared the rowing boat hire business was no longer in operation. I should ask Hilda about that; it was such a lovely thing to do on those long summer days when we were kids. So sad they were no longer here. Maybe I could raise the topic in the Swansneck Messenger? I could write an article to ask if somebody would want to start up the boat hire again.

A couple of Mallard ducks waddled up to my feet, then quacked in disgust as I didn't have bread for them. They soon lost interest and sauntered off to a shady spot, burying their heads within soft downy feathers, to settle down for a snooze.

I gazed at the lake and my mind floated back to its deliberations.

Vinnie. Why hadn't I considered the scrappy notes I'd

found at the pigeon loft before now? I'd pushed the paper into my handbag the other day, telling myself I'd get a chance to study them while at the shop. But events had overrun me. I hastily rummaged through my bag.

Ah, there they were. I treated them with respect and smoothed them out on my lap.

THE CLOCK IS TICKING

THIS IS THE START—NOT THE END

Vinnie definitely wrote these. I recalled the simple capital letter print he used, both on the darts team notice board at the pub, and the darts tournament schedule handed to Mrs. Horridge.

So what did the cryptic pigeon messages mean, and who had received them?

Bert?

No matter how I tried, I couldn't make Bert and the messages connect. So I considered the other people at the loft.

Nick? I knew little about him but remembered he was taking his wife out to an anniversary dinner in Preston on Friday evening. So if asked, that would be his alibi. I wasn't aware of any connection between Nick and Jack either. Although, if my other deliberations drew a blank, I'd consider broadening my investigations to include Nick.

Tim?

I sat up on the bench with a jolt. Tim, Amy's father, at last, a connection between random puzzle parts.

Jack—Vinnie—Amy—Tim.

I read each of the cryptic messages again, but this time applying known connections between these four players.

THE CLOCK IS TICKING...

I thought about the wording. A clock, a time clock perhaps—like those used for the pigeon races.

Tim belonged to the pigeon racing set and Vinnie drove for the conveyor company the Racing Association contracted to transport the birds to the release spot. The fastest birds won prize money and even a car in national races. Perhaps Vinnie had ensured Tim's birds did well?

But they couldn't win every prize from the Association races; that would be too obvious. I had heard about betting syndicates. Although if Tim and Vinnie were fixing pigeon races, neither of them could place bets on the birds themselves without suspicion. So was Jack placing bets for the group? Had I uncovered another of the Nabbs' money making scams?

I applied the same train of thought to the second message...

THIS IS THE START—NOT THE END...

The end of what? Had somebody tried to end something? Had Tim threatened to pull out of their racing scam and his partners were not happy about losing an income?

I shook my head. I couldn't see Tim involved in a betting scam with the Nabbs as his partners in crime. That didn't add up to the person I'd found Tim to be. He was a hard working family man, not a petty crook.

Okay, I told myself. Drop the birds from your thoughts. Nobody ever got murdered over a pigeon race.

I needed to try again, but this time I had to come up with a different angle to connect the four names.

THE CLOCK IS TICKING... Ticking toward what? What other event was nearing when I found that message on Friday morning?

The wedding!

Hmm. I considered the love triangle I'd discussed with Greg.

Amy had a crush on Vinnie, and even though he didn't appear to reciprocate her infatuation—Jack still seemed jealous. Hence their argument.

Nevertheless, Amy went on to marry Mark Drinkall, so what was the point in sending messages to Tim? That made little sense.

Out of the corner of my eye, I noticed the ducks stretching their wings. They had awoken and waddled back to check me out, not realising I was the same person who didn't have food for them on their last attempt. They were not as shrewd as Derek. I smirked. Derek would have known it was a waste of time to try begging from the same person twice.

Then, as though somehow aware I was thinking about him, Derek gave one of his loud cries. His piercing call... eeeoww, eeeoww, eeeoww broke the afternoon stillness, causing other birds on and around the lake to make their own calls. It seemed like a cacophony of conversations being transmitted throughout the park. Then, just as quickly as it had begun—it stopped.

The raucous interruption made me think about Derek. Why had Bert allowed him to get into the allotments and cause so much damage to the vegetables? A slip up as serious as that just wasn't like Bert. He knew the allotment holders relied on selling their produce to the hotel chef, and that he'd demand perfection. Half pecked food just wouldn't make it onto the restaurant plate. I know Bert felt ill on Friday morning, but still. He knew full well the level of destruction a bird like Derek would do if let loose in there. He'd be like a kid in a sweet shop...

I got up from the bench and tiptoed back across the manicured lawn to reach the band stand. From there I stole along the path toward the aviary. I wanted to see Derek if he was there...

I neared the aviary and saw that Agnes had indeed been around with the bird seed. There was a flurry of birds and even a cheeky pigeon or two taking advantage of the free-for-all. A pair of geese honked to chase them away, but the pigeons were way too cool about their mission. As a breed, they'd been through several world wars, so a few honking geese would be no setback. They just hopped to the other side and continued pecking.

I stood and watched their antics, and then from around the far side of the aviary, Derek appeared. He strode with that confident manner he had, his iridescent blue and green plumage shimmering as he dragged his long tail feather train behind him. The little top-knot crest on his head wobbled as he spotted Agnes headed to the palm house. But Derek was late to the feeding party today, and I watched him trail after Agnes toward the palm house hoping to get something.

It was only when Agnes removed Bert's jacket to hang it inside the palm house door, that I noticed Derek's reaction. As Agnes closed the door behind her and left, Derek stayed fixated on the jacket, staring at it through the glass panel.

Then it hit me.

Derek didn't follow Bert... he followed the jacket.

To him, the jacket represented bird seed. And who was it that always wore the jacket? Well, until a couple of days ago, Bert, but in the last few days, it had been Agnes.

I quickly headed for the main park gate, wanting to get home... this was a whole new revelation.

I sensed the jigsaw puzzle falling into place.

CHAPTER TWENTY-SEVEN

I put the kettle on, made a big pot of tea and sat down at my little yellow kitchen table. A sense of excitement ran through me. The answers were within me if I could just drag them out.

I placed the pigeon messages on the table, opened my notepad, grabbed my pen and got down to business.

THE CLOCK IS TICKING

I felt sure this referred to the wedding.

But why use pigeons to relay threats? Because it would be spooky to receive a threat via one of your pigeons? Perhaps the sender wanted to play nasty mind games on the recipient? Plus, Vinnie's job provided easy access to the birds.

So who was the intended recipient? Definitely Tim, I concluded. He was the only person at the lofts with a direct connection to the wedding.

I sipped my tea and jotted down those notes.

Okay, so why would Jack and Vinnie be so interested in the impending nuptials? I didn't think either of them would be overly concerned about losing Amy to another man. And from what I'd heard in the village, the Nabb family's only concern was getting easy money.

I chewed on the end of my pen.

Blackmail was easy money and blackmail was the crime

I'd thought linked Jack to George. Although wrong on that point, I had it from Kim's own lips that Jack was blackmailing her to carry out the bar fraud. So it seemed, blackmail is—was—Jack Nabb's modus operandi. He was a leech on Swansneck society, and he always kept an eye open for an opportunity to suck blood from new prey.

So, if his final victim was Tim, what hold did Jack have over him that would make him pay up to any demands?

I glanced down at the four names I'd written across the top of my pad. And one jumped out at me.

Amy.

If you wanted to get at Tim, you threatened Amy. His weak spot was his angel—Amy.

But what would he use for a blackmail threat? It would need to be something that would destroy Amy's plans... and her plans were to make a good match with a solid and respectable man.

I finished one cup of tea and poured myself another; the action reminding me of Nelly Higson's comment at the Tearooms. She claimed Amy *"Was a bit of a one,"* and Marilyn had said Amy *"Had a thing for older men."*

I tapped my pen on the table.

Did Amy have a secret past? Had she been involved with multiple unsuitable men before taking her mother's advice to heart and settling for Mark? Perhaps Amy did something a *nice girl who plans to marry an aspiring accountant* shouldn't do?

If Jack had indisputable proof of such misbehaviour, threatening Tim with its exposure would be a license to print money. And Tim would be his printing press.

I looked at the second message... I'd picked this up on Saturday morning, the morning of the wedding.

THIS IS THE START—NOT THE END

Had Tim paid Jack to keep his silence? If so, this second message clearly told Tim the payment was not final—it was just the start of bleeding him dry.

But Jack was already dead by Friday evening, so the Saturday message couldn't have been from him. The message was in Vinnie's handwriting, so it must have been from Vinnie. As the truck driver, he also had the opportunity to send it. Was he trying to keep the Nabb family business alive, perhaps? Did he consider the Tim money tree too good an opportunity to let go?

I noted these thoughts down on the pad. I was getting more puzzle parts, but they still didn't fit into one cohesive picture. What was I missing?

Tim said he'd been stuck in a traffic jam at the time of the murder. I tried to remember the details of what he'd said at the lofts—when he'd become animated about his terrible week and I'd become bored. I frowned. He'd said there was an oil tanker spill that caused the delay.

Didn't Marilyn say she saw details of the jam on the TV news? So Tim could have seen that too.

Was Tim lying about being stuck in that traffic?

I pushed away the remains of my cold cup of tea and stood. A change of outlook might change my thought processes. This small kitchen could constrict my imagination, and I needed my full range of faculties right now. I entered the front room and brushed aside the net curtain to peer out the window. The memory of Bert and Derek walking to the allotments flashed before my eyes, combined with my new discovery—that Derek would follow the jacket no matter who wore it.

Out of the blue, the puzzle fell into place and I instantly knew what I should do.

I checked my watch. It was past four o'clock. I hadn't realised it was so late. But as I'd already arranged to see Tim at 4.30, the timing was perfect.

Although, I didn't want Billy to be at the lofts.

I dashed back to the kitchen and dug my phone from my

handbag, suddenly realising I didn't have Billy's contact number, or Peggy's. Hilda had relayed my earlier messages, so my only choice was to ask her to contact Peggy and delay Billy's visit until another day.

I quickly tapped out a text message to Hilda, then pulled DI Kenon's now tatty card from my bag and dialled his number. It went straight through to voicemail.

"Hello. It's Jenny Bradshaw. I need to speak to you. I've uncovered vital information regarding Jack Nabb's murder."

Again, I glanced at my watch. It was four-twenty and I needed to get a move on to meet Tim. If I missed him, he would be on his way to Belgium... and I didn't have to be an investigative genius to fathom that he wouldn't be back. I hesitated. Not able to recite all the details of my breakthrough in a voicemail, so I gave DI Kenon the pertinent facts.

"I believe Tim Yates is the killer, I've already arranged a 4.30 meeting at the lofts... so can't wait to talk with you." I babbled. "He's planning to leave Swansneck at five o'clock, going to Belgium. I'll do my best to delay him. Please meet me at the lofts."

The message was garbled, but there was nothing I could do about that now. I grabbed my handbag and made for the door.

CHAPTER TWENTY-EIGHT

Breathless by the time I reached the lofts, I rounded the corner and saw Tim already there, bending to close the latch on his loft door. For a stupid fleeting moment, I wondered what would happen to his pigeons when he went on the run.

Tim straightened up and smiled broadly.

"Hi, Jenny. There's no sign of Billy yet, but there's still time..."

"Ah, yes, about that," I said, catching my breath, wondering what on earth I should say to delay him.

"It's Billy, you see," I drawled. "He sent me a text. He's not coming, changed his mind about taking on the birds." I shrugged. "Kids, eh?"

"That's a real shame. I was looking forward to meeting him. Oh, well." He checked his watch. "Time to get going then."

I panicked at my stupidity for giving him an opportunity to leave. Think, quick!

"While you have a moment, Tim, would you check my birds, please? They may be sick."

"Really? Well...there have been some alerts about bird flu..." Concerned, he walked along the row to reach my loft. "Let's take a look at them..."

He unlatched the door, and upon entering the restricted space of the loft, a flurry of wings and preened feathers filled the air.

The flapping and anxiety of the pigeons disturbed me and their unrest seemed to the point of hysteria. I felt guilty for ignoring them this morning.

Tim calmed them and inspected each bird like an expert.

"Nope, they seem fine. Nothing to worry about." He came back out of the loft and closed the latches. "You need to give them food and water today though. It's been so hot and dry."

I nodded and sought to get my mind back on track. What to say next?

Another idea dawned on me.

"Tim. I wanted to ask you a favour."

"Yes?"

"It's about Bert."

"What about him?"

"Well, Agnes must be under tremendous stress now he's been arrested, poor lady. So I was thinking..."

I watched him as I spoke of Bert; he was agitated and repeatedly checked his watch. I sensed my suspicions were right, but I needed to keep up these delay tactics.

"So?" Tim asked.

"Nick has already volunteered to care for Bert's pigeon loft, so, I thought we'd also volunteer to help out. You care for the aviary birds each evening after work, and I'll see to Bert's allotment."

He clenched his teeth.

I kept up the pretence.

"You have amazing knowledge about birds, so you're the best man in the village to take over from Bert. Just for the time being." *Until they discover he's innocent*, I said in my head, then continued. "I know you're going away to Belgium for a few days, but I could tell Agnes you'd be happy to help her out on your return."

Tim was now looking downright angry. My stomach lurched. Had I pushed the helpful neighbour act too far?

"But the allotments... They must still be out of bounds for

the police investigations?"

"Oh no, I was down there the other day. All signs of the police have gone, except for their big boots having trampled all over stuff, that is." I tried to sound exasperated by the inconvenience, like Lilly Halliwell with seven L's.

"But wouldn't the other plot holders take care of Bert's allotment?" Tim's voice was irate, although as to why I wasn't sure. I wasn't asking him to attend to Bert's plot.

"Well no," I said. "They're far too busy replanting their vegetables after the destruction and mayhem caused by the police and Derek." As soon as the word Derek passed my lips, I knew I'd said too much. My confidence had gotten the better of me, and I watched Tim's face drain of colour.

"What makes you think Derek was in the allotments?" he said, raising one eyebrow.

"Well, I, err... it was a guess," I stammered.

But he didn't believe me, I could tell.

I tried to swallow. My throat was dry and rasped like sand paper. I dredged up a little saliva to keep me going. Where was DI Kenon? Had he got my message? Oh God, what had I done?

"You know, don't you?" A steel-like hardness entered Tim's grey eyes.

"Know? Know what?" I said innocently and backed up a step closer to my loft.

"Don't play daft with me, Jenny. You're a bright girl. Tell me what you know."

I had no choice but to confess. Still, I needn't give him the version I believed. I could present him with one of my alternative, incorrect versions—to buy me time.

"You received blackmail threats." I said as levelly as I could muster. Then, with a deep breath, I pulled the two little scraps of paper from my handbag and handed them to him. He glanced at them and let them drop to the floor. They floated down from his hands like feathers in a light breeze.

"I know Vinnie took part..." I began. "The notes are in his handwriting, and he had access to your birds during the races and training runs."

Tim straightened. "You're quite the detective, aren't you, Jen?" He curved his lips into an artificial smile. "So what did you deduce from that..?"

"That you were all involved in a pigeon racing scam, to make money from betting." His eyes bore into mine as I spoke. Like an eagle, he watched for a flicker of hesitation from his prey.

"But Vinnie wanted Jack out of the picture," I stammered. Unnerved by his eyes, I sought to misdirect him further but struggled to find a continuation to my lie that worked. I floundered. I was in a serious mess, and from his expression he knew it.

"And..?" he enquired.

"And you wanted out of the betting scam... But they wanted you to stay... That's what the messages mean."

He gave a derisory laugh. "Is that the best you can do? You honestly believe I'd kill someone over a pigeon race? I'm shocked you have such a low opinion of me."

"I don't have a low opinion of you, Tim," I squeaked. Did he notice he'd just admitted to killing Jack? I prayed he hadn't caught that important fact.

"But bravo, Jenny," he said, giving me a slow hand clap. "You should go on the stage with an acting ability like that." He took a step closer. "Now one more time, eh? With feeling..."

My shoulders sagged. It was useless, so I relented.

"Jack and Vinnie wanted to extract money from you. To protect Amy from the—"

"Truth?" he finished for me.

"Well, yes, I suppose you could put it that way," I answered, although I wasn't sure what he meant by it. "Mark would have refused to marry Amy if he knew, and that would have ended Sharon's hopes for her future."

"And what do you care about Sharon's hopes for Amy?" he barked at me. "What about my hopes for her, eh?"

Previously his anger had simmered beneath the surface. Now it had erupted.

What was Tim saying? He inferred something completely different to what I'd said. I shook my head in confusion but had to continue. I prayed I'd hear police sirens soon. I had to keep Tim talking, so I tried another approach.

"You were under a lot of stress before the wedding, Tim," I said softly to defuse his rage.

"Stress..? Stress..!" he exploded. "You wouldn't know the meaning of the word. Nobody could understand what I experienced in the weeks before the wedding..."

I kept my silence although my eyes spoke volumes to him as they grew to the size of pies.

"Working overtime every day, slaving like a dog to make enough sales to boost my commission. I had wedding bills to cover and was in debt up to the hilt. It was impossible to meet the demands he made."

"He? Don't you mean *they*?"

Tim narrowed his eyes and his forehead glistened with beads of sweat. "You know I mean Jack. You've already guessed that far."

I swallowed hard. "Well, it wasn't so much guess work as information gathering," I whispered. But why I felt the need to improve his opinion of my fact finding abilities was beyond me.

"Information? Please enlighten me."

I hesitated, not sure if I should say my next thought, but judging by his expression, I had no choice.

"That... that... Amy had a thing for older men," I faltered. "That she had done things with men Jack could prove..."

"You're off the mark there." He gave me a twisted grin, then stepped closer to whisper in my ear. "Try again."

His breath was hot on my cheek. I attempted to swallow, but my throat rejected the concept.

My mind darted around all the solutions I'd tried earlier today, seeking to grab one and reveal it to Tim.

What about Jack being in love with Amy? No, it wasn't a workable reason for blackmail, so I didn't even voice that idea.

Tim's closeness unnerved me. I took a step back, but he stepped forward to keep the same distance between our faces. I tried a different approach.

"You're dedicated to your family... to Amy..." I dropped her name hoping to soothe his threatening behaviour. "Everyone knows you'd do anything for your Amy..."

The tactic worked, in that his eyes softened and he smiled. "My Amy. That's just the point. She is *my* Amy, and I treated her as my angel. I promised her wedding day would be the best day of her life. But he would have shattered that promise..." His eyes darkened again.

I tried to clear my throat to speak with clarity, but I was so dry I only croaked. "You gave her that day, Tim. You didn't break your promise to her."

Desperate to get away from here and at a loss what else to say, I edged back again, only to hit the wire mesh of my pigeon loft. I'd backed up as far as possible so turned my head to look away from him—to seek an escape route. But he read my mind.

"Do you really think I can let you go... now that you know the secret?"

"But that's just it, Tim, I don't know, honestly I don't. You can see that by the stupid theories I've given you."

He leaned forward and hissed into my ear like a serpent. "But you worked out I'd killed Jack, and that's enough."

In a heartbeat, I understood what he meant by *enough*. My blood pulsed through my veins. It was obvious; once he'd confessed the murder he'd also have to silence me, just as he had Jack.

I had no idea how to escape him, but I had to keep him talking; so I tried to justify his actions for him.

"But, you only killed Jack to protect Amy... from the truth." Still clueless as to what this mysterious truth was, I kept going. "Tim, did you believe the truth would have put a stop to Amy marrying Mark? Is there anything in today's world that people haven't already seen on the internet?"

Tim looked perplexed for a moment then shook his head. "The Internet? Ah! You think the blackmail was about porn videos?" He pushed his face closer to mine then inclined his head and smiled. A shocking, twisted smile. "Wrong again, my little detective, try harder."

I was getting exasperated by these enforced guessing games. I'd grasped at every crazy theory that had crossed my mind. It was as though he was demanding me to get it right. But then I wondered if the delay was a good thing for me. Although it seemed I was now in the same situation Kim had found herself in with Jack Nabb. Damned if I did and damned if I didn't.

He seized my shoulders. How else could I appeal to him?

"What about Sharon? She... she..." I wasn't sure where I was going with that. "Jack was blackmailing you, Tim, nobody would blame you... Except for Sharon maybe, she'd have said you should have..." As I uttered the words, his grip tightened. His fingers dug deep, and in a flash, I knew I'd discovered the secret.

I stared into his eyes. "It's Jack... isn't it?" I whispered. "Jack is Amy's father."

He didn't have to deny or confirm it. The black thunder that tracked across his face was confirmation enough.

"Jack threatened to tell the whole congregation at the church." Tim spat the words into my face. "He swore he'd tell my Amy that I wasn't her biological father and that she was a Nabb." He lifted his eyebrows and gave a sardonic smile. "But Jack didn't expect the worm to turn, did he?"

I gasped.

"In the beginning, I would have given Jack what he asked, but as each day arrived, he raised the amount I had to pay. I tried to find the money, but it was futile. I'd never get the amount he demanded in time."

Tim glared at me, a man pushed beyond the brink. Jack Nabb had been stupid to imagine he could do that to someone and not expect a backlash.

Tim continued. "I contacted Jack and told him to meet me at the allotments. On that Friday it would be deserted at five o'clock because Bert said he was too sick to do his work at the park, let alone his allotment. I told Jack to meet me at Bert's shed. Nobody would see us talking there."

Tim's nearness showed every degree of his strain. Tension coiled within him as he confessed what happened that day.

"I intended to tell Jack I couldn't make the full payment in time. That he'd get the rest at the end of the month." Tim broke off and gave a little nervous laugh. "In my stupidity, I believed it would be a one off payment..."

His expression changed to fury, a pale flabby cheeked man driven to murder. Holding my breath, I gaped at him in horror.

"I told Jack I couldn't pay him everything before the wedding, but he just laughed at me. I pleaded with him, but he wouldn't wait—said he'd reveal everything at the church."

I stared at Tim speechless, rooted to the spot.

"You must understand..." Tim pleaded of me. "Jack was being totally unreasonable. I told him, I'm only an ordinary working man for heaven's sake, where was I going to spirit a lump sum of money at a moment's notice?" Tim's voice was both desperate and exasperated. "It was when I called Jack the lowest life form on the planet that he took a swing at me." Tim's face paled. "I blocked his punch and pushed his force back at him. He lost his balance—fell backward—and hit his head on those rockery stones. It was instant. There was no going back."

I let out my breath. His description of the scene was vivid. The hard, sharp rockery stones. Despite the sweltering heat, my blood chilled.

"But why implicate Bert?" I murmured. "Why would you do that?"

"It wasn't my first reaction," He looked deep into my eyes. "That was your fault..."

"Me!" I squeaked. How can he twist this onto me?

"Yes, it was you... you and that florist; you were on the corner when I reached the allotment gate. I couldn't leave without being seen by you. So I had to use the river stepping stones to get to the park. It was the only way out."

My eyes widened as I thought of the same stepping stones we'd played on as kids. But we had used them as a game of mischief, not a game of murder.

Tim continued his warped concept of it being my fault, my fault that Bert was now languishing in jail.

"You provided the time I needed to stop panicking. During those minutes that felt like hours to me, I realised something. When someone discovered Jack's body without an obvious reason for his death, the police would ask too many questions. They'd dig so deep they'd find out about the blackmail and expose the secret." His eyes took on a meek, almost innocent expression. "It wasn't anything personal against Bert. We were beside his shed, so it was only natural. The Nabbs were petty thieves. No surprise if they were up to their old tricks. So I went into the palm house to get Bert's jacket and cap and picked up a trowel in there too. Then I walked out of the main gate and down Park Road, just as Bert does. When I reached the allotments, I jemmied the lock on Bert's shed." He paused, seeming to relive the moment he'd seen the body for the second time. "I'd planned to get back to the park via the river again, but I hadn't counted on that damned peacock." A twisted smile hovered on his lips. "I wasn't aware Derek had followed me, you see—that he'd come through the gate behind me and was pecking away at the vegetables. I knew I couldn't leave him there... had to get him back to the park, or he'd blow my whole plan. Bert would never have let Derek get in through the gate, everyone knew that. So I led him out, locked the gate and headed back to the park, but this time over the footbridge. I returned the jacket, cap, and trowel to the palm house and left the park by the main gate again."

I couldn't fathom the lengths he'd gone to, all to pin his horrible crime on Bert.

"Didn't you consider what would happen to Bert?" I exclaimed.

Tim shrugged. "Oh, he'd be hailed a hero. An old man who caught a known petty thief breaking into his shed and fought off an attack. Self-defence. Any court in the country would be full of sympathy for Bert and let him off with a suspended sentence. He'd have been okay."

Even though I understood the warped theory behind Tim's logic, it still wasn't right. The stress could have killed Bert, and Tim would have had two deaths on his hands... or should I consider that to be three?

Tim still held a firm grip on my shoulders and sensed my body tense against my last thought. He gave me a shake, causing my handbag strap to slip from my shoulder, and the bag clattered to the ground. I peered down at it and fleetingly wondered how to reach my phone to call for help. But that was impossible. I looked back at his face, and like an alley cat challenge, we attempted to stare each other out. Suddenly he whipped one of his arms around the back of my neck and clamped it about my throat, and then twisted my body to hold me partly behind him, a shift that rendered me helpless.

His forearm pressed against my wind pipe. When I tried

to make a noise he applied more pressure, a move that informed me if I tried to shout out, he would strangle me for sure.

Nevertheless, I didn't make it easy for him as he pulled me away from the lofts. What did he plan to do to me? It didn't take long before I his intention became clear.

He dragged me behind him, my head in a wrestler's arm clamp, and I stumbled backward as he marched forwards— towards the river bank.

The low undergrowth that covered the span between the lofts and the river bank was not wide. It wouldn't be long before I faced the sheer drop to the exposed rocks.

I twisted and struggled as much as his strangle hold permitted. The dust I kicked up from the dry earth clouded around us, and he coughed as he hauled me toward the edge. I would never survive being thrown onto the huge jagged rocks of the river bed.

Then I heard a boy's voice shouting my name.

"Jenny! Where are you? Jenny... Sorry I'm late... Jenny!"

Tim stopped, but we had reached the river bank, I sensed he was preparing to twist me around and push me off the edge. I tried to shout back to Billy, but Tim's strangle hold tightened. Panicking I struggled to break free then I suddenly remembered his limp since the wedding reception. While I was still behind him, it would be my only chance.

I lifted my right leg as high as possible and aimed the hardest heel kick I could muster into the side of his knee. In an instant, he dropped to the floor with a howl. I'd hit my target. My action caused him to release his hold around my throat, and I dashed back to the lofts to reach Billy. I tried to yell to him, to tell him I was here. I didn't want him to leave, but my parched throat was raw.

"Billy!" I shouted, over and over again, but it was only a croak.

I emerged from the shrubbery, to find Billy standing

there, shock etched on his face. Then his eyes fixed on something beyond me. He was looking toward Tim. I grabbed Billy's arm and tugged him back with me to reach the lofts.

Would Tim try to take on the two of us?

But Tim had come to his senses, and instead of confronting us he half-ran, half-hobbled toward the far side of the bathhouse, making his escape to the road. Then as he rounded the corner and out of sight there was a loud clatter and a scream of pain.

"My bike!" yelled Billy, tearing from my grasp. He ran to where Tim had gone from sight.

"Billy... no!" I screeched, but it was too late. The boy was around the corner like a prize Whippet.

I caught up to Billy, only to see him standing stock still and staring down at Tim.

As he'd made his escape, Tim had run straight into Billy's bike. It was lying on the ground and among the twisted metal spokes was Tim's leg, splayed at a painful, unnatural angle. He groaned in agony.

Billy didn't understand what he'd accomplished. He just looked over at me with a guilty expression.

"I'm sorry," he said in a childish, flat voice. "My mum's always telling me off for leaving my bike on the ground."

I gazed at the young boy who'd inadvertently saved my life, my ears failing to register the wail of police sirens, the slamming of car doors and the shouting of police. Then, jolted me out of my daze, I whirled around to see a familiar face.

DI Kenon.

CHAPTER TWENTY-NINE

I sat in the beer garden of The Flying Shuttle with DI Kenon on Sunday afternoon. Although I'd already given my statement of Friday's events, he'd asked if we could meet, and we agreed on the pub beer garden.

I sipped a long cool sarsaparilla through a straw. The soft drink seemed in keeping with local tradition and the virtuous beliefs of Cornelius Swan. His stern, sober statue regarded us from across the village green, where over the centuries it kept watch over his small empire.

DI Kenon eyed me with concern. "How are you feeling now?"

"Better, thanks. Physically, I have a few bruises, but it's more the shock of it all..."

"You truly had us on this one," he said with a wry smile. "We didn't suspect Tim Yates at all."

"That's hardly surprising. His motive stemmed from a well-kept secret."

I considered George Lees and Kim. Through my village connections, I was now the holder of their secrets too. But I'd made promises to both Hilda and Kim that I couldn't break. It was best to let the threat of exposed secrets go with Jack Nabb to his grave. There was nothing to gain by telling DI Kenon about them.

"I'm sorry about the delay in getting to you on Friday. I

was in a briefing at Preston Police Headquarters so I didn't hear your voicemail until the meeting finished."

"But I couldn't wait..." I said. "My meeting with Tim was already arranged for 4.30. If I hadn't shown up, we'd have lost our chance."

"You were taking a massive risk though." He wagged his finger at me and frowned.

"My only intention was to stall him until you arrived... to prevent him leaving the country."

"I wondered about that. You know, I'm not sure if you were stupid facing up to him alone, or brave."

"I'd prefer to think of it as brave, thank you very much."

DI Kenon smirked, entertained by my judicious choice from the two available options.

"We took Tim into custody—after he'd been to the hospital and had his dislocated knee strapped up, that is."

"And Bert?" I asked.

"Released, once we had Tim in custody—and your statement about his confession..."

A childish yell filled the air, followed by a squeal from a little girl. DI Kenon instinctively looked away from me, to check all was well.

For a brief moment, we watched the girl tumbling on the grass near her father.

"This brings me to another question I have for you..." he said. "What made you put all the pieces together as you did?"

"I can't take all the credit." I laughed. "It was Derek. He's the one who saved Bert!"

DI Kenon regarded me with disbelief. I needed to explain the comment, so he didn't decide I'd finally lost what remained of my common sense.

"I'd been strolling around the park when I noticed that Derek doesn't, in fact, follow Bert. We were all convinced he trailed after him because he was so devoted. But in reality, Derek follows the jacket as his food comes from the pockets. It was at that moment I realised there was truth in Agnes's alibi for Bert. Agnes is just not a lady who can lie—her nervousness would get the better of her—even if her husband's freedom depended on it. And then I knew, anyone could have put on Bert's jacket and cap and pretended to be him."

DI Kenon shook his head. "You are kidding me, right?"

"No, honestly, it was Derek who alerted me to the truth. Although, when Tim wore the jacket he didn't consider Derek would follow him either. As he, like all of us in Swansneck, thought Derek only followed Bert." I shrugged. It even sounded crazy to my ears. "The problem was Derek had falsely confirmed for everyone—including you, the police—that it was Bert who'd walked down Park Road around the time the murder took place."

"So Derek dropped Bert in it..." said DI Kenon.

"And then pulled him out again..." I added quickly. Derek was my hero; he'd helped me to save Bert from prison.

"We questioned Sharon Yates," he continued, taking a gulp of his cool lemonade. "She confirmed the background to Amy's true paternity, just as you said in your statement. She admitted dating Jack Nabb, back in the day and found herself pregnant at nineteen. Even if Jack had suggested he'd do the right thing by her—although she doubted he would—she didn't want to marry into the Nabb family. So she never told him of her pregnancy. Sharon began dating Tim, and when she realised he was a decent bloke, she told him she was having Jack's baby. As she'd suspected, Tim said he'd marry her and take the baby as his own."

"Well, that certainly explains the life advice she gave to both Amy and Marilyn," I mused.

DI Kenon raised a questioning eyebrow.

"Sharon told them to look for a good man," I explained. "How they should not use passion as the deciding factor when choosing a life mate." I gave him the abbreviated version of Sharon's lecture.

He nodded. Whether he agreed with Sharon's take on relationships or not, he didn't volunteer. He picked up his glass and drained it.

"Another?" he asked as he stood.

"I've got to admit, I am still suffering from a parched throat, DI Kenon." I twiddled the straw in what remained of my drink and melted ice cubes.

"Please... less of the DI Kenon... it's Dave." He smiled. "After all, we are neighbours."

I returned his friendly grin. "Okay, in that case, I'll have another sarsaparilla please, Dave..."

He disappeared into the pub to replenish our drinks and I watched the father and child run around the green. I thought about Tim and his protective instincts toward Amy. His passionate need to protect his family was now the reason it would be broken apart. I wondered how Amy was taking the news—and then remembered she was still on honeymoon in Dubai. Poor girl had a lot to take in on her return.

Dave placed fresh drinks on our table and sat down again.

"We've arrested Vinnie, by the way," he said. "We're charging him with blackmail."

"Really... even though it was Jack who threatened Tim with the fatherhood secret?"

"Yes, Vinnie was an accomplice. He wrote the messages you had found at the loft. He knew what his brother was up to and helped him carry out his demands with menace."

"I was wondering why Jack had waited until now to blackmail Tim. Why not sooner? It's been over twenty years since Amy's birth."

"I questioned Vinnie about that. He said Jack was always on the lookout to make money—but hadn't known Amy was his child until the village was abuzz about the flashy Yates wedding. When he saw Amy talking to Vinnie, and found out who her mother was, he put two and two together and came up with the plan. Apparently, Jack's thinking was that Amy couldn't be Tim's child because she didn't have his pale colouring. Amy has Jack's dark curly hair and the sallow Nabb complexion."

"But still... That's a weak supposition. Children are born with different colouring to their natural parents all the time. Sometimes it can even skip a generation."

"You know that, and I know that, which is why it's all so sad."

I didn't get his point. "Sad? Why do you say sad?"

"Vinnie said they took a punt on Tim and only knew for sure that Jack's guess was right when their first message hooked him." Dave Kenon shook his head. "If Tim had ignored their first message—if he'd stood up to them and told them to get lost—Jack and Vinnie wouldn't have pursued him. They'd have assumed they'd got it wrong and moved on to some other poor sod with their scams."

"Hmm, I see your point," I said. "Tim's willingness and sheer passion to protect Amy from the truth was his downfall."

"There's that word again... passion." Dave nodded. "I suppose crimes of passion can present themselves in different ways." He brushed his hand along his chin, thoughtfully. "Although, I don't think Tim committed pre-meditated murder," he said, more to himself than me.

"What makes you say so? You heard his car alarm, which was part of his created alibi wasn't it? That, and being stuck in traffic on the M6 all afternoon."

"Yes, but they were created after the fact. I don't believe he had them in his mind before he met Jack at the allotments. He created them on the fly after Jack died. Once he'd implicated Bert by using his jacket, he realised he needed something to cover himself. So he opened his car to set off the alarm close to six o'clock. And it was easy to say he was in that traffic jam, as it was reported all over the news

Friday evening. After that, nobody gave him a second thought as a suspect. With no obvious connection between him and Jack, why would they?"

I had to agree, it didn't appear pre-meditated.

"Tim admitted he planned to leave the country permanently," Dave continued. "Once the wedding day was over, he booked the trip to Belgium. With several job applications and interviews arranged over there, he was fairly confident he'd get an immediate job due to his business contacts. So, you were right, he had no intention of coming back on Monday."

"But what about Sharon, did she know everything?"

"They both deny she had any knowledge of the blackmail or the murder, although we have no proof either way. It's my guess that Tim kept Sharon in the dark when he was being blackmailed, but after he'd killed Jack, he told her what happened so she didn't block their sudden move to Belgium. Sharon seemed quite agitated when we interviewed her. Even though she planned to go with him, I think this whole situation has left her shell-shocked."

"And their home, would they have simply left everything behind?"

"No, they planned to have Amy ship everything over to Belgium when she returned from her honeymoon. Tim was going to tell Amy he'd received a fantastic job opportunity that was too good to miss. In truth, he thought it best to get out of Swansneck now, while he wasn't a suspect."

"So when he showed such willingness to take Billy under his wing as his mentor..."

"You provided him with a good cover story. Tim agreeing to mentor Billy made it more believable he would only be away for a few days." He finished his drink. "Oh, I meant to ask you, the lad... Billy... Why did he show up when you told him not to come?"

"Ah, yes, I'd tried to stop him coming, but my message

didn't reach him. It was a text trail between Hilda and Peggy. I should have guessed they'd drop the ball on that!" I laughed. "But their lousy abilities with technology actually did me a favour."

"Saved your life, is how I'd phrase it," he said bluntly. "From what Billy told us you were about to meet your maker. He couldn't see you when he arrived, but he spotted your handbag on the floor at the coop and decided you must still be around there somewhere. Then he saw the dust clouds near the edge of the river bank."

"That must have been when he shouted for me—which distracted Tim."

"Allowing you do a karate style kick..."

"Hardly, but I see what you mean!" I laughed at the reference and then thought about the pigeons. "Nick contacted my dad last night, and volunteered to mentor Billy so he could take care of my, Dad's, Wilf's birds." I smirked. "Well, whoever they belonged to, they are now Billy's. Nick will be a good teacher. The Swansneck lofts are a village tradition. Young blood will carry it into the future."

A chime alerted me to a text, and I extracted my phone from my bag to check it out. It was from Hilda, inviting me to Sunday lunch. I replied, accepting her kind offer.

It was strange, when I'd arrived in Swansneck only two weeks ago, my fear had been that Dad and Hilda would be clingy and possessive, and that I'd feel trapped. With the arrogance of youth, I'd felt certain they'd want me with them all of the time, and I'd have no life of my own. But the opposite was the case. They'd forced me out of the bakery and made me find my way within the village. Now, I was the one grateful when they said they wanted to see me—grateful that I was again part of the Swansneck family.

I looked over at Cornelius Swan's statue. For the first time, I understood what it truly represented—not greed, or power—but a man with a vision for a community.

And now, with my Hat Shop soon to expand into vintage clothing, allowing me to express my passion for fashion, plus the planned facelift of the Swansneck Messenger, I realised—this was only the beginning.

THE END

GLOSSARY OF BRITISH TERMS

Allotments
An area of land divided into smaller plots. Each plot is then rented to an individual for growing vegetables or flowers.

Bay window
Architectural term: A window that sticks out from the outer wall of a house and usually has three sides. It forms a bay within the room.

Bloke
A man often considered to be a masculine, ordinary type of guy. "John is a really nice bloke."

Brassed-off
Exasperated, disgruntled or annoyed. "I'm really brassed off, I've been waiting in this queue for 30 minutes."

Cheeky sod
A light-hearted reprimand to someone who has crossed the line or is being presumptuous.

A brazen person who gets away with things no one else would. "He's a cheeky sod asking the boss for time off."

Cheeky sod usually refers to males, **cheeky mare** for females.

Chin wag
To gossip. "Let's get together for lunch and have a chin wag."

Coo-ee
A high pitched call shouted by females to attract someone's attention.

Cheese and onion pie
A savoury pie, with an upper and lower pastry crust, filled with a blend of melted cheese and onion.

Crap
Derogatory term, meaning bad or rubbish. "The bird table you made is crap." Or, "What you just said is a load of crap." The word is mildly abusive or insulting.

Dado rail
Architectural term: A decorative waist-high moulding fixed horizontally around the walls of a room. Often, the wall above the dado rail is then painted a different colour, or wallpapered.

Eccles cake
Originating from the town of Eccles in Lancashire, England, an Eccles cake is a buttery, flaky pastry filled with currents and sprinkled with sugar. But in 1650 they were actually forbidden by the Puritans! Oliver Cromwell decreed in an act of Parliament that anyone found eating a currant cake would be imprisoned. Fortunately, by the time of the Restoration of the Royal Family, the cakes were allowed once again.

Fells
Hills in the Lake District region of North West England are called Fells.

Full English breakfast
A substantial fried breakfast usually consisting of: eggs, bacon, sausage, grilled tomato, mushrooms and toast. Sometimes baked beans or fried potatoes are added.

Hot Pot
A Lancashire Hot Pot is savoury dish of lamb stew topped with slices of potato. A Hot Pot pie has an additional pastry lid.

Knick-knack
A small, worthless ornament. "The shelves in her room were covered in knick-knacks gathering dust."

Model Victorian Village
The fictional Swansneck village is thoroughly researched and based upon the *model industrial villages* that were built by rich Victorian industrialists of the era. The term *model*, means it demonstrated better living conditions for factory workers – although their homes were tied to their jobs at the mill. There were only a few of these 'model' villages built in England, mainly in the north, for textile mills and soap factories. The practice ensured a stable workforce, who couldn't leave their jobs without becoming homeless.

Novelty teapot
A decorative, ceramic teapot, often designed to resemble something else, or to be amusing.

Picture rail
Architectural term: A decorative moulding fixed around the walls of a room approximately 18"/50cm from the ceiling. The wall above the picture rail is painted, while the wall below is covered in wallpaper. The purpose of the picture rail was to enable pictures to be suspended from it, so as not to damage the wall surface.

Picture rail shelf
Architectural term: Positioned as the picture rail above, but it is a shelf, not a decorative moulding. Collections of decorative plates or ornaments were displayed on the high shelf.

Plot
The smaller section of land within the allotments. A gardener would rent and attend to his own plot.

Privy
A toilet located in a small shed outside a house or other building.

Rate of knots
Originating from the speed of a boat: knots, and can refer to doing something in a hurry. "She completed the task at a rate of knots so she could go home early."

Sash window
Architectural term: A window with two framed panes of glass, one above the other. The panes can be moved and slid open by operating a sash pulley mechanism. This style of window was generally fitted in Victorian properties.

Secret Service
Equivalent of the **CIA** or **MI5** in the UK.

Tearoom/s
A sedate establishment originating from the Victorian era for the purpose of 'taking tea'. Afternoon tea would generally consist of small triangular sandwiches, sponge cake or fondant fancies, and a pot of tea.

Victorian/ Victorian Era
The Victorian Era refers to the years of the reign of Queen Victoria in Great Britain: 1837 to 1901. Clothing, furniture and buildings are often referred to as Victorian in their design.

Whippet
A breed of dog descended from, and strongly resembling a small greyhound. Approximately 20"/50cm tall. Due to its keen hunting instinct and speed of chasing small game like rabbits it is also known as the poachers best friend. A lovable, affectionate breed also used as a therapy dog.

About the Author

V.S Vale was born in Lancashire, England, with family connections to the textile and clothing trade going back four generations. She has worked in the fashion; interior and jewellery design industry most of her life. In addition to this, she spends much of her time writing, and loves creating a fictional world inhabited by entertaining characters.

Having enjoyed the process of writing her first novel so much, she decided to make it a series of books, all centred on the gossipy, tight-knit community of Swansneck village.

Living in a seaside resort on the Lancashire coast, when she isn't working or writing, she enjoys walking on the beach with her little terrier-cross dog, Pepper. She also walks in the pinewoods close to her home, hoping to catch sight of the elusive red squirrels in the treetops. When time allows, she visits some of the many great heritage houses of England, and imagines the life stories of the people that once lived there.

"I'd love to hear if you enjoyed reading this first book in the series, and would be delighted if you left a review on the platform where you purchased it. I appreciate you taking the time. Many thanks!" V.S. Vale

Coming Soon....

POETIC POISON

Swansneck Village Mystery Series Book 2

www.vsvale.com

Be sure to visit my website to receive an exclusive copy of **Old Mother Bradshaw's Cook Book**, featuring the Lancashire recipes enjoyed by the Swansneck characters! It's free when you join my newsletter... PLUS you'll be first to hear about brand new releases, sneak peeks and exclusive giveaways.
You'll also find links to follow V S Vale on social media:

Facebook: https://www.facebook.com/vsvaleauthor/
Twitter: https://twitter.com/VSValeAuthor
Instagram: https://www.instagram.com/vsvaleauthor/
Pinterest: https://www.pinterest.co.uk/VSValeAuthor/

Made in the USA
San Bernardino, CA
23 November 2018